Between Brothers

Stasia Black

Copyright © 2023 Stasia Black.

All rights reserved.
No part of this publication may be reproduced, distributed, or transmitted in any form or by any means, included photocopying, recording, or other electronic or mechanical methods, without the prior written permission of the publisher, except in the case of brief quotations embodied in critical reviews and certain other noncommercial uses permitted by copyright law.

This is a work of fiction. Similarities to real people, places, or events are entirely coincidental.

I pull out my phone for some perspective from some of my favorite influencers who remind me that 'impossible' is just a word.

Then I sigh again when an alarm goes off, telling me I only have another fifteen minutes here before I have to get back and take Mom to her doctor's appointment. She can drive herself, but as she tells me constantly, "You're lazy enough; you might as well be good for *something* and take me to my appointments."

Which she has a lot of. Not because there's anything actually wrong with her at a spry sixty-one, but she's a hypochondriac with good insurance, so between the doctors and her weekly hair appointments, we spend a lot of time on the road together. And there's nothing worse than being locked up in an enclosed space with a woman who loves to pick at all your flaws.

"Did you go for a walk yesterday? Really, Lauren. How do you expect to lose weight and find a man if you aren't even *trying*?"

Or, "Why don't you come in with me to the salon? That frumpy look isn't going to get you any jobs. Employers respect *presentation*."

My mother's the kind of woman who puts make-up on to take mail to the mailbox. She cannot fathom that I, her daughter, her life's great embarrassment, leave the house in leggings, a T-shirt, and no make-up. It's why, though she expects me to drive her everywhere, she tells me to stay in the car instead of coming in with her to the actual appointments.

"I have a *reputation* in this town. And everyone remembers you like you used to be. Back in high school when you were so pretty and making such good grades."

She meant back when I had an eating disorder, and she *still* shamed me relentlessly for my weight. It eventually landed me in the hospital, which embarrassed her to no end. "Why do you have to be so dramatic about everything?" she cried when she came to visit me. "Why can't you be normal like everyone else's daughters?"

So it's with dread that I look down at my laptop as the minutes creep closer. These short outings I steal for myself away from her feel like the only times I can breathe. Which feels ridiculous at my age.

Sometimes, I just want to *scream* because of it all. Life was not supposed to turn out like this.

I always dreamed of finding adventure. Of traveling the world. Of doing *something* with my life instead of all this absolute *nothing*—

My thoughts are interrupted by all the people around me breaking out into screams. I look up from my notebook to see them falling over themselves as they flee the plaza.

What the hell? I blink in confusion. Especially when I see some people stop running to take out their phones and aim them at the sky. Finally, I look up.

And my mouth drops open. What the hell?!!

A muscled man descends from the sky, huge black wings extending from his back, flapping as he comes down.

He drops right into the center of the plaza, hands held out, a huge, slightly wild grin on his face.

"Mortals, behold!" he shouts. "Your god is here among you!"

If my chin wasn't on my chest before, it is now. The man is shirtless as he faces us, a hood over the back of his head—a mere shred of material because it's been cut to accommodate his wings. He's still holding his huge, muscled arms outwards, hands up, though he looks anything but welcome or friendly as his voice continues booming out. "Your god seeks a consort. Volunteers may line up now before me and bow down so that I may choose amongst you."

It's like something out of a Marvel movie. The costume is elaborate—well, I'd say it was a costume, but how did he *fly*? It has to be a magician's trick, right? Didn't David Copperfield make the Statue of Liberty disappear or something? Is there a jetpack on his back, hidden by the huge wings?

Within moments, security guards approach, pointing Tasers out in front of them. "Lay on the ground!" they shout. "Get down, now!"

The winged man chuckles in their direction and, hands still held outwards, makes a white-blue light erupt from his fingertips, arcing back and forth between his hands. I gasp as I hear the faint crackle of electricity.

"Stop that!" shouts one of the guards, and I hear fear in the man's voice. More people run away now, though they keep their phones up as they go. I stay where I am, trembling and frozen. I'm not sure if it's because I'm scared or because something is actually *happening*.

Nothing but bad or boring things happen in my life. Maybe this is bad. It's probably terrible. And yet, I'm transfixed.

I was just praying to God, and here comes a man from the sky proclaiming he *is* a god.

One of the guards shoots his Taser, and the white-blue light arcing from between the self-proclaimed god's hands shoots out, deflecting the little prongs. Not only that, but the light travels back up the wires of the Taser and lights up the handle in the guard's hands. He screams out, his body seizing at the shock. He drops the fried Taser even as he falls over, still shaking.

Another security guard promptly turns and flees. "I'm calling the cops," he shouts over his shoulder.

Everyone else has fled the plaza for the safety of the surrounding buildings at this point, the rest of the guards included. Which the winged man seems to realize at the same time I do.

He looks around, hands finally lowered, white-blue light dimming. "Well, who will be my consort?"

Then his eyes fall on me.

And on impulse, I do something very, very foolish. I raise my hand.

He smiles.

And starts walking toward me.

Oh shit.

What am I doing? What have I done?

I drop my hand. But it's too late. His sights are already set on me.

Chapter Two

LAUREN

He comes straight toward me. Wow. Um. He's really tall. And those are a lot of muscles.

I shake my head, and when that doesn't seem to deter him, I lift my hands and shake my head and gesture to dissuade him. "Whoa. Whoa. Sorry, momentary impulse move. Just go on to the next person."

He just grins. "You are a beautiful female. You will be a prize consort."

Consort? Um, can I call backsies? But what is this guy really gonna do, just pick me up and fly away with me? I mean, *ha*. He might have muscles, but I'm more than a big girl. Plus, whatever jet pack or magic trick he used to get here surely won't work a second time. Because I don't *actually believe* he's a god. Do I?

But up close, with the way he's angled, I can see his wings and where they're attached to his back. They look even more realistic. Either that, or he's got a really good special effects crew.

"I choose this female for my consort!" he says loudly, proclaiming it to the mostly deserted crowd and then reaching down for me.

"Whoa, whoa, whoa," I say as he hefts me to my feet. Damn, he's shockingly strong. He immediately bends down and scoops me up with one arm under my knees and one beneath my back. I yelp as I'm cradled against his chest as if I weigh nothing. My arms scramble around his neck as I feel his feet leave the ground. "Wait, wait, are you real?"

He nods, his grin too wide. "As real and as close to a god as this world knows."

"Will you hurt me?" I ask desperately.

For the first time, the wild grin falls from his face, and I notice something like concern cross his features. "Consorts are sacred. No one must ever hurt a consort. Ever."

He leans in, and I blink, foolish and overwhelmed to not notice how handsome he is. The hood was shading his face before, but yeah. He has strong, handsome features and he's just really, really um. . . gulp. . . *male*. He gazes down at me, his intense, stormy gray eyes locking me in place. "I will never hurt you."

Shouting erupts from the other end of the plaza, and his head swings in that direction. Mine does, too, and I see police start to flood the plaza.

"Our courtship comes to an end, beautiful consort," he says.

"What does that me—?"

There's no time to finish my question because before I've even taken another breath, he bends his knees slightly and then rockets us up into the air.

I scream. And scream and scream and clench my arms around his neck so tight I have to be choking him. His arms just tighten against my ample curves as we rise faster than any man-made jet-pack could ever accomplish, his huge wings coming to life and cutting through the air around us.

Oh my god, is this real? Is this actually happening?

My heart isn't just in my throat. It's bypassed that. It's in my mouth from how fast we're suddenly accelerating. A low, thrumming blue light erupts around us and breaks a bit of the freezing wind resistance. I clench my eyes shut as I press my face against his huge, warm chest.

Wasn't something like this what I was just wishing for? Praying for, even? Adventure. A... *gulp*... man? I feel a crazy rush in my ears. The world isn't safe. This man is very, *very* unsafe.

We're flying higher now and faster.

Oh my god! Part of me believed by talking to him, I was just stalling until help arrived. Only a small percentage was actually contemplating running away with him. Or—flying away with him, as it were.

And now—

Oh god! The plaza is getting smaller and smaller below us.

And I'm being flown off to god knows where by... well, someone who believes he *is* a god. And just might be.

Chapter Three

REMUS

My plan is going well. Of course it is. I am Remus, destroyer of cities, a very clever god of war.

Naturally, my stupider, less talented brothers had a harder time acquiring consorts than I did. I always suspected it would be the case were I ever to try.

But there was always the obstacle of the ball and chain tied around my neck—or rather, to the back of my head—my Siamese twin, Romulus. No one can imagine what it's like to have a face on the other side of one's head, unseen without the aid of mirrors but always ready to wake when I am sleeping and second-guess any plan I try to make.

It's never been fair to share a body with him. He's always ready to whip around and snatch control just when things are getting interesting.

For example, when I began making plans to go take a consort

from one of the humans' cities months ago, Romulus knew what I was doing. He sleeps when I'm awake and vice versa, and we know what the other is up to because of our shared memory. He's able to spy on me, which is how I found myself locked back up in the dungeon during my waking hours. The same dungeon he locked us in for two hundred years rather than let me free to play out all my schemes.

Only one of my other brothers cared for my plight.

Layden alone came to me in the dungeon and offered me a solution. The youngest of us, he took pity on me because he knew how capricious our other brothers could be. He was long absent from our sides and no longer the sweet little brother who would blindly go along with whatever Abaddon decreed. He had also learned much during his time away. Not just magic. He met dark beings, a secret I believe he shared with only me.

And he gave me an elixir so that I might keep my mind separate from Romulus's.

Outwardly, both Layden and I played the obedient brothers and gained our freedom to move about the castle. I promised to give up my schemes of stealing a consort for my own. Layden pretended to be content to be among family again.

Together, we plotted.

After months and months of being good little boys, and along with Romulus's assurance that he had me in check—ha, as if he ever could leash his better half—we got the rest of them to agree to go on vacation.

So I took my opportunity, and now I am holding the most beautiful, sumptuous of females in my arms, carrying her back to the castle to make her mine.

She has even stopped screaming. Well, almost. Every so often, a little squeal erupts, but mostly, she buries her face against my chest. She is so warm, pressed close to me. Had I known it would feel like this, I would have found a way to take a consort much, much sooner.

The excitement growing in my chest makes me feel giddy in a

way that I have not felt since I won the Battle of the Three Emperors against the Austrian-Russo forces in 1805.

Back then, the prize was only more war and bloodlust. Now, it is the curiosity and wild adventure of having won a consort of my very own. After thousands of years of war, I have known enough bloodshed to have slaked my bloodlust.

A consort, though? A consort is one thing I have never known.

Finally, the land below begins to be familiar. My wings flap strong against the northern wind, and I bring us down. It is summertime, and so for a short while, the land below is not covered in snow and ice but rich, verdant greens and browns.

And there, like a great sturdy stone rising up from the landscape beside the glittering blue lake, is my home.

I spiral us down toward the castle tower, sending out the runes that open the forcefield shielding us from any unfriendly intruders, and enter through the window of my bedroom.

I feel the female jolt in my arms as I touch down on the floor, but her head doesn't lift from my chest. When I look down at her, her eyes are still clenched shut tight.

In the corner, the fire crackles. In spite of my warming rune shield, the air up high can be cold when moving so fast, and I know a human's temperature can be fickle. So even though it makes the room uncomfortably warm for me, I set the fire going before I left to seek my prize.

"We are here."

Her arms around my neck do not unclench. Her face is beautiful, and I smile at her, so near, clinging to me so tightly. I do not mind continuing to have her lush body in my arms.

Suddenly, her eyes pop open, and she looks around.

"Jesus Christ! Am I not actually dreaming?"

Her head starts to shake, and she peels her arms from around my neck and wiggles as if to be set down. I sigh. All right. I put her down on her feet. She wobbles a little, but my tail immediately flicks out to surround her waist and steady her.

Her eyes go wider as one hand tentatively reaches down, her fingertips skimming across my leathery appendage. "Not a dream," she whispers, as if to herself.

I try not to let my eyes roll back in my head from how good it feels to have the female's fingers stroke my tail. "Are you steady, little one?"

Her eyes shoot up to me. "Uh." She blinks as our gazes make contact. And then she looks around, her head swinging this way and that. "Holy crap, are we in a *castle*?"

My tail reluctantly unravels as she strides to the window, puts her hands on the sill, and looks out. She looks astounded at everything she sees. "I can't believe this," she whispers again, head slowly shaking. Then she whips back around to look at me. "Wait, okay, so if this isn't a dream—and this is all really, really detailed in a way I'm not sure my subconscious could dream up. . . I mean I don't even *know* this much about castles. . ."

She looks from the room, with its big four-poster canopy bed and sumptuous rugs, back out the huge, open window.

"Where *are* we? There's no city, no lights, only forest as far as I can see. I mean, is this real? Or did I get knocked out and put into an experimental AI simulation?"

She sticks her hand out the window to feel the breeze.

I have a curious consort. Beautiful and curious and full of vivacious life. I am fully intrigued and delighted by her.

"I am called Remus. It is good to have you here, consort. What are you called?"

She turns back around to look at me. "But seriously. Is this for *real,* real?"

My eyes narrow. What does she mean? "What other real is there?"

She laughs and turns around. I think I could become addicted to the sound of her laugh. "I mean, is this just a computer program or—" She reaches out now to touch the stone walls. "It all feels real. Cool to the touch. So are we in another, I don't know, *realm*? Are we still in my world even?"

Her eyes track back to me, and I feel a sizzle that goes straight through me when her gaze connects with mine. "Your realm, yes. Just removed from the humans. Safe from their eyes and tracking devices."

Her eyebrows go up.

"So it's a *magic* castle?" she squeaks. "I wanna see everything."

I pause. This feels too good to be true. Immediately, I am suspicious. "Why? So you can find a way to escape? Because we are in a place far from other human dwellings. There is nowhere to run."

The smile falls from her face, and she crosses her arms over her chest as she takes a step back from me. "Well, that's ominous as fuck. I thought you said you wouldn't hurt me."

"I would never harm a consort," I bark, and she takes another step back.

I grit my teeth and stretch my neck. Fuck. Romulus tends to wake up when I get agitated, always ready to take charge of my screwups and save the day with his calm, cold logic. I tug my flask from my pants and chug a small swill. The liquid is bitter, metallic almost, and a little salty on my tongue, but it does the trick and sends my twin back to dreamland. I am fully my own again.

My consort eyes me warily, and I see the distrust her distrust.

"If there is one thing I have learned to value above all others, it is the health and well-being of one's consort. I will see to your happiness here. I vow it." I lift a hand to my chest over my heart. She may not know me yet, but in this, I am earnest. It feels strange to show earnestness when I wear so many other masks for everyone else. With her alone, perhaps, I can be real. Or as real as a monster such as me can ever manage.

Her tense stance loosens slightly. Her arms stay crossed even as her shoulders lower a bit. "Trust is earned," she says.

I nod. Ah, so my consort is wise as well as beautiful. I am happy to discover this.

She bites her lip. "My name's Lauren."

"Lo-Ren," I pronounce, then grin. "Lo-Ren consort, it is my heart's delight to have you here."

I hold out my arm wide to the doorway of my bedroom, gesturing toward the rest of the castle, hoping it will delight her as much as my room has. "What would you like to see first?"

Chapter Four

LAUREN

I don't know quite what to make of him. This man claims to be a god but, at the moment, he feels much more like a man. Well, one with wings and a tail anyway.

What do I know though? I don't have the best track record with men.

But we're not thinking about that right now. I've stepped into something that resembles a fairytale at the moment, and one doesn't clutter that with bullshit memories of the past. At least not right now. Right now, I want to be lost in this moment and completely forget my past.

Because what I wanted, what I've *really* wanted—even though I never knew how to pray for it—was to be free. Free from all the bullshit of my own life. And somehow, miraculously, that freedom has been delivered in the form of a seven-foot tall, muscle-bound, handsome if wild-eyed, bewinged god. And the tail, I can't forget about the tail. Even now, it twitches in the air behind him like a playfully curious cat.

Only as I watch him watching me do I remember he asked me a question. What do I want to see first?

"Everything!" I exclaim.

He grins wide, white teeth flashing, and holds out a hand toward the door. "I'm not sure our castle is as magical as you might wish. Our father had lavish tastes, but my brothers burned many of his things after an. . . er, extreme disagreement."

"You have brothers?" I ask. "Are they like you?"

He coughs a little, and the hood he's still wearing falls back from his face a bit. He tugs it into place again. "We were all given different. . . ah, gifts by our father. So no, not like me." Then he grins, the big one that splits his face, one eyebrow quirking up as he flirts with me. "I assure you, I am quite unique. And you have gotten the best of all the brothers."

I laugh at that. "Oh yeah? Maybe I should judge for myself. Where are these brothers of yours? Or do you all have your own castles?"

He waves a hand dismissively. "They're on vacation with their consorts. Well, my youngest brother does not yet have the joy of companionship because he's just returned to us."

I shake my head, not quite following all he's saying. "But they're all gods, like you?"

"As I have said," he steps nearer and dips his head closer to mine. "None are like me, little Lo-ren."

His closeness sends my heart suddenly racing, and my breathing quickens. I spin away and head for the door. "You said you'd show me everything. I'm ready." I hustle out the door, but I swear I hear him chuckle behind me.

Pushing open the heavy wooden door, I step out into a hallway. I still can't believe I'm in a real castle.

Traveling to Europe and visiting places where castles exist has always been on my bucket list. But it's also something I sorta never believed would ever happen for me. Cross-the-ocean plane tickets are expensive, as is travel in general. Hell, I've never even been to the ocean!

I lift my hands and trail them along the walls as I walk. The stones *feel* old. Older than anywhere I've ever been in the States. Light filters in from huge windows at the end of the hallway, and when we reach it, there's a spiral staircase heading both directions.

I turn around to Remus. "Which way, up or down?"

"If you want to see something magical, then go up. Three flights."

I feel a little thrill at every wild step into the unknown I'm taking. Continuing to hold onto the walls, because obviously, a modern convenience like railings don't exist in a place like this, I head up the stairs.

Now, despite what my mom thinks, I *do* actually try to go for a walk most days. I handle the steps, and I'm only breathing slightly heavier by the last set of steep stairs. There's a misconception that big girls are always out of shape, which pisses me off. It's just one of the things people get wrong about folks like me.

Remus comes up behind me and smoothly dips a hand to my back for a moment. "This way."

I suck in a breath at the touch, but he's pulled his hand away and is walking ahead of me. I stare, trying to muffle my gasp as his folded wings bob and his tail continues to flip back and forth, occasionally brushing the walls. He still has on the hood covering his hair, and my eyes drop without meaning to his tight backside.

His pants have a buttoned opening for his tail to emerge, right where his spine and tailbone meet, but they're quite form-fitting everywhere else. Ahem. I jerk my eyes away as soon as I realize I'm staring.

I look around. Unlike the floor we came from, the top of the stairs leads to a single, huge, round room, and I can only guess that it's the top of a castle turret. Sunlight spills in through the countless windows that line the walls, the tint of the glass panes making the light change colors as it passes into the room.

"The story of where I come from."

The room is empty but for an extravagantly intricate mosaic in the center of the floor. The picture and design of the mosaic are unclear at first, but as I step back and move to angle myself correctly, it becomes clear.

My breath catches.

Flaming angelic beings of white and gold, all with wings like Remus, except pure white in color, not black. The beings are gathered in a huge rectangular hall, flanking each side. At the front is some sort of fire or power source that's so bright it's a burst of white.

"What is this?" I breathe out.

Remus just says, "Watch."

I frown, confused, but before my very eyes, the mosaic begins to move. The little tiles shift and change colors. I yelp and step back against the wall, right into Remus's chest. He chuckles and slips an arm around my waist to steady me but doesn't remove it even once it's clear I've got my balance.

And there's something comforting about his touch as I watch in wonder at the tiles shifting. The great hall remains, but all the angelic beings change, filtering out of the hall like a ceremony has finished.

Then, another figure enters, slightly different from the angels. A little less bright. A little more human-looking, but still with white wings. Like something in between a human and an angel.

Unlike the angels standing tall, wings flared, this figure lurks. He sticks to the shadows. Head swinging this way and that, tiles shift and ripple so that it feels like I'm watching a pixelated movie. He steals up toward the bright fire at the altar, dipping his hand in and pulling some fire out. Then he flees back down the aisle.

Once he gets to the end of the aisle, the tiles ripple, and the scene changes to follow the figure down a slightly darker hallway and into a room that has a rippling blue mirror in its center. He looks behind him once. And then jumps through the mirror.

Again, the entire mosaic ripples, tiles exploding in a mesmerizing rainbow of colors, as the man-angel in the center clutches the bright white burst of fire to his chest.

And then the entire picture goes white, so white I briefly close my eyes, and when I open them again, the man has landed in a crouch. He still holds the white fire against his chest, but he's landed on verdant green grass. He stands up triumphantly, lifting the white fire above his head, and his wings flare outwards.

The picture freezes there, and I breathe out. "What did I just see?" I blink, only now realizing Remus's hand is still around my waist.

I spin and, not wanting to step on the magic mosaic, hurry back around the perimeter of the room to the door.

Remus follows, and once we're at the small foyer at the top of the stairs, he tilts his head back toward the room. "That was my father's monument to his proudest moment when he stole the spark of life from the gods so he could become a god himself. When he came here to Earth, he forged his children with the stolen fire, implanting the godspark in each of us."

He bangs his fist against his chest.

My eyes widen. Well, that answers that. If I believe in a magic floor, anyway. "Oh," I manage. And then, "Wow."

"Yes," he nods down at me and stands a little taller as I look at him. "Wow."

I shake my head and smack his chest lightly. His, um, bare chest, I remember as my fingertips graze against his skin. "You're too full of yourself." I try to turn away from him, but he snatches my hand and holds it there against his chest.

"I feel very full when you are here at my side, Lo-Ren consort."

Swoon.

Wait, what the hell am I thinking? Not swoon. I've made this mistake before, falling for a guy who seems too good to be true. The thing about guys like this is that there's always a catch. Usually some gigantic red flag that's been waving in my face the whole time.

Just then, I realize that Remus's hood has come a little askew. On impulse, I reach up and snatch it off the back of his head.

And yelp in surprise when he bends down to grab the hood back.

"Oh my god!"

Remus immediately lets go of my hand and backs into the corner to hide what I've already seen.

"How is there another face on the back of your head?" I squeak out.

"I did not want you to see that yet," he snaps, not looking as confident for the first time since I've met him. He grits his teeth and stretches his neck in a way that looks painful.

"W-what is it?" I ask, hoping I don't sound judgmental but knowing I'm failing.

Remus pulls a small flask from his pants pocket, takes a sip, then stretches his neck again, settling back with a sigh. When he glances back at me, he looks more settled.

"Meet my twin brother, Romulus," Remus says calmly.

"Your tw— Why isn't he moving?!" My heart thumps hard, the fairytale-like wonder of everything falling away as I'm washed with a dose of the reality of what's just happened. I've essentially been kidnapped by some god-like creature with wings and—and *two faces*! I mean, yes, I might've volunteered to be kidnapped, but that's neither here nor there at the moment!

"He's sleeping."

"Does he ever wake up?" I walk forward and grab Remus's shoulders, trying to turn him around so I can get a better look at the other face, but he blocks me by keeping his chest toward me. His hands cinch me around the waist, and astonishingly, he lifts me and deposits me several feet back.

I make a startled noise as my bicycling feet meet the stone again. He doesn't let go of my waist, and just like earlier, my heart speeds up at his closeness. I blink, trying to clear away the haze of hormones his nearness stirs up. Wasn't I just telling myself it was time to come back to my senses? *Not* swoon!

"He's not going to wake up for a long time," Remus says.

When I inhale and ask, "What does *that* mean?" all I smell is *him*. Maleness and clean musk and good lord, it's been too long since I've been touched by a man.

Remus only grins, a wild glint back in his eyes. His hands linger at my waist, squeezing slightly, and I swat at them. I'm very aware of the feel of him squeezing a little more before he lets go.

"Don't worry, little one; it's only you and me at this party for as long as we can manage."

"Nothing you're saying makes sense!" I declare.

"But you don't want boring, do you?"

"How do you know what I want? Maybe I'm fine with boring. Boring is *safe*."

He just scoffs. "Safe? What fun is safety? There's no adventure in safety." He leans in, grinning that too-wide grin. "And you're a woman who wants adventure, aren't you?"

I narrow my eyes at him. "You know nothing about me. Or what I need."

He's staring right at me, and I notice that his eyes are a dark, dark gray. His face is chiseled, beautiful and unnerving, with thick lips and a smile that seems to curve too wide so often, like the Cheshire cat.

"Oh, I want to hear all about your *needs*." The way he says the last word makes it sound... gulp... sexual.

I blink, my mouth going a little dry. Is he flirting with me? I've forgotten what that feels like. "Can we get back to the part where there's a sleeping twin on the other side of your head?"

"Are you hungry?" he asks suddenly. "I bet you're hungry. I know a place that makes the most delicious meals."

I frown as he pulls back. Is that a reference to me being thick? My last boyfriend used to say passive-aggressive crap all the time, especially in front of his friends when we were out and anyone mentioned food. Like, oh, she's *always* hungry, and there'd inevitably be a snigger from someone.

But just because it's the only problem I've had in life that has *yet* to find a permanent solution doesn't mean one *can't* be found.

He locked me in a dungeon for two hundred years. It only seems fair that I've found a way to send him nighty-night for. . . well, as long as I can find a way to manage. And, after meeting the fair Lo-Ren, I've suddenly become even more mightily motivated.

As I near the city, I use runes to cloak myself. Unlike my dramatic entrance in the human town square earlier, I'm back to skulking about their world.

Unfortunately, they have some of the best toys and food. My stars, the *food*. Especially this city where I drop down now. Ah, Paris. Even under Napolean, in the midst of the blockades, the city of light never truly lost its shine.

I drop down to a familiar spot in the 5th arrondissement, where I have a large black trench coat and hood stashed. It's painful and scrunches my wings, but *ce la vie*. I curl up my tail to hide it and try not to grin at passersby as I take to the streets. They seem to find me disconcerting if I let my full grin stretch. I've tried to be careful with Lo-Ren thus far, too, but my perfect little consort has been taking everything in stride.

I sigh happily as I allow the runes to fade when I'm amidst the crowded, busy streets. I hate to leave her at the castle alone for long, so I pop in quickly to *La Tour d'Argent* to pick up the food I ordered earlier. They always say to plan for success, so I ordered ahead. It turns out some of these new toys the humans have thought up during my long confinement—phones especially—have their uses.

Once I have the food, I'm in the air again and on my way back to my prize.

I'm eager to see her.

And to see how she did with my little test.

Yes, I am confident in my obvious perfection, apart from the little issue of my parasite, and she *did* volunteer as all Earth females ought to when presented with the opportunity to be consort to a god. Yet I have been acquainted with these foolish mortals enough to know that when they meet a Horseman of the Apocalypse, as they have so adoringly named us, they also have a tendency to flee. Or wet their pants in fright. It really varies on the day.

So, I thought I'd give my sweet pudding cup a little test. To hear Abaddon tell it, his Hannah-wife fled him the second he let her out of his sight. Not that she got very far.

My motivation has made my flight short, and soon, I'm opening the runes back to the castle and walking through the door to the dining room. The table my brothers and I made sits long and proud in the center of the room, already set for a dinner I don't expect to be having any time soon.

I've been through enough skirmishes to expect when setting the test how it will go.

Needless to say, I am not surprised to see that my Lo-Ren is not seated obediently waiting for me. But perhaps I am a twinge disappointed, which *does* surprise me.

However, in the next moment, I'm grinning. Because there's nothing I love more than a chase. Perhaps it was unkind not to warn her that there's one rule of monsters: if you run, we chase. Then again, I intentionally showed her the moving mural upstairs.

I figured I might as well paint us first as angels rather than give away my true nature right off the bat.

But if chase I must... My grin stretches. I rub my hands together and feel my tail rise excitedly in the air behind me as I drop the large bag of food on the table.

Just then, the furthest door leading to the bathing room opens, and Lo-Ren steps out. "Oh!" Her features brighten. "You're back already!"

I freeze and blink, trying to dampen my grin. She... didn't run? Didn't even *try* to escape? Even after seeing Romulus? My heart thumps a little oddly in my chest as she walks toward me, looking completely calm.

"What'd you get? Please tell me it's not sushi." She makes a face. "I would have told you if you'd given me half a second before taking off like that. I've tried to get into the whole raw fish thing but just can't make myself like it."

I blink some more. I am rarely the one taken off guard.

Finally, I manage to blurt a word. "Duck." And then a string of words follow. "From one of the finest Parisian restaurants, famous for the dish. I've been going there for. . . many years." *Centuries*. At least some establishments among these mortals have staying power. "With olive tapenade, a cheese plate, and the finest Beaujolais."

She just continues staring at me pleasantly, our eyes making contact in a way that continues to unsettle me. I look away first, breathing out heavily as I begin to pull the food from the bag. The wine is nicely chilled.

Lo-Ren comes near. Closer to me than people usually like to stand.

"Wow. It all smells delicious. This is actually really nice. And I love wine and cheese." She sneaks out a hand and grabs a slice of cheese, popping it in her mouth as I pour wine into the goblets at the table.

I want to ask her why she didn't run. Or at least try. I know it would have been futile, but humans have never been known for their excellent logic skills. Their instincts are barely above that of animals. Freeze, fight, or flight. I've seen it a million times in battle. When faced with fear, those are their three instincts.

But then another thought stalls me. Is she truly not afraid of me?

Who *is* this creature?

Is she somehow as mad as me?

"Why are you grinning at me like that?" she asks, pausing with another piece of cheese halfway to her mouth.

"No reason," I say and pull out the last entrée. Using utensils on the table, I transfer everything from cardboard boxes to the elegant tableware Abaddon told Kharon to buy for his bride.

It truly was a lovely little wedding at the start of summer, and I'll admit it stirred my jealousy and made me decide it was time once and for all to find a consort for my very own. If even the *Thing* could find a female companion, then surely it would be nothing for me to do so, parasite or not.

I grin at my Lo-Ren as our feast is laid out before us. Ah, but one last detail to make it perfect.

Pointing my finger, I use a couple of runes to light the candles standing in the middle of the table.

Lo-Ren gasps. "I'm not sure I'm gonna get used to that any time soon."

I scoff. "That is the least of my skills, and *that* is what impresses you?"

She shrugs. "Well, the flying was sure... *something*." Her eyes widen at the last word, and she lets out a little laugh. "I gotta say, when I woke up yesterday, I certainly couldn't have imagined that I'd be sitting in a castle having a Parisian dinner with a god today. The universe, she's got jokes."

I lift my glass. "To the universe."

She half-nods, half-shakes her head. "To the universe."

Then, we both take bites of the succulent duck. Her eyes immediately go wide again as she chews. Will I ever get used to how expressive her face is?

"Holy shit," she says after swallowing. "That's so fucking good!"

I smile at her pleasure. "I told you they were famous for the duck. They've had quite a while to perfect the recipe."

"What's a while?" she asks, immediately cutting into another bite. "How long have you been ordering from there?" Before lifting the fork to her mouth, though, she takes a sip of wine.

I laugh at the way she phrased the question. "They've certainly had some staff changes, but I've been going there since they opened in 1582."

She coughs, spitting out some of the wine. "What?" She coughs some more, lifting her napkin. "Did you just say you've been going since—"

Oh, I am having fun now. "1582. It's the oldest restaurant in

Paris, at least that's still around. So as I said, they've had some time to perfect the recipe."

"Holy shit." She lifts the wine goblet and drinks far more than a sip, her wide eyes on me the whole time. "I mean, I've always had a thing for older dudes." She wipes her mouth again with the napkin. "How old are we talking here?"

I grin. "What is it you mortals say? Age is just a number?"

"Yeah, and we know even when we say it that it's bullshit," she says. "So, how old?"

I shrug. "I genuinely couldn't tell you. Kingdoms rise and fall. My brothers and I remain."

Her eyes, already wide, get wider.

I gesture to her food. "Don't let it get cold. It's an insult to waste the best food Paris has to offer." As one who often went hungry when traveling with my youngest brother, I ought to know. But I decide not to toss everything on my sweet, wide-eyed consort at once.

Her eyes linger on me, but she eventually tears them away to look back down at her plate, eating the bite of duck she'd cut earlier. Her body relaxes a little as she chews. Not even my apparently shocking revelation can distract her from the pleasures of the dish, which delights me in a way I can't quite describe.

I, too, am particularly fond of the pleasures of the flesh. I take a long sip of wine, watching her.

"So tell me more about this particularly long life of yours," she says after swallowing. "And your brother." She picks up her wine glass and gestures toward the other side of my head. "Tell me about him."

"I have a lot of brothers," I transition smoothly. "Too many, some might say."

I ignore the tightening of my jaw and instead tell her about Abaddon, the eldest, always sure he was the gods' gift. And Thing, who lately renamed himself Kharon after he met his wife, Ksenia.

"Layden's the youngest. Good with gadgets and computers. You'll like him."

She pulls out a small, square device from her pocket. "Good, I was wondering if there was Wi-Fi here cause I can't get a single bar of cell reception. Do you know the password?"

I stare at her blankly, just like all of us tend to do when Layden starts going on about the strange pieces of plass-tick that light up in his hands. When did humans go and get so clever with their tools? Millennia of them barely figuring out what to do with fire and the metals they dig out of the ground, then you get chained to a wall for two hundred years, and they've gone and made the whole world light up.

She rolls her eyes. "Never mind. You said they're on vacation? When do they get back?"

I wave a hand. "Enough about them. Tell me about *you*."

"Me?" she laughs. "Pretty sure my boring life isn't going to interest a dude who's been around for thousands of years."

"But you are my consort," I declare. "All of you interests me. I want to know your past so I may know what has shaped you and brought you here to this moment."

She takes another bite of her food and averts her eyes.

I frown. Hannah-wife is happy to chatter about herself, but I suppose Thing/Kharon's consort is slower to open up. Unless you get her talking about her favorite subject, which consists of the types of blades best for killing a man. But I have a feeling it is not a former life as an assassin that keeps Lo-Ren's lips shut so tight.

"Why will you not speak?"

When she looks back at me, her dark eyes seem lit with some fire I cannot understand. "Is this how it works in your world? You demand people jump, and they ask how high?"

I think back to the rest of my dealings with mortals, and though she has mentioned a particularly peculiar request, I answer honestly. "Yes."

Her mouth drops open. "And that's how you expect this to go with me?"

I frown again and blink. "You are a mere human, and I am a god. So it would be wise for you to do as I command."

A squeak comes out of her as she leaps to her feet. "Are you serious?"

Though I am fond of humor, especially at one of my brothers' expense, I was not making a joke. Yet, I sense the danger possible in how I respond. Which confuses me because things had been going so well up until now.

"Sit down," I say reasonably. "Let us finish this meal and continue speaking as nicely as we have until this moment."

She makes a scoffing noise, picks up her napkin, wipes her mouth, and then tosses it furiously down on the table. "No, *thank you.*"

I sense the thank you is not sincere and narrow my eyes. "Why have you become so intractable?" I question. "I was expressing interest in your past. I thought that would please you."

She puts her fists on the table and leans in, once again making strong eye contact. But whereas before, there was a sizzle when our gazes connected, now there is a hard challenge there. "Sure. But first, you have to tell me more about the sleeping guy on the other side of your head."

Heat floods my chest, and I take to my feet as well, mirroring her stance across the table. "That's none of your concern."

"Ha," she cries. "So it's fine for you to command me to tell you things, but I can't ask about the elephant in the room?"

"My brother is hardly an elephant."

"You know what I mean!"

We glare one another down. And then she snatches up the wine bottle and strides away from the table toward the stairs. "I'll be spending the rest of the evening in my room."

When I start to follow her, she turns around and glares at me. "*Alone.*"

The word rings out in the room, stopping me in my tracks.

I'm left dumbfounded as she and her gorgeous, swaying hips stomp away from me.

Chapter Six

LAUREN

The gall of that man! God. Guy. Whatever.
To think I'd just open up and spill my guts cause he said so. Hypocritical bastard! I knew he was too good to be true.

I take another long swallow of the wine. And then giggle. I know it's got to be some sort of sin to swill wine this expensive. The last time I drank wine straight from the bottle, it was Two Buck Chuck. I'd just dramatically stomped out of my boyfriend's apartment, which we shared, with a suitcase full of my shit and gone to a hotel.

Which I could only afford for one night.

But that one night, I got drunk off my ass, promised myself I deserved *so* much better, and swore that things could only look up from there. Right?

Ha.

Hahahahahahahahaha.

I moved back in with my mom after racking up a week at the hotel on my credit card and coming to my senses that I had nowhere else to go. After a month with her, I was back at my cheating ex's door, begging for another chance because I was so miserable with her. I figured maybe a nice-ish cheater with a three-bedroom in Uptown was better than my childhood bedroom and a hateful mother tearing into me every time I walked into the kitchen.

Lemme tell you, I thought that was rock bottom.

Nope.

Rock bottom was learning he'd already moved the new bitch into the master bedroom and thrown out the rest of my shit when I didn't come back for it after a week. We'd been together seven years.

Seven years and all I got was a heartless boot to the curb when he upgraded.

Oh, and did I tell you? The cherry on top of that shit Sunday? I worked at his company doing everything from books to marketing and advertising and even dropped out of college to help before getting more and more drawn in. But on paper, I'd only ever be an Administrative Assistant. And with all the names I called him upon finding I'd been replaced with a skinnier, younger New Bitch, I knew there was no way I'd get a reference letter, so yeah.

Here I am.

Twenty-eight. Unemployed. No degree. Living with my mom because I'd been stupid enough to let some asshole use me up and toss me out.

No, I do not want to tell the handsome new guy who's swooped in and carried me away about my shitty past.

I take another swallow, whining when the last of the liquid runs into my mouth and there isn't anymore. I shake the bottle over my gaping mouth, only to elicit a few more drops. Then I roll over on the bed.

I'm doing such a bang-up job of not repeating history.

A handsome, obvious wreck of a guy shows up asking for volunteers to be swept up, and what bitch is all, *I volunteer as tribute!* Ding ding ding, ladies and gentlemen. *Me.*

I'm pretty sure my therapist would say something annoying and wise like, *Well, if you start to notice a pattern in your behavior, maybe that's something worth paying attention to.*

Can I help it if I'm attracted to assholes?

I grab a pillow and yank it over my face, screaming into it.

Sometimes, we're attracted to the most familiar dynamics. Again, my therapist's voice. I drag the pillow away from my face.

Oh dear God, please tell me I have not run away from one narcissist only to head straight into the arms of another.

I sit up and feel the wine slosh in my stomach. I let out a long, unladylike burp and giggle. Damn, that's some good wine. I feel very, very buzzy. Which is a cute word for drunk off my ass.

Usually, at this point in my few and far between, give-into-despair-and-drink-a-bunch-of-wine moments, I'd turn on a sappy Netflix rom-com about some lonely lady buying an inn somewhere or moving back to her hometown only to find some handsome carpenter waiting to woo her.

I look around the bedroom. Yeah, it's nice with all the lush carpets and nice furniture, but my millennial brain is freaking out for the lack of *screens* around here. Or at least a good, trashy romance novel. But I usually only read those on my phone.

I stand up and only wobble a *little* before falling back on my ass. At least the mattress is a soft landing. The second time, I totally manage to stay on my feet, even if I have to hold onto the wall to steady myself.

I'm bored. And hungry. What kind of asshole brings you to his castle and doesn't even show you where the kitchen is? Yeah, yeah, fly off to Paris and get you some Michelin-starred dinner from the fanciest and oldest restaurant in the city, blah, blah, blah. How about you show a bitch the kitchen so she can get her own midnight snack? Should be the number one hospitality rule; everybody knows that.

I get to the door and head down the hallway, both arms out so I have a hand on each wall to steady myself. Luckily, little lights turn on in my presence to light my way. Thank fuck, cause I woulda made it like three feet in the dark before giving up, and I really could do with some bread or something to soak up the wine in my stomach.

But then I get to the stairs and remember how stupid-far up in the air we are.

I slump against one of the walls and let out a long-suffering groan.

"Whyyyyyy?" Half of me wants to sit down and go down the stairs on my butt like I did when I was a kid. But I realize it might take a while if I go down the whole way like that.

At least I'm not at the top of the turret like earlier. And it turns out that keeping a death grip on the stone walls and carefully stepping sideways works because I make it down each level. And then I have to explore because, hello, no one showed me where the damn kitchen was.

Logic tells me it'll be on the main floor or one below. Cause like, *Upstairs, Downstairs*, right? Does a place like this have staff? As I head down the stairs into the cooler basement, I get shivers, wondering who might be in service to a god with two faces.

But when the lights flick on as I step through the door, my heart rate slows down. It's just a regular-looking kitchen.

I wasn't sure what I'd find. Maybe an open fire or something to match the rest of the castle's medieval feel?

But this kitchen looks super modern, like something out of a restaurant. There are shiny stainless steel countertops, every appliance you could want, and several large double sinks. Plus, if I'm right. . . that's a walk-in fridge in the back. For the first time in hours, I smile.

I crack the door and grin wider. Oh, hell yeah. It is a well-stocked walk-in with everything from a small supermarket's worth of fresh fruit and vegetables, along with a lot of other stuff. Meat, eggs, fish. And desserts. Cake. Cheesecakes of several varieties. Damn. Someone's got a sweet tooth.

Putting a hand on my rumbly stomach, I know I'm not really in the mood for anything sweet, so I pull back out of the fridge and turn around. Right beside the walk-in, I thought I saw—yep, a small pantry area full of all sorts of artisan-looking breads. Perfect.

I grab some fluffy sourdough and head back into the fridge for some cold cuts and mayo. Finally, in the cool basement kitchen, I make myself a sandwich.

Right as I open my mouth and take a bite, guess who shows up in the doorway?

That's right. Big asshole with wings and a tail.

I only choke a little on my bite, but then, determined to be cool after our last interaction, continue chewing and don't hurry at all.

He stays in the doorway, a dark silhouette in the otherwise brightly lit room. "I'm glad you're making yourself at home," he says.

I can't read him. For once, he's not smiling, but he doesn't look upset, either.

If it was Michael, my ex, he'd be sending some sort of signal that he was still mad at me for my *outburst* earlier. That was what he called it when I did or said anything he didn't like. An *outburst*. His subtle, not-so-subtle way of keeping me in line so I was the perfect little girlfriend who worked her ass off to please him at all times.

I arch an eyebrow and catch even more of an attitude, determined never to be that weak woman ever again.

"I got hungry," I say, my mouth half-full of food. Another thing that Michael hated. *Half-masticated food should never be seen.*

He was a guy who had a lot of *shoulds* and *should-nots* for the women he dated.

I take another big bite of my sandwich.

Remus only tilts his head and watches me with what looks like interest. "I'm curious to learn all about your wants and desires. I realize it may be. . . difficult for me to always. . ." His eyes stay on me, but I feel the reticence in his manner as he tries to say what he's trying to say, something I can sense is unusual.

I swallow my bite. "What's difficult?" I ask a little less belligerently. Maybe all the wine in my system is softening me a little toward him. And knowing that if it was Michael, he'd be doubling down on the assholery.

"My acquaintance with humans has been in very particular contexts. I think I may need to. . . alter some of my ways. I might not always know how. Is it fair to ask for patience? I really do want to get to know you."

I let out a deep breath. I didn't expect this. "What context was that?"

He shrugs. "Battle."

My eyebrows go up. I don't know what I expected of a being thousands of years old. That he just hung out at this castle the whole time? But him being a warrior. . . My eyes track over his gigantic shoulders and huge, muscled thighs. Yeah, that makes sense.

"What kind of battles? Cause I've never heard of you, and I feel like the history books might have made mention of someone as, uh, unique as you."

His grin comes back, cracking wide as he laughs.

"Oh, I'm sure you know my work. My brothers and I were there with Hannibal of Carthage, Alexander, Ceasar, and Genghis Khan. Anywhere blood was to be spilled and power to be gained, we were there to shape the destinies of men."

I stop chewing and just barely manage to swallow my food. Uhhhh. "So you like. . . spilling blood?"

His grin goes wide, teeth a little menacing as his gaze gets a faraway haziness to it. "Armies marching as far as the eye could see, the smell of adrenaline and battle fury in the air as men are roused to war. And then, all that pent-up energy finally *released* with the first arrow launched and the clash of warriors or infantrymen. Then comes chaos, barely leashed as the tide turns back and forth as men fight for their lives and other foolish notions like nation and honor. In truth, they were merely pawns in a far more glorious game."

I pull back. I'm a pacifist. "How can you say that? They were *people*."

He blinks, returning to the present moment with me.

"Is that how you see me? Just as a pawn in some game?"

He shakes his head. "No, Lo-Ren. That is my past."

"One you obviously miss."

His eyebrows narrow. "It was what I was made for. My father crafted sons that he might know power on this plane of existence."

"And the only way he could get power was by killing people?"

"War is how men gain power," he says, looking at me like I'm foolish or naïve not to understand that.

I throw my hands up. "That's such a—a—a destructive, *male* thing to say! What did your father need all that power for anyway?" I ask, disgusted. "Just so he could fight another war and kill a bunch more people? What did it ever get him?"

Remus laughs as if I just don't get it. "What do you mean, what did it get him? He won influence. He whispered in the ears of the most powerful men on earth. They won wealth, riches, and kingdoms and created empires! The world you now know is because of what my father, brothers, and I *did*. We created civilizations."

I cough out a disbelieving laugh. "You mean you *destroyed* civilizations. You're only talking about war, not peace."

Remus waves a hand away. "Peace was what happened until the next war when another great leader rose up."

"Are you serious? What about the great leaders who were able to maintain peace? Don't you get that that's what actually makes a leader great?"

"Expanding a territory is what makes a leader great. Conquering so that you have created an empire from the stretch of one sea to another is what makes a leader great."

"If war is so great, why aren't you still out there leading battles and whispering in the ears of generals?" I ask, fists on my hips. I can't believe I ever went along with such a, a *barbarian*.

He waves a hand again, reaching for a bottle of whisky and uncorking the top. He drinks straight from the bottle like I did from the wine earlier. "I decided to retire. Even the most celebrated generals deserve to rest at the end of their great service."

"Who did you ever serve?" I spit out.

He looks straight at me. "Myself." But then his eyes drop as he takes another long swig. "And my father, I suppose." I remember the stealthy figure stealing fire from the angels.

"And where is he? Off with your brothers? War criminals on vacation?"

Remus slams the bottle of whiskey down on the counter. "My father's gone. Damned to Gehenna if there's any justice in the place we sent him back to."

"Really? Is that what you want? Justice for all the lives you've taken?"

In one sudden swoop of wings, Remus flies across the kitchen so he's standing in front of me, crowding my space. He slams a hand against the wall above my head, and I gasp as he looks down at me.

"You've found out my secret, little consort. I'm not a good man. In fact, I'm a very, very bad one. I don't care about morality or right and wrong."

He bends his head down over me, eyes piercing mine. As much as I want to squeeze my eyes shut against the magnetism of his pull, I don't. God help me; I stare right back even as my body begins to tremble from his nearness.

"But maybe you don't want a good man," he whispers, voice low. "Good men are boring. And I'm beginning to suspect that underneath that sweet, good-girl exterior is a woman who wants more than the safe and boring things a normal life has to give her."

He leans down even more so his thick lips brush my temple at my hairline. "Life with me won't be safe. Or expected. I want to do things to your body that will have you shuddering and gasping my name. I want you trembling and aching and begging me for more even though you're already spent."

A quiver wracks through my body at his filthy words and the images they're conjuring in my mind.

He leans down more, slightly to the side now so that his whisper is right against my earlobe. "I want to grab the luscious flesh of your ass in both of my hands and drag you up and down my cock until you forget your own name because you've been crying out mine for so many hours straight."

I gasp, and it comes out something like a squeak.

Hot air and the brush of his lips against my ear have me quivering and drenching my panties, my eyelids fluttering as he continues to speak low. "Then and only then will I permit you to give in to your pleasure, clenching and bursting apart while acknowledging me as your one true god."

Chapter Seven

LAUREN

And that's how he leaves me. He doesn't push like some men might, leaving me to question everything I ever thought I knew.

What the hell was my life a week ago? *Yesterday?*

Is this really me?

Because as wild and as insane as it may be, it's yesterday that feels like the dream world. This feels *real*. Like my life was waiting to begin, and earlier today, in that plaza by that fountain, it finally did.

And not because I met some man.

But because when something shocking and unusual finally happened to shake up my boring, dead-end, tragic fucking life, I didn't run with everyone else to safety.

I jumped off the edge of the cliff when there was every chance jagged rocks or sharks waited below.

I'm not the girl who leaps. I'm never, ever the girl who leaps.

When I met Michael, I was a shy girl who was one year away from graduating with my Library Sciences degree when a few girlfriends dragged me out to a bar for my twenty-first birthday. I'd commuted to college all three years and had never been much of a partier anyway, so it was one of the few times I'd ever drunk alcohol.

When my bestie started flirting with a group of guys—who turned out to be Michael's friends taking *him* out for finally getting his start-up off the ground—I never thought the cute guy with the good haircut and bright smile would ever look *my* way. Not when I was out with who I considered to be my much more attractive friends.

I didn't really leap that night. The alcohol loosened me up enough to giggle at his jokes and lean in flirtily when he sat down beside me and started telling me all about his new company. I thought it was luck that I got laid on my birthday by such a good-looking guy. Even if most of that experience was comprised of him pumping inside me twice, then crawling up the bed to jerk himself off all over my face.

When he contacted me the next week to ask if I wanted a summer internship at his company, I was only excited about the experience. I didn't see it for the narcissist-seeks-bait ploy that it was.

God, I was such a sucker.

He saw how weak I was. Then he got free labor for the summer and free ass to go with it.

Was he cheating on me the *entire* time? That question has tormented me when I let it. Michael liked what was comfortable. He'd recently moved out of his mother's house, too. And I cooked, cleaned, and did his laundry because he was just *so* stressed out with the start-up.

But I had a boyfriend! We lived together, and he *loved* me; I was a *vital* part of his business. He told me so all the time. At first, anyway. I was still paid a pittance wage, and he'd never *officially* gotten around to changing my title to Operations Director because he was "so busy." But that was the way of genius. He was about to start another money-raising round with investors and was so stressed out. I needed to help him de-stress and keep the team more focused on the next product release than ever before.

I slam my hand against the mattress I'm lying on with the lights off. Ugh! I'm supposed to be living in the moment, not letting that bastard take up another ounce of my brain space. I hate that I still think about him. I hate that he still has the ability to affect me. I never wanted to be this woman pining over a guy, especially now I know what a rotten person he is.

I idolized him for so long. I *believed* in him and all the bullshit he peddled. And then to realize that the nagging in the back of your mind that *maybe* something was off was right all along? The things you questioned him about but he always had an answer for. His way of turning questions back on you to make *you* feel like *you'd* done something shameful by even asking him in the first place...

It crushed your faith in... kinda everything.

He was a lie. I'd been with a stranger the whole time and was a fool. The whole shape of my world was busted.

And I went back to live with Mom, who was a different kind of rotten.

Well, I wasn't quite sure what to make of this world anymore.

But then, when something wild and magnificent and dangerous showed up, I knew I was ready to take the leap. Yes, I wanted to escape the life I was living, but I also wanted to believe in... *something* again. I wanted to believe in something magical, even if it didn't turn out to be something good.

Wasn't that what adventure was supposed to be?

Not always lollipops and yellow brick roads.

Sometimes, there were dark and dangerous woods. Always scintillating to read about but maybe a little more terrifying to live.

Had there been some terrifying moments today? Hell, yes. Being flown up into the sky without the comforting walls of an airplane at a speed no human should ever experience, magic blue light or not— Yes, that was fucking terrifying. Getting back to this castle and realizing just how big he was, that I was alone and had allowed myself to be whisked off to a secondary location... Terrifying.

But then Remus had been kind.

Arrogant, out of touch, blood-thirsty and maybe a teeeeeetch sociopathic, but also oddly gentle and considerate.

And way too sexy for either of our good.

He looked at me in a way Michael sure as hell never had.

I have a suspicion that if Remus and I ever... well, I think it would involve more than just a couple of pumps. What would it be like to be with a man who could stay hard? Because I have a feeling the arrogant god could.

I slap my hands over my eyes. Dear God, why do you do this to me?

Now I can't get the thought of Remus out of my head. And what Remus might be like... down there. He has a tail and wings. But the rest of him is so human-looking.

Then again, there is another face on the other side of his head. Like a whole other... person? He called him *brother.*

I furrow my brows in thought. Does that mean there are... *two* down there too?

I shake my head and realize, yup, I'm officially feeling all that wine. At the same time, my hand creeps down my stomach, and I realize I also don't care. It's just me, myself, and I here in this room, along with my fantasies of the firm body that was inches away from me earlier while he whispered filthy things into my ear.

My fingers slip beneath the waistband of my jeans.

And further still.

My questing fingers find my curls and hesitate. Am I really going to—

But then I remember the low rumble of his voice. *I want you trembling and aching and begging me for more.*

A gasp escapes my throat as my middle finger finds my swelling clit. God, I'm already wet just thinking about him. Just remembering. A shudder goes through my body as I start to move my finger.

He said he hasn't had much experience with humans. Would he know how to be gentle with my body?

But then, he didn't push earlier when plenty of regular guys would have. And he promised never to hurt me. Plus, this is just the safety of my fantasies.

So I allow myself the space to imagine him gripping my ample ass just like he promised. Really relishing in just how much junk I've got in my trunk. Tracing his hands around my hips, squeezing me as he went.

Michael occasionally gave lip service to "not minding" that I was a bigger girl.

But the way Remus looks at me... Like I'm exactly the type of woman he prefers. I remember that beauty standards throughout the ages have been very different from our twenty-first-century ones. The appreciation and lust burning in his eyes when I left him felt so real, so *palpable*—

I twist onto my side on the bed, curling around my hand that's more urgent against my clit now.

He's strong, too. He could handle a body like mine.

Would his fingers know how to get me worked up like this? Would he be curious about how to get me wet? Are his words just empty promises, or would he put me on the bed, spread my thighs wide, and kiss down my big, soft stomach, exploring me with that wicked tongue of his?

A pleasured squeak comes from my throat at the mental image, and I bury my face in the pillow. I feel my orgasm coming far faster than when I usually touch myself. Then again, I don't typically have such striking, immediate inspiration.

I imagine Remus somewhere in the castle right now and wonder if he's thinking of me. I imagine him in his bed right now. Is he nearby?

Is he... touching himself, too?

I bite the pillow, and my fingers slip down further toward the opening of my pussy. I imagine his huge body lifting over mine.

Feeling his hardness against my flushed, wet flesh that's so, so ready for him.

Is he imagining the same thing while he clutches his hand mercilessly around himself, heart-thumping as he milks himself to the thought of thrusting inside me?

"*Remus*," I whisper-moan into the pillow and finger-fuck myself until I come.

I'm breathing so hard afterward, so awash with pleasure, I think I'll never fall asleep. But after the wild release, barely pulling my fingers out of myself to rearrange the pillow, I'm out within minutes.

Chapter Eight

REMUS

I inhale the scent of her released desire from outside her room, every muscle straining to break down the door and burst into claim her.

My nose may not be as enhanced as my brothers', but it's still far superior to any mortals. I intended to simply walk past her room like a good boy. But who am I kidding? I'm not good and never have been.

And when the scent that hit the air when I whispered in her ear suddenly saturated the hallway outside of her door, there was no way not to stop. I lean my head against the wood of her door and inhale with all my might.

Only to hear her little squeal and realize, *fuck*, she's pleasuring herself.

I'd riled her up, and she was finishing the job.

My hands clench into fists, and it takes discipline I rarely display to stay in place. I grind my teeth as Romulus threatens to burst awake and steal the moment from me. The bastard's always taking advantage of any moment of surprise or stress.

I grab the flask from my hip and take a swig.

The salty, metallic liquid barely hits my throat before I feel the zing of clearer awareness, fully awake and back in full control of my own body again. I smile because I've never wanted to be present more as I lean against the door, inhaling and listening with my enhanced senses.

I stay there all the way until she gasps my name, and an extra flood of her scent hits me like a blast.

Then I stumble back from the door, overwhelmed with need. I turn and storm away silently.

But I won't give myself the same relief. No, I want to linger at this knife's edge of arousal until she screams my name while allowing *me* to pleasure her. Not just the thought of me.

I swing back around and reach for the doorknob, close, *so close* to shoving the door open and stomping inside.

But then I remember my previous experience with human females.

That is, my nonexistent experience.

It is not as if I haven't wanted to lie with them before. But unlike many soldiers, I was always disgusted by the taking of females as plunders of war. And whores were so terrified by me, even if they'd take my coin, it immediately softened my cock.

The thought of a woman who gasps my name with pleasure instead of backing away from me in fear or disgust has me so hard. I did not shelter her from who I am, and still, she writhes at the thought of me on the other side of the door.

Silently, I press my palm to the cool wood, the rest of me all heat. She is a precious treasure, unlike any I have met.

But one must be careful with treasure, or it will break.

I must tread slowly.

As much as I hate it and as much as it is not in my nature, I must have patience.

So I turn away with a wide grin, looking forward to a long night of sleepless torture, imagining all the ways I plan to make her squeal once I break through her defenses. Because patience is a two-way street. Perhaps if I continue to tempt the fiery woman as I did tonight, I will not have to wait so long after all.

* * *

The next morning, I knock on her door, ready with beignets and coffee from Café Du Monde. She opens the door, looking so beautifully rumpled that I want all sorts of things that go against my new determination to slow things down. Don't scare the beautiful woman.

I feel hope and something else I'm not accustomed to—fear. Fear that this could so easily be fucked up.

Yes, I am a god, but I'm beginning to see that this possibility of her wanting me back is as thin as a spider's gossamer string in the dewy light of morning. Because I am also a monster, and she is delicate. So, so delicate. I do not have a history of being good with delicate things. But I will be now.

I hold up the bounty I have procured for her and delight in the way her eyes light up with surprise as she looks at the logo on the paper bag.

"Did you really get this from—?"

"A little flight to New Orleans is a good stretch in the morning."

Her eyebrows arch high as she takes the coffee from my hand and inhales the steaming brew.

"I thought you might like to take a walk by the lake today. Explore the grounds a little."

"I'm not even dressed yet."

I take my time looking her up and down. She only has her T-shirt on, her thick, curvy thighs and calves exposed.

"Hey," she says, moving behind the door. When I glance back at her face, her cheeks are flushed, but her eyes are still bright. I'm reminded of the long night I spent replaying every little noise she made and the scent of her pleasure that lingered tortuously in my nostrils.

I was glad for the long, cold flight in the early morning hours to get my body back under control.

"Thanks for breakfast. But you do realize if I'm going to actually stay here, I'll need more than just food?" Her voice is sharp, like she's trying to make up for the way my gaze affects her body.

"Anything you need, you have but to ask."

"I need clothes. And a toothbrush. You know, the basics? And I will so murder you if you bring me back size six clothes or some bullshit like that."

I frown. Hmm. I have never thought about purchasing a woman's clothing or how to go about it. But I see what she means. For all I have thought about getting myself a consort, it does turn out there were certain... practicalities I have overlooked.

But she is here, and that is all that matters.

"I can have you a complete wardrobe by tonight," I say confidently. "And anything else you need. Just make me a list."

What I have learned, no matter the era I live in, is that money can triumph over any difficulty. Whether it be gold bars, paper scripts, or these plastic cards that connect to bank accounts, wealth is always the true king. And my brothers and I have accumulated our fair share over the years.

Romulus saw the wisdom of investing our wealth in Italian banks in the early seventeenth century, the returns of which have made us one of the wealthiest, if most famously secretive, families in Europe. Romulus also arranged for a human accounting firm to be the face of the family.

But over the years, I knew Romulus had expanded interests with the investment firm, connecting to a fixer who could take on odder requests, such as when we needed new kitchen appliances and other modern conveniences delivered to an empty warehouse in a remote Finnish town, one with no video surveillance. Then Thing or Abaddon would pick them up and bring them back here.

She frowns at me from beyond the door, then closes it in my face.

I have waited for her all night. I do not mind waiting a little longer. I close my eyes, and my keen ears listen as her soft feed pad away from the door. I hear the rustle of the bag as she opens it and her little, stifled moan of pleasure as she bites into one of the beignets. Oh yes, I feel that noise all the way down my entire body. I determine at this moment to introduce her to every pleasure I can imagine. To memorize her every sensuous sigh and gasp that I can introduce her to.

I wish she had not closed the door between us and that I could see her face as she devoured the pastry. I would give away half my wealth to see the look of ecstasy that accompanied that little moan.

Patience.

I have to stifle a groan of my own. I am bad at patience. It is not one of my virtues. Not that I have many of those anyway.

A slight slurp as she sips the coffee and a bite into the pastry again with a softer sigh this time. How she tortures me. Does she know?

I breathe out.

I don't think she does. She's unconscious of how sumptuous I find her, I think. Of how much restraint I must expend every moment I'm in her presence and what punishment it feels like to have this door between us.

What feels like hours later but is probably only twenty minutes, I hear her feet pad toward the door again.

My breath catches as I step back.

Apparently, not quickly enough because when she opens the door, she gasps in surprise to see me there. "You're still here. Have you been waiting the whole time?"

I think about disseminating for a moment, then opt for the truth. "Where else would I be?"

She blinks rapidly for several moments, then looks down at the floor. This is when I notice, sadly, that she's dressed herself as she was yesterday, in the blue pants that outline her legs so deliciously.

I cannot say I am sad about these modern fashions. The pants women wear now leave both so much and so little to the imagination as they detail the entire shape of a woman's legs. I am entirely entranced by her shapely curves and again must tear my eyes away so I am not caught staring.

"Did you make a list?" I ask.

She notches her chin higher. "I did." She shoves a piece of paper toward me. I recognize it as the stationary from my desk. The ink is sloppy from my ink pot and not correctly blotted.

I note at the top of the list is modern pens and a journal. Then, a long list of items, everything from a toothbrush and toothpaste to bras and clothing items with numbers and letters beside each that I can only assume delineate sizes but may as well be gibberish to me. I trust that the human fixer will be able to decipher the code.

"Excellent," I say, waving the paper to help dry the ink before folding it and putting it in my pocket. "Now, shall we take in the grounds?" I hold out my arm to her. My demeanor is calm, but her eyes look behind me, and I realize my damn tail is giving away my happiness at having her so near, whipping back and forth in the air.

Sometimes, it has a mind of its own. With a little concentration, I manage to get control of it. It curls forward, the tip of it settling at the small of Lo-Ren's back as she takes my arm, urging her forward.

She gasps a little, looking behind her but not pulling away from the touch of my tail. Or my arm. In fact, I might say she tightens her hold of me as we head down the stairs.

We've certainly come a long way in a short while.

In no time at all, we're on the ground floor. I lead her through the large, arched dining room and push open the front of the castle door. I feel pride in leading her across the threshold, which is an unusual feeling for me. Sadistic joy, happiness at the expense of others, nihilistic rage at the pointlessness of life—those are the emotions I'm familiar with.

But this? Pride at having a beautiful woman on my arm who seems to *want* to spend time with me?

My chest feels weird and squishy, and my throat is a little choked up.

She slept in, and the mid-morning sun is dappled as it streams through the tall trees onto the lake by the castle.

"It's beautiful," she breathes out, squeezing my arm a little tighter as she tugs me forward at a quicker pace. I easily keep up with her smaller legs as she hurries toward the lake. It's summer, but the cool breeze keeps it from being hot.

I'm mesmerized by the feel of her beside me as we head to the edge of the lake.

"The water's so clear!" she exclaims, looking away from the lake for only a moment to gaze up at me in wonder. Then her eyes are back on the lake. "I didn't think water could be so clear. Look, you can see the fish swimming!"

I can only stare at her. I've seen a thousand fish in my life. But only one of *her*.

"I never imagined it would be like this," I say.

Her eyes shoot back to me and get very wide. Searching. "What do you mean?"

I feel my brow furrow. "Taking a consort. I thought I knew all the feelings there were in the world. But you make me feel things that are"—I put a hand to my chest to emphasize the strange sensations she makes me feel there—"*new*."

She cocks her head sideways. "Good new or bad new?"

"How can you ask that? You mesmerize me every moment. I never thought a human could bewitch a god, but I am completely under your spell."

Her eyes search mine, moving back and forth, and for a moment, I swear she's drawing closer, breathing in and out so deeply that her bosom heaves closer to my chest with her every inhale.

Until she suddenly yanks back and shakes her head.

"I can't be sure if you're real. If any of this is real," she exclaims. "I mean, sometimes it feels so much more real than my old life I left behind. But then you say things like that."

"Like what?" I ask, baffled.

She tosses up her hands, looking back at me. "Things that sound *too* perfect. Like something out of a movie or a romance novel."

I frown. "And this is bad?"

"No, I mean—I just don't know if it's *real*."

"I won't lie to you," I say, closing the space between us. "I'm many things, but I am not a liar. I'm telling the truth when I say I've never felt like this before."

I grab her hands and place her palms on my chest. "This is real. You are real. *I* am real."

She steps even closer as her palms press against me. "I can feel your heart beating," she whispers.

I look down at her as she lifts her face to me, and we're mere inches from each other.

"Do you feel it, too?" I ask. "This draw between us that feels like crackling lightning?"

She's close enough that I can feel it when she trembles. "Yes," she whispers.

Fuck patience.

I bend down and press my lips to hers.

She gasps into my mouth, so soft and sweet.

I feel a spark light inside my entire body. Lust and the need to devour her. This is what it must be like when the gods strike you with lightning.

I cup her jaw, my hands moving to tangle in her thick hair as I kiss her more deeply. Her mouth opens to mine and though I am not capable of it, I swear I die in that moment as I'm swept away in her sweetness.

How can the mating of mouths feel *this* good?

One of her hands is still pressed against my racing heart, while the other grabs the waist of my pants. I grow stiff and hard as I pull her in closer.

She groans into my mouth, fingers fisting against my bare stomach and the worn leather of my pants.

I want to mate her. I want to bear her down to the soft grasses and fuck her sweet cunt so, so badly. I want to tear open my pants and release my stiff cock—

My tail whips restlessly in the air behind me. Gods of the Great Hall, I want it so badly.

I want it so badly... and *yet*.

My hand still in her hair, I tug away from her questing mouth.

She lets out a little protesting moan. And I want to bring her back into me even more.

She's blinking, and for a moment, our eyes search each other. Her lips are berry pink from our kisses. And more than anything, I want her to trust me. To know that all I want is her pleasure.

"May I explore your body?"

Her mouth drops open. "I—W-what?"

"I want to free you from these clothes and explore every inch of your body with my tongue and lips."

"O-oh." She pauses in silence, breaths coming quickly.

Have I pressed for too much, too fast? Dammit, I was supposed to have patience. But before I can withdraw my request, she looks around as if to ensure we are alone and then pulls her shirt over her head.

I grin, awash with a flush of joy at every new inch of her flesh that is exposed to me. But she is not nearly bare to me yet. Another contraption covers her voluptuous breasts, soft mountains that I immediately want to cover with my hands.

She sees where my eyes are. "D-do you want me to take my bra off?"

I swallow and meet her gaze. *Patience*. "I want what you want," I say low, stepping closer to her and dropping my lips to the soft skin of her shoulder.

How, *how*, can skin be so soft? I inhale her, and she shudders as I skim my lips over to her collarbone.

"Holy shit," she whispers low. "How can you make me feel like this when you're barely even touching me? Usually I don't let anyone touch me without the lights off. But you make me feel..."

She's trembling and so warm. Her arms twist around behind her, and the thick cloth securing her breasts suddenly loosens.

I pull back slightly in surprise as she slides the straps down her arms.

I'm transfixed as the cups drop away from her ample chest, and all the air blasts out of my lungs when her huge, swinging teats are revealed.

Immediately, my hands take the place of the cloth cups. She's so deliciously heavy in my hands. Heavy but soft at the same time, so round and full.

"I know they aren't the perkiest," she says, eyes down.

"They're perfect," I breathe out, my voice husky from trying to hold back my wild lust. "I can't imagine any more perfect."

I move around behind her back so that my hands can cup her fully, my thumbs and fingertips toying with the pebbled nipples that peak her perfect, full breasts as I embrace her. I've never touched anything more womanly, and I've never felt more male.

My cock is fully hard in my pants, and she can't help but feel it jamming into her equally ample ass as I nestle my lips against the nape of her neck and start laying kisses there. Apparently, she doesn't mind because she presses her round ass back against me, delighting in how she affects me.

She pulls her long hair to the side so I have better access to her neck.

Ahhhh, yes. To have a female delighting in *my* touch... it's headier than any alcohol or drug I've ever tried. The way she gives herself to me...

My teeth nibble her flesh, and she whines, a little high-pitched needy noise that's so exquisite, I want to live in this moment forever.

"Remus," she whispers. "Remus."

And then she flips around to face me and throws her arms around my neck. At first, I'm surprised and worried about her hands making contact with Romulus. But my hood stays in place, and her fevered eyes are only on me as she lunges forward, bare breasts pressed to my chest as she kisses me.

In this moment, there is only her and I.

I'm allowed what I've never been allowed before. To simply be myself, taking what I want.

And all I want is her.

I welcome her embrace, though I do redirect her arms to my waist, where I feel more comfortable. She secures her arms to me and tugs me in so close her soft bosoms smush against my chest. The feel of her flesh against my flesh—*fuck*—and then her lips are on mine again.

It's not like before. Not gentle, fleeting kisses, me pulling passion from her.

No. Her passion is wild as she kisses me. Her lips and tongue seek and take, and now we devour each other with the same passion. She will drive me wild. She will drive me beyond control.

My hands want to be everywhere exploring her. Memorizing the moment and her curves. The feel of her against me. I massage down her shoulders to her waist, where I squeeze her, then I get to her hips.

And encounter her pants.

I pull away from her lips only long enough to demand, "I want to see *all* of you. As you *are*."

She nods, immediately knowing what I mean, and together, our hands fumble to get down her stretchy coverings, peeling them off and revealing the acres of gorgeous, creamy flesh I but glimpsed last night.

I twist and take us down to the ground, flapping my wings once so that we have a smooth, soft landing. She squeals in surprise as I lay us down, one of my soft, feathered wings beneath her as an extra layer of softness between her and the grassy ground.

And then, starting at her ankle, I begin to kiss up her skin.

As if to entice me even more, her skin becomes softer as I kiss up to her knee, then softer still once I make it to her thighs.

I'm so attuned to her that I hear her intake of breath, a sharp contrast to the warm summer breeze blowing against our skin and my feathers.

At first, her legs are locked tightly together. So I kiss right up the seam of them. As her little sighs continue, her legs begin to relax, and I massage up her calves and pause at the sweet flesh above her knees.

She's so achingly soft. Though she still has the flimsy fabric covering her sex, her scent is strong and intoxicating up close. I open my mouth as I kiss her thigh, sucking and scraping my teeth just the barest bit over her soft skin.

She shudders beneath me. I feel her everywhere. Even the denser nerves in my wing she lays upon light up at the feel of her responsive movements. I suckle her skin ever more hungrily, and her hands come to my shoulders, fingernails digging in. Urging me upwards as her legs relax open.

I want to rip the fabric away from her sex. Looking up, I see a large wet spot, and her scent is heavier in the air.

I lift up from between her thighs.

"I want to taste you here," I growl.

She looks down at me, and for one second, her breath hitches. But then she nods frantically. "Yes, please. I want that, too."

I grin wide and then, using my hands and teeth, tear away the lacy fabric separating me from her mysteries. She shrieks a little but only widens her legs further.

And then I'm there, breathing over her glistening pink sex, hungering like a wolf to devour her.

First, I inhale, for once feeling a modicum of the patience I pretend to possess.

But only because when it comes to this perfect pleasure, I will not rush. No, I will not rush my first taste of this finest wine.

I lick straight up the center of her. Which makes her quiver and almost knocks me over with the wild, feral scent of her.

When she doesn't immediately begin to squeal the little mewls like I heard through her door last night, I intuit that I must learn the ways to touch her. So I lift a hand experimentally, tentatively touching the flushed, pink folds of flesh.

She curves her body in toward me. As if she's shy. But her hips also move. Seeking.

I've never been tentative in my life, so I make my fingers bolder, pressing my palm against her flushed sex and exploring with multiple fingers.

I can't quite tell what I'm touching just by feel. But I know when she starts to respond to me, and I feel little nubbins amongst the softer, moist flesh. When I rub, she begins to make noises, and her hips move even more. Oh, I like that. I like that quite a lot.

Trying to memorize where my fingers are, I keep moving them and rubbing her, desperately ignoring my own shaft pulsing achingly in my pants. More of her scent perfumes the air.

I must have my mouth on her. I must taste the scent that's been torturing me.

Finally, I drop my head between her legs, and she opens wider still to me, welcoming me in.

I lift my finger from the upper part of her sex, where I was rubbing a nubbin of nerves that seems to have her quite excited and replace it with my mouth.

If I thought she was excited before—

Her legs immediately lock around the back of my neck when my mouth closes over her there, and I start sucking. She tastes delicious, and I cannot believe she's actually allowing me to suckle her in this bare, intimate place at the center of her. It's so animal and intimate at the same time.

I grasp her ass and pry her open wider to me as I get acquainted with her, laid before me like a feast.

I am not a proper man, and I do not know if there is a proper way to do this. All I know is that now that I have my consort in this position, and she is enthusiastic to be here, I want her to be encouraged to come back for more. And more, and more, and more.

I leave one of my fingers in between her legs and continue to explore. With her legs locked around my head like this, her sex is amazingly open to me.

I always knew females had an opening here; I'm not a complete fool about the mechanics of how sex works. But to press my forefinger all along her drenched entrance while I suckle at her bundle. . . I'm amazed at the way she starts to go wild all around me. Especially when I slip my finger inside her—oh fuck, *inside her*—and pull back against the upper ridge of her pubic bone. . . Then I tug back against my mouth, where I lick and kiss and tongue her—

She screams. And I mean screams so loud I almost let her go, except her nails are digging into my shoulder and her hips buck against my face in a way that makes me think the scream is a good thing. So I keep going. And the scream rides up the scale to an octave I'm not sure many mortals would even be able to hear.

She bucks and bucks against my mouth until she finally goes still, that high-pitched whine still coming from her throat.

Then, she collapses against the grass, only the tip of my wing beneath her now because we were both so vehement in what we were just doing.

She breathes hard like she just ran up all the flights of stairs and back down again at once. Several spasms rock her entire body, which has otherwise gone slack, one of her legs falling down from around my neck, the other remaining there haphazardly.

I smile wide and lick my lips, savoring in her juices.

"Holy shit," she finally breathes out, her other leg sliding off me. I catch it just in time and help lay it gently to the ground.

Her chest rises and falls, her bottom still beautifully bared. Her flushed sex winks at me from between her legs.

"Holy shit," she says again, breathily. "I didn't expect that."

"I cannot say that I did either," I chuckle, laying down beside her and cradling her to me.

She blinks shyly up at me and then buries her face in my chest. "I can't believe we just did that." She covers her face with her hands.

I frown down at her. "Why do you hide yourself?"

I reach down and lift her leg so that she wraps herself around my hip. Torture to my stiff cock but also everything I've ever wanted, even if I didn't quite know it until this moment. She comes willingly, snuggling her body around me like a blanket. But she keeps her face covered.

"Lo-Ren. Why do you hide your face? May I not see you after the pleasure we shared?"

She drops her hands but just smooshes her face against my bare chest instead. "I've just—No one's ever—" She shakes her head and buries her face tighter against me.

I blink in confusion at her half-sentences and run my fingers through her hair. "What do you mean, sweet consort? Speak with me."

She sucks in a deep breath and exhales against my sternum. Still not looking up at me, at least she speaks. "It's never felt so *good*. No one's ever made me feel like this before."

I grin over her head and wrap my arms around her to pull her more tightly against me. "I have only begun to make you feel good things, Lo-Ren."

I feel the shudder that goes through her body at my words, and a deep quake of happiness resonates inside me. Though my lust is still high and unquenched, this feels perfect, just as it is.

Holding my Lo-Ren in the summer breeze by the lake, under the shade of the tall pines. I may not be able to travel to the other realms like my brother Kharon, but I now know what paradise is.

Chapter Nine

LAUREN

Can life actually change this fast? All that day and the next continue to be so amazing. We spend them talking. Eating. He shows me an amazing bath with tons of jets and leaves me to lounge. He gives me time alone that night, not pushing even after what happened by the lake.

He ordered me what feels like a whole wardrobe of clothes that he flies in along with dinner the following day, designer fashions that I'm shocked by. It's all the things I asked for and much, much more, and I do a little fashion show for him because it's so exciting to try everything on. Everything fits exquisitely, even though I didn't think some of these companies made things in my size. How did he have them tailored to my measurements *that* quickly? The expense must have been insane, but I can't deny that it feels amazing parading around in a silky Yves Saint Laurent nightgown while we stay up all night talking.

We talk about everything. Well, almost everything. He tells me about his brothers, Abaddon and Kharon—who apparently used to be named *Thing*—and about their consorts. Abaddon's just had a daughter who's got wings and tiny little horns like her father and to hear Remus tell it, is an adorable little hellion.

He tells me about his cruel father and how they've all just really started to be a family again. He tells me about his youngest brother, Layden, who recently returned after they thought him dead.

He tells me about everyone in his world except the twin on the back of his head.

"Why won't you talk about him?"

"He doesn't matter." Remus waves a dismissive hand.

I make a face. Outside, the sun is just coming up. We've talked all night *again*. Just talked, even though, with the way he's sitting so close to me on the bed, I've been secretly going nuts, replaying his mouth on me by the lake about every other second. Which is why I feel tired but also punch-drunk with lust as we continue *talking*. Plus, I'm way too fascinated with everything coming out of his mouth to pay attention to my heavy eyelids. "He must have mattered at some point. He's part of you."

He just shakes his head. "All that matters is right here." He holds me tighter, his dark eyes searching mine. "You. Me." He drags his hand down the line of my hip and tugs me closer to him. "*This*."

"What?" I roll my eyes, hiding an internal shiver. It doesn't help that he always walks around without a shirt to display his six-pack abs. "Sex?"

"No." He shakes his head. "This closeness between us. I've never known this before, and it's all I want. I want to live in this space, just me and you."

"But there's a whole world out there, and it's going to come knocking at some point."

His lips drop down to brush against mine as he says, "But not right now."

And I easily give into him as he begins drugging me with kisses, nibbling on my bottom lip as he massages my waist with his strong, sure fingers. Dragging me into him as we lay down sideways on the pillows, facing each other. My leg lifts to wrap around his hip, and his wing sweeps over me, cocooning us. My heartbeat starts to race, and suddenly, I don't feel the least bit tired.

Maybe he's right. Maybe the rest of the world can just disappear for a little while longer.

Maybe there can be just me and him. And *this*.

God, I want this to be real and not just the escape I'd hoped for. I want this to *last*. I want the realness. I'm starting to not just want to escape but an actual life here. A real life. *This* life, with this person, the little bits he shows of me at a time.

All the good things I'm feeling and the endorphins swimming around my body feel intoxicating as Remus holds me. He's always finding a way to touch me. While we go for walks, or while I was baking cookies yesterday after the lake. I mean, sure, it's great that he can get fine cuisine from anywhere in the world, but a kitchen that nice deserves to be cooked in. And I love baking; I've always found it relaxing.

This morning, he asked if I trusted him, and when I said yes, he took me flying.

I immediately backed away, but he laughed and reminded me that I said I trusted him. "I'll go slow," he said, "so you can really *see*."

It *was* different. He held me to him just as tightly, and his tail wrapped around me for security. His wings were like a paraglider above as we coasted over the most beautiful countryside. The greens of the trees were so green, the sky so blue. The lake below glittered like a sapphire.

My breath was taken away by the magical experience—and by the terrifying heights—but strangely enough, I *did* trust him, even after knowing him for such a short time.

When we dropped back down to the earth, and my feet hit the ground, I still shyly clutched his arm as we walked back to the castle.

These last few days have been like the most amazing extended date. I can't explain it. It feels like I've known him forever, even though I just met him, and our worlds couldn't be further apart.

And maybe because of that closeness, I want to leap on him and take him back to the ground every other moment. I want to explore his body the way he did mine by the lake and ask him a thousand questions. I want to understand his mind and see if any of the things I'm thinking about him are real or just a wild romantic figment of my imagination.

Because more than anything, I want him to be real. I want *this* to be real. Which is probably just wishful thinking.

"You are quiet," he says, breaking the long silence between us as his wings drop, allowing the rest of the world back in. The sunrise turns a brighter pink through the window behind him. "What is happening inside your head?"

I laugh and drop my head bashfully. At the same time, I'm very aware of my leg around his hip, opening myself to him.

"Well, actually, I was sort of wondering the same thing. What we did by the lake. . . and just all of this. Getting to know you. This has all been a really intense experience. I'm wondering. . . who you are."

He frowns in confusion. "I've told you and shown you. I'm Remus, god-born from the life spark stolen from the Great Hall—"

"No," I laugh. "I mean, I'm starting to get that. Not that I can really wrap my head around it, but I get it. I'm talking about who you are." Suddenly self-conscious, I pull my leg back, pressing my hand to his chest instead. He captures it, holding it there. I try to keep breathing as I continue, "On the *inside*. Who is Remus? What kind of person are you?"

He frowns again. "No one's ever asked me that. I have only been myself. Brother to my brothers."

"Who would they say you are?"

I flip my hand to take his hand. He looks down at our hands in surprise, and I almost pull mine back, embarrassed, but then he squeezes it before I can.

He moves close so that there's barely any space between us on the bed. I can feel the heat of his hard body. When I dare to glance up at his face, I don't miss the smile there, smaller than the wild grin he sometimes has. As if he looks... contented. At least until he begins to speak about his brothers.

"My brothers might not have the kindest words to say about me." He winces, pulling back again. I'm both frustrated and enticed by what feels like a tug-of-war between us. We've been so close all night, but just when I think he's about to make a move, he doesn't. "Battle was the only language our father understood. Brothers fight, naturally. And our father thought we could only become the best if we fought the best—which was each other. Our epic battles could span days, weeks, months, even in the worst cases, and destroy huge swaths of land before our father finally declared a victor."

"Months? Just fighting each other?"

He nods as if it's the most ordinary thing in the world. "Lately, it has been different. We have been... more friendly. But that's new. We're all very strong in different ways. And our father was very demanding." His mouth twists down.

"But what about when you weren't fighting. What was your family like, then?"

He frowns down at me, as if he doesn't understand my question. "All I've known is war."

"Is that... what you *want*?" Some of the nice feelings in my belly start to fade, and I let go of his hand.

His eyebrows draw together and he immediately reaches to take back my hand, interlacing our fingers in between our chests. Does he notice I'm breathing heavier, my breasts all but busting out of the lace-topped nightgown as we face each other on the bed?

"I want *you*." His eyes glance toward the window. "The world, it seems, has changed. Perhaps my brothers and I are no longer needed. Perhaps it is time for softer things. For consorts and. . ." His face scrunches up as he makes a face. "*Peace*."

I laugh. "Don't look so disgusted by the thought of peace. It's nice when things are quiet." I toy with his hand, my fingers playing with his in the small space between us.

He shrugs, still looking a little disappointed. "I was made for war. I wouldn't know what to do with myself during peace."

"Well, when were you last in battle?"

"It's been well over two hundred years," he says a little wistfully.

"What have you been doing since then?"

"My brothers and I have been having a long dispute."

"For two hundred years?" I ask, shocked.

He shrugs.

"If you destroyed a bunch of land when you fought for months, what happens when you fight for two hundred *years*?"

"It wasn't a fair fight because my brothers locked me in the dungeon for most of it. I've only recently been freed."

My jaw drops. "Are you joking?" How did he tell me all about his brothers yet leave this little bit of the history out?

He looks at me and laughs, his fingers toying with mine again. "Don't look so shocked, little consort. We are brutes and don't pretend to be anything else. But my eldest brother was tamed by his consort, who convinced him to let me out."

I cock an eyebrow, entirely unsettled and also fascinated by this conversation. "Is that my job? To tame you?" I reach a finger out and run it across his eyebrow, the liquid feeling in my belly heating up again. How have we been on this bed for so long without him making a move on me? Does he not want to? I retract my hand.

He shoots me a sideways glance, and that wide, wicked grin slides over his face. "You couldn't tame me if you tried." He tugs me against him by my waist, his dark eyes burning down into mine. "I've tried to give you time, but I hunger for you. May I again lick you until you shudder all over my face?"

Well, it's good to know I'm not the only one who's been thinking about it.

My sex contracts at his words and the hardness I suddenly feel pressing into my belly. Does he only want to lick me again, or will there be more? It feels like we've had days and days of foreplay, and I'm already so on edge.

I bite my bottom lip so I don't beg for him to *fuck me, god yes, fuck me!*

"You are so beautiful," he exhales, running the fingers of his left hand through the slight tangle of dark hair at my temple.

I frown. *He's just telling you what you want to hear so he can fuck you.* Dammit, I hate the old voices in my head. I want him to fuck me! But when those old wounds get triggered...

"What is this?" I breathe out as he presses his hips against me. Hard. "What are we doing?"

We've talked so platonically all night and all of yesterday and yesterday night that I wondered if I imagined what he did to me at the lake.

"Isn't it obvious?" he asks, leaning down to kiss me. Finally, oh god, *finally*. He's so huge he blocks out all the new morning light.

"What do you mean? What's obvious? That you want to fuck me?" I bite out. I don't know if I ask the question belligerently because I'm suddenly freaked out by the proposed intimacy or because I feel like he's been luring me into a false sense of comfort with all this *talking*. It's probably just all my old insecurities flaring. I want him so, so bad I'm thrumming with the need, but I'm also terrified of being taken advantage of again.

Remus glowers at me. "No. Not fucking you."

I can't help a little thrill from running down my spine at him even uttering the words. "What, then?" I gasp.

He's all but on top, hovering over me, wings flaring again to block out most of the light so that we're in shadow. If I didn't trust him so much, I'd be intimidated.

I do, don't I? Trust him?

I suck in a quick breath.

"This," he says in a low, growling breath, "is me and you. Nothing more, nothing less." He lowers his body to skim his chest against mine. "Nothing happens here that you don't want." He swoops down so that I can feel the warmth of his next words right over the tip of the thin, silky nightgown covering my breasts.

"But also, whatever you want *can* happen. If you want my tongue to explore slowly, oh so achingly slowly, every curve and crevice of your body, that's certainly what I want. If you want to be massaged and licked, inside and out, that, my dear, is what I had in mind when I sat down on this bed with you last night. It's been in the back of my mind the entire time we've talked of other things because the scent from between your legs drives me mad with want. What do you think about that?"

I think some sort of incoherent high-pitched noise comes from the back of my throat in answer.

I nod and flip over so that my stomach faces the mattress. "Sure. A massage sounds great."

I hear a chuckle from above me. "A massage, eh? That's what you choose from the menu I proffered?"

Being facedown and not having to look him in the face might give me a tad more hutzpah because I dare to say airily, "A massage to start with, anyway. I've had a very trying few days being yanked all through the air this way and that."

"Oh, you have, have you?"

I shrug. "You're the one going around offering massages."

I'm not ready for how close his lips are when they suddenly whisper behind my left ear. "Any excuse to get my hands on you, little consort. Will you take off your coverings for me? I want to see you."

I slip the small straps of my nightgown off over my shoulders, and he drags it down my back until it gathers at my waist. At first, I think he'll stop there. But no. He demands, "Up," and I lift my hips.

Then his big, cool hands drag the silk down my bare ass. I enjoy his hiss of surprise at the fact that I'm not wearing any underwear before he's got the fabric down my upper thighs and slipped off my legs completely.

I'm absolutely naked, face down on the bed. My fingers fist in the fabric. Just a massage. Right. I only want a massage. Excitement gathers in my belly.

His big, cool hands come back to my shoulders, slightly wet with some kind of sweet-smelling oil. He doesn't do any usual massage I've ever had before. Using his palms, he just starts to rub. He's at my shoulders, but somehow the massage is already sensuous. I don't know how to describe it, except maybe in the way he digs in his fingers, trailing at the end after his palm has dug into my muscles. Deep, too. He's not just playing on the surface.

He's getting *real* acquainted with my body. And then there's the way I can see it clearly affecting him. He's not an impersonal masseuse at a spa. I turn my head to watch as his whole body bends over me, his soft fingers digging in and rolling. The concentration on his face, along with the pressure of his knowing hands—*damn*.

I about come from that alone. Especially when he works his way to my lower back, deeply grasping onto my hips like he's a moment away from flipping me and riding me hard.

When he lifts to get more oil on his hands, I take a huge breath and flip onto my back. I want to cover my eyes, but I'm trying to be strong. I'm trying to be better than the girl who fled her cheating boyfriend and allowed herself to believe it was *her fault* because she wasn't pretty enough. I want to be all that I am and be her proudly.

So I bare my breasts, and I don't cover my eyes, and I at least pretend that I'm proud and believe that I'm as beautiful as he proclaims I am, even if half of me is horrified he'll run or say something beneath his breath that will break my heart. I try to remind myself that he seemed to like what he saw the other day at the lake. But insecurities war with my attempt at reasoning. At the lake, I was being wild and spontaneous. Here, there's far too much time to think.

He gets rid of the excess oil on a cloth on the nightstand. Then, reverently, eyes on mine as if checking in to make sure I'm still with him, he hovers there without touching.

I nod even as I hold my breath.

But then he cups both of my breasts, hefting them in his palms as if to feel their full weight and shape.

"They're real," I say, then feel stupid for saying it. If there's one thing I'm proud of, it's my big, round boobs. Silly, since the only reason they're so big is because *all* of me is so big. But hey, I've always claimed they're my best feature, and assholes have liked them in the past.

"They're glorious," Remus says, holding them fully in his hands and kissing each nipple carefully.

But then he completely bypasses them and starts massaging down my stomach to one of my fat rolls.

"What are you doing?" I squeal, sitting up and unconsciously covering my breasts.

He looks confused. "Worshipping and massaging every inch of your glorious flesh."

My mouth drops open, appalled. "Well, not *there*."

Remus's eyes look down my stomach, the last place I want him looking, and I let go of my boobs, all but doubling over to keep him from zeroing in on what I look like. "Stop it! Don't look at me there!"

Remus's eyes come back to mine, completely bewildered. "Why not?"

"Because," I sputter, reaching over and dragging the sheet up over myself. "That's not a pretty part of a woman. Go out into the hallway while I put my nightgown back on."

"Wait. Why can't I look at you there? It is as beautiful as every other part of you."

"Don't be ridiculous," I say. "Don't be a liar."

He sits up straight. "No one accuses me of being a liar. Not even you."

"You need to be more sensitive!"

"Why do you cover yourself and not believe me when I try to worship your beautiful body?"

Which is when I burst into tears.

"Lo-Ren!" he exclaims in shock, moving up the bed. He reaches out for me, but I twist away, giving him my back and curling away from him. I wait for him to leave. Michael hated it when I cried and would disappear until I got myself together. That will be good. I liked the way Remus was looking at me before he—

I cry even harder, putting my hands to my face as if I can hide even more. If I can just have a moment—

That's when one of Remus's strong, firm arms curls around my waist from behind. He's climbed into bed at my back, and for a long moment, he just holds me. I cry harder, tensing. But then I relax back into his body.

When he bends his forehead to the back of my neck, I hiccup and grab his arm, squeezing him tight as he holds me. He's surrounding me, and I feel so safe.

Finally, he speaks. "Tears mean you hurt. I did not mean to hurt Lo-Ren. I often saw my father's consort cry. I swore I would not hurt you, and yet I have made you cry."

I shake my head and twist in his arms to face him. His words pierce my chest.

His arm curled around my waist holds me tight, and our heads are close on the pillows as we gaze into one another's eyes.

"It's not you. It's a lifetime of other people's actions that hurt me," I whisper.

He scowls and then demands, "Who? I will punish them."

I laugh and press my face to his chest, essentially wiping my tears off on him before pulling back and looking into his searching eyes again.

"There are too many to count. Society. Mean girls at school growing up. My mother."

He nods at this, understanding coming into his eyes. "Parents can be cruel."

"I mean, I know somewhere deep down she loves me." I roll my eyes. "Deep, deep down."

He shrugs. "This hurt is unforgivable. You are *perfect*." He says this last bit vehemently. "But you just tell me wherever you would like me to touch you and not touch you, and I will listen to you. I do not want to resurrect old hurts."

How? How does a man from a world so different from mine still know the perfect thing to say? Because, unlike other guys I've known, his words aren't rehearsed lines. He seems to be discovering this as he goes, so genuinely. And it means everything, this connection growing between us.

With my free hand, I reach out and trace down his arm from his shoulder to where he hugs me at my waist, right below my breasts. With a deep inhale, I reach for his hand and tug it down so that he's touching my lower belly.

He smiles so sweetly, his dark eyes searching mine. His hand begins massaging me there, and for a moment, I'm appalled. But then I breathe in and out and focus on the feel of his touch.

His every movement is so sensual as he kneads my body. Digging in with his palm and then his fingers tugging backward needily. Especially as he moves around toward my hips and ass.

His very *touch* makes me feel beautiful and wanted and desirable. I believe he's telling the truth when he calls me beautiful because of the look in his eyes and the need in his fingertips. A little groan escapes my lips. Because I need him, too. The feelings that had been doused are roaring back to life between my legs.

Without thinking about what I'm doing, and for once giving into the feelings in my body, I lift a leg to wrap around his hip and pull him into me. It was playful when I did this earlier. But now, it's with purpose. I feel his hardness there within his pants: thick, long, stiff, *pulsing*. Further proof of his desire for me.

Another noise comes from my throat, higher-pitched. Oh my god, I want him so badly. He makes my whole body go liquid.

He palms my ass with his huge hands and starts to massage it. Roughly. Needily. I arch my hips up against him, so satisfied when I get a short, needy little grunt out of him.

"I want you," I gasp, leaning up to kiss him.

He kisses me passionately. I can feel his need, his teeth nipping at my bottom lip before he suckles it, and then his tongue toys with mine.

I pull away, gasping, my hands squeezing his waist as I arch my core against his hardness again and look into his lust-clouded eyes.

"I want you," I repeat. And just in case that wasn't enough clarification. "I want you *inside* me."

Chapter Ten

REMUS

I freeze at her words. Does she truly mean it? Is she ready to mate? But then, as if hearing my unspoken question, she reaches between us for the button of my pants. She seems to struggle with the button, though, and I am no fool. My cock has been straining so long against my leathers. I reach down eagerly to help her.

I am only sad her glorious hips pull back to give us space to work the line of buttons, especially difficult because of my swollen member. She giggles, and it is such a musical, sexy sound. Every bit of her drives me to the point of being undone. I only dreamed of what it might mean to have a consort, and still, I could never have dreamed up Lo-Ren.

Finally, my buttons are undone, and I am not sure what to do next. But Lo-Ren, my glorious, gorgeous Lo-Ren, boldly reaches down.

I hiss as her fingers close around my shaft, tugging me free from my soft leather pants. Her eyes widen as she pulls me out, and for a moment, I fear I am too different from what she is used to. "Am I... normal to you?"

She squeezes me harder, her leg coming back around me so her moist warmth cradles the tip of me. "You're *perfect*."

Her curled hand moves up and down my shaft, and I jerk in her hand, feeling light burst outward from my spine in a manner that takes my breath away. Behind me, I feel my tail start to whip back and forth furiously. She giggles again and bites her bottom lip.

Is she nervous? My own heart pounds in my ears. I want to recapture her trust in case it is wavering.

I lift my hand to cradle her jaw. "Beautiful Lo-Ren, my Lo-Ren. Are you here with me?"

Tentatively, her eyes lift to mine, and I see her soften. She nods. "I'm with you," she breathes out. "I want to be with you in every way."

Eyes locked, still holding my shaft, she positions me so that my tip nestles against her drenched, tight little opening.

We both react at the contact. I gasp, and she shudders, shuffling closer so that I slip a little ways in. Her body grips around me, holding me and inviting me. My cock stiffens even harder, a thing I wouldn't have thought possible.

Her brown eyes seem greener now, with little flecks of gold, as she looks at me with such trust and glowing need. I want to answer her need with my own. I want to satisfy her and discover this intimacy and wild, giddy pleasure between us.

As if of one mind, our hips shift, hers widening to allow me in further, right as I'm seeking entry.

"Fuck," she hisses out, "you feel so good inside me."

My fingers clutch at the back of her skull with need as my cock stretches inside her tight little pussy. I imagined a thousand things about what sex might feel like. Usually quick, horny scenarios involving careless whores over the centuries, even though I never could bring myself to go through with it, picturing the disgust in their eyes after they accepted my coin. I imagined the way they would laugh to their fellows as they retold the story of the misshapen monster they'd charged extra to fuck that night.

I never thought consummation could feel like this—so natural and with such connection to the woman receiving me. It's overwhelming as she gasps, her face straining in pleasure as her fingers scrabble at my waist, tugging me to her like she wants even more of me.

I feel like I'm splitting her open, even as wet as she is. I pull back and thrust forward, and she moans in pleasure. So I do it again and —*Fuck*, that feels *so* good.

I grit my teeth with pleasure. Then I stretch my neck, my whole body clenching tight as my cock fills to bursting with my next thrust.

Which is when I realize that, dammit, this pleasure has me on the edge of losing control.

I shake my head to gather my senses. No. No. Not now. I can't lose control to my twin brother now. This moment is mine.

She is *mine*.

I ignore my worry and open my eyes, focusing on Lo-Ren. My Lo-Ren.

I blink and kiss her again, drowning myself in her taste and our connection. This is *ours*. Hers and mine. No one can take it. Not even *him*.

I shift us, rolling so that she's on her back.

"Yes," she moans, rolling with me and opening her legs even wider. Surrendering even as she puts one hand on my ass, pulling me into her. Her hand travels further and finds my tail. She doesn't even hesitate. Her hand wraps around the base of it, and she tugs, just like she did on my shaft.

It drives me mad, making me thrust in with less delicacy, which makes her moan beneath me even louder. She's so tight. So fucking tight, clenching all around my cock. I never imagined—

"Oh," she cries with my every thrust. "Oh, oh, *oh*," each one higher pitched than the last. "Yes. God. There. Right there."

She tightens around my cock and, with the hand not squeezing my tail, squeezes her own lush breast. She's the most astonishing, sexy sight beneath me as our bodies come together and apart.

But I want more. I want closer. I grind my teeth against the pleasure threatening to light up my spine and the pressure in my balls.

I won't let go. Can't let go.

I bend my body over hers, elbows on either side of her, and I clutch her jaw with one hand, forcing her to look into my eyes. She's been a little lost in her pleasure, but both of us come back to one another. Even as she continues to quake below me, her mouth open in shocked pleasure, her eyes wide and wild.

"I claim this body," I whisper, my entire body straining as I mate her slowly, intentionally. A torturous thrusting in and out so that both of us can feel the entire path of my cock as I drag in and out against her plump, swollen flesh.

She spasms around me, the highest-pitched squeal coming out of her throat as she reaches her climax, her hips thrusting up and down against me spasmodically.

I continue to hold her face in my hands, clenching more than ever. "You and I will be one forever."

She nods, tears of pleasure flooding her eyes as she arches into me, fingernails digging into my waist and tail. "Forever," she squeals before her eyes close, and she begins to shake uncontrollably with her climax.

I can no longer keep my control. *I'll be able to stay with her*, I tell myself as I lose the last shred of my grip. The pull between us is strong enough. *For once, I'll be able to stay.*

In a flood, I hold tight to her, memorizing her face as the force of my own peak slams through my body.

I feel it. For an instant, I feel every inch of the pleasure and connection. I see her pleasure-flooded eyes as she opens them, and we share it. We are together in the most intense moment two beings can share, like an eclipsing sun.

I feel the light of heaven, of wholeness, and for the first time in my life, I know true peace.

And in the very next moment, it's all yanked away as darkness falls, the heavy shade of sleep taking me as my brother swings in to replace me.

I only have the briefest fraction of a second to feel the horror of all I haven't said to my beloved before there's only darkness, and I feel nothing at all.

Chapter Eleven

ROMULUS

Twisting back into consciousness is always a little disconcerting, but no transition has ever been as shocking as this one. I mean, I'm used to picking up after my brother's messes, but—

I'm on top of a beautiful woman, and we're—

I pull out of her tight cunny and shudder with another hit of my body's release, even as I know how wrong it is.

The woman scrambles back and yanks her covers up over herself.

"Holy shit, who are you?" I ask, leaping off the bed. And wondering exactly what the hell my brother has gotten me into now.

"He said you'd never wake up!" she cries.

He said *what?* I snatch my pants from the floor and yank them on.

I briefly close my eyes and search our shared memory to find out what the hell my brother's been up to, but it's... blank. Wait. That's not possible. It shouldn't be possible.

"Bring him back!" she shrieks.

My eyes pop back open. "It doesn't work like that. What did he tell you? I'm Romulus. Did he tell you about me? Who even *are* you? How did you get here?"

The sheet of the bed tightly wrapped underneath her arms, she breathes out hard, fluffing some of the dark chestnut hair out of her face. She scoots up until her back is against the headboard and takes a moment to rearrange a pillow.

"How could you— How could he— How could he just leave like that?" she says, obviously very upset. "When we were in the middle of—"

She tugs the sheet tighter around herself.

I sigh, dragging a hand down my face and shuddering. Because *fuck*, I can still feel the aftereffects of what my brother's just been up to with this body. It's a line we've never, ever crossed before. For good reason.

I thought he and I had an unspoken agreement. Obviously, worst case scenario, swapping midway would be upsetting to whatever partner we might have. But apparently, after being locked up for two hundred years, Remus decided it was time to get his jollies off.

"Where did he even find you?" I ask. I glance around. "Look, I'm sorry if he didn't fully explain all this." I gesture to the dual faces of our head. "If you just tell me how much he owes you, I'll take you back to wherever you're from—"

Her mouth drops open. "How much he *owes* me? You think I'm a —" She hisses out, and she might as well be breathing fire. I can only look at her in confusion. Wait, is she not a prostitute?

I hold up a hand. "Just wait a moment."

I try harder to seek the memories of what has happened during my sleep. I frown, eyes closed, really trying. But again, there is nothing. My eyes pop back open to see the woman furiously pulling a nightgown over her head.

"Maybe he wouldn't talk about you because you're such an asshole," she mutters under her breath.

My mouth drops open. Is she kidding? Everyone knows I'm the *good* one. "What lies has he told you?" I demand.

She spins around to me. "Remus never lied to me once."

I scoff at that. "He obviously didn't tell you about me."

"I knew you were there. Just sleeping."

"I never sleep for long. We swap back and forth all the time. You couldn't have spent much time with my brother. So you'll forgive my assumptions." I glance toward the bed. "But I can't imagine anyone who wasn't getting paid for the effort sleeping with him after only knowing him at most a few hours."

Again, she looks furious. "I've known him for—" She looks pissed, but her cheeks also get pink. "Three days. But they've been a really long, intimate, intense three days."

I frown. "Three days." I shake my head. "That's not possible." I mean, there was once a tense forty-eight hours during the Battle of Thebes with Alexander the Great where he held me back so he could unleash chaos and hell on the enemy, but beyond that, the most we stay ourselves is usually twelve hours at a time.

She arches her eyebrow, hand on her hips. "So now you're calling me a liar in addition to a whore?"

"I don't know," I bark, dragging a hand through my hair again. "I mean, *no*. I just don't know what's going on. If you aren't a call girl, where on earth did my brother find you?"

She throws out her hands. "He flew down to a fountain in the center of my city and, ya know, asked if anyone wanted to volunteer to be his consort."

"He did *what*? Flew down? In front of humans?"

"Yeah, it really freaked most of them out. They ran away. Well, a lot of them pulled out their phones," she waves a hand, "but most were running away in fright."

"Including you?" I ask.

"Oh, well, I . . . didn't run." Her cheeks turn pink again, and not for the first time, I notice how incredibly attractive she is. My pants are tight, responding to her in ways I never respond to females. Not that there are ever females around to respond to. But I certainly don't react to my other brother's consorts this way.

Which reminds me of what she just told me.

"Wait, you didn't run?" I blink in confusion before I finally get it. "Are you telling me you actually volunteered for my brother's madness?"

I'm sure she'll laugh off my statement and tell me that my brother chased her as she ran, kidnapping her and bringing her here.

Instead, to my utter shock, she just nods. "Exactly. I didn't run. I volunteered. I'm Lauren by the way." She holds out her hand.

"Why would you volunteer?" I ask, completely befuddled. "Couldn't you see what he was?"

"Well, I couldn't tell you were on the other side of his head at first. He was wearing a hood. But I could see the wings and tail. I was," she shrugs, "intrigued."

"Intrigued?" My voice leaps an octave. "A terrifying, half-mad being drops from the sky—"

"He said he was a god," she pipes up.

"Even worse! And you volunteer to be his consort? Did he even wait to get you back to the castle before ripping off your clothing and molesting you?"

I'm horrified as I take in the crumpled bedding and disheveled hair. Have they been abed the entirety of the last three days? Is *that* what kept me asleep for so long?

Her hands are at her hips again as she stands tall, glaring at me. "You sure make a lot of assumptions. And you know what they say about people who assume things."

I just look at her, bewildered. "No, what?"

She narrows an eyebrow. "You just make an *ass* out of *u*," she points at me, and "*me*."

I smirk without amusement. So she's clever. Or thinks she is. She has no clue what she's volunteered herself into the middle of here.

"My brother broke about a hundred rules. We don't reveal ourselves to mortals."

"Why not? If you are gods."

"Because we like our quiet. We're retired."

"Why?"

"Because this isn't our world. It never was, and we have no business affecting the mortals or their affairs."

She huffs out a breath. "Wow, how noble of you. 'Cause the way Remus tells it, you used to get all up in human affairs. Running our wars and secretly guiding empires for like. . . thousands and thousands of years."

Reckless! Sharing so much with a human. I'm going to kill my brother. If there was a way to slice his face off the other side of my head without killing myself in the process, I would have done it long ago.

He really thinks he can just go steal himself a consort. Even if this one volunteered, I share half this body, and a consort is an absolute impossibility for a creature like us! Something my brother knows very well.

"What else happened at this fountain? You volunteered, and then he brought you here?"

"It was amazing," she sighs, a smile on her face. "I'm really surprised I was the only volunteer, actually. Especially when he said the part about him being a god. I don't think a lot of people took him seriously. I mean, I sure didn't, not at first. And then when the cops came, and everyone started running, well, I figured I must be half-crazy to stay there, but—"

I hold up a hand again, the other going to my temples. How much damage has my brother done, and how has the rest of my family not come home to put him in check yet? Obviously, Remus deserves to be locked back up in the basement for these infractions.

I need more information, though. "And you say that was three days ago? So, for three consecutive days, you've been with my brother, and this is the first you're seeing me awake?"

She nods wide-eyed. "He told me all about your other brothers, but he wouldn't talk about you."

I sneer at that. Did he worry saying my name would summon me? How *has* he managed to stay awake so long, though? Hearing that my brother has suddenly figured out how to keep me asleep for *seventy-six hours* is more than a little alarming.

Now that I think about it, of course, he made a play to get a consort. Ever since Abaddon and Kharon got theirs, he's wanted one.

Well, I'm awake now, and it's time to go about my usual job. Putting back into order all the things my brother has thrown into chaos.

I look at the beautiful sex-goddess of a woman, sigh, and say what must be said. "It's time to get you back home."

Chapter Twelve

LAUREN

I stare blankly at him. "Oh, so you're the funny one, is that it?"

He glares down at me. "I'm being serious."

I decide then and there that I don't like his face. It's more normal than Remus's and less angular. Remus has a human face, too, but it's like all his features have been *juuuust* a little stretched. His handsome jaw is just a touch too wide. His forehead angled deep. And his grin, that wild and wicked grin of his, is unnerving when he lets out his full Cheshire cat grin.

But he was *my* wild man. And while I don't think he was the kind of man who could ever be tamed, in our intimate moments together, it's like he was discovering what it felt like to genuinely connect to another person for the first time, just like I was. And it was such a powerful connection, I can't help but be furious at this sanctimonious twin who's suddenly taken his place—face so different—and yet body the same.

I'd been having the longest orgasm of my life, connecting on both a physical and *spiritual* level with Remus as he made love to me. There was nothing else to call it except making love, him clutching my cheeks, our bodies so cemented together as he demanded and I gave.

I'd never known such body-quaking pleasure could exist, especially just from penetrative sex. But it was like his shaft dragged along every spot inside me and lit me up from a thousand places at once. And watching his face when he finally gave into the pleasure I could tell he was fighting...

I saw the wild shock of euphoria hit as we locked gazes, bodies singing together, chests heaving as we cried out in perfect pleasure.

But then, in a flash, fear crossed his features, and his hands stiffened and went lax around me as his head spun around one-eighty. Then suddenly, a different man was on top of me, eyes wide as he immediately pulled out, even as I instinctively clenched to pull the familiar body I hadn't finished milking back in.

That was enough of a shock, but then came Romulus's words.

And now, he's telling me he's going to take me home?

I spit with all the venom inside me, "You'll take me home over my dead body."

Romulus stares at me incredulously. "But you can't stay here."

I cross my arms. "I'm not going anywhere until I talk to Remus again."

Romulus gives me a cold stare. "He's not here. I am. And considering all he did while *I* slept, I'd say it's about time for me to clean up his mess."

He takes a step toward me, and I dodge around the bed, getting low and holding my arms up. "I'm serious," I growl. "I bite." I snap my teeth at him.

Romulus stands up and stretches his neck, frowning as he feels along his collarbone. "Yes, I can see that."

I make an angry noise. "Not like that. I hate you. I'll bite your finger off!"

"It'll just grow back."

"Wha—" I scoff, at a loss for words at that. I cross my arms back over my chest. "Don't you think you should wait until your brothers get back from vacation before you make any hasty decisions?"

He tilts his head at me, the expression on his face changing as he nods. "Well, little girl." I bristle at how patronizing he is. "At last, you say something sensical. I'll get Abaddon here, and he'll know what to do. At least he'll back my play because, obviously, the logical thing to do is to put you back exactly where my brother found you."

"Hey!" I snap. "Why don't you start trying not to be an asshole, like... *now?*"

He narrows his eyes at me, then strides for the door. Which is another kick to the gut.

"Wait!" I call, and he stops.

He starts to turn around, but I wave for him to stop. I don't want to see Romulus's stupid face. I reach up to Remus's sleeping features and caress his face. He looks calm in sleep. Unlike himself. Remus never looks calm. He's always riled about something and so alive. He's the definition of alive.

I reach up and kiss his sleeping lips, whispering, "Come back to me, my love."

Romulus doesn't move for a long moment after I pull back, and for a second, I hope his stillness means they'll switch back.

But no, he reaches for the door and then stomps out, large wings swooping behind him, tail near the floor rather than playfully dancing in the air like usual when Remus is in control.

I follow after him. "What am I supposed to do now?" I ask.

"Wait," he says before slamming the door shut in my face.

Chapter Thirteen

ROMULUS

Come back to me, my love. Her soft voice whispering those words to my *twin brother,* of all people, haunts me as I run down the stairs.

All Remus knows is war. He was never good at the art of sweet words or manipulation. That was our father's domain and, on occasion, mine. I could manipulate for tactical advantage like no one else.

Remus was only ever the chaos. He could burn fury and contention in men's hearts that made them lust for blood. He could turn kinsmen against kinsmen, lighting up a personal quibble that had nothing to do with the battle at large and stoke their bloodlust so they'd slay one another on the spot, though the battlefield was two leagues away.

So there is only one true reason he's brought this beautiful woman to our castle.

He has done it to torment me. To allow me to feel the touch and embrace of the most beautiful woman and then have her turn away in disgust right *after* the climax of my first-ever sexual encounter. Because he is a sadistic fuck and always will be.

He is no one's *love*, and the sooner this woman realizes it, the better.

Abaddon will be my ally in this. He will see the danger in Remus's reckless actions, betraying our presence to the humans. If I'm lucky, he'll agree to another two-hundred-year sentence in the dungeon.

Yes, it means I'll also be caged, but at least I know my family will come speak to me when I am awake, and I'll still have my studies. Layden has been showing us all sorts of devices that connect the whole world on computers with little screens. He declares the entire world can be held within the palm of one's hand. I will have time to study this new world of his.

Order will be restored.

And Remus will be punished. I allow myself a small smile at this and breathe out as I pull out the phone from the library desk on the second floor. The library was an addition Hannah asked for, and we've been slowly filling it with tomes and comfortable furniture.

Hannah likes to be in here while Raven plays. It was a bit of a hairy week while they taught Raven not to fly up, rip the books off the shelves, and tear into the books with her sharp little fangs, but Abaddon was patient with his small daughter. I've been quite impressed with the transformation of my eldest brother into an understanding father.

I punch in the phone number Abaddon was insistent that I memorize upon his leaving. Did he intuit there would inevitably be an emergency, leaving only me and Remus behind? I promised I could keep my brother in check for their weeklong vacation, but I could not even manage three days.

I lift the phone to my ear and listen to it ring. Perhaps he will not answer. Do I want him to? I am never happy to discuss failure, but we can only begin to fix a problem once everyone knows about it.

It rings and rings. I sigh, about to set it down, when it's answered with a gruff, "What?"

"Abaddon."

"What's wrong? What's happened?"

"It's Remus," I answer.

A heavy sigh comes across the line. "Of course it is. What's happened?"

"He's taken a consort."

"What?" Abaddon roars. "Why didn't you stop him?"

"I wasn't awake in time. You need to come back home. He also made a spectacle in front of some humans."

"A spectacle—In front—Where?" Abaddon demands.

"I'm not sure. I forgot to ask."

Then I hear voices in the background and some shuffling. Finally, a couple minutes later, Abaddon comes back on the phone. "Dammit, Layden's found the video of it already. It's all over the human's internet. We're on our way back."

"Good."

I go back upstairs to tell the woman the good news. Except right when I step on the stairs, my nose lifts and my ears attune. There's activity in the kitchen. She's left her room. Hmm. I suppose she does have two legs. I'm just surprised she knows her way around.

I head down the stairs and poke my head into the kitchen. She's bustling around, her hair pulled back from her lovely face, grabbing ingredients and tossing them into a bowl.

Seeing her, I feel a strange slug in my chest. She's so beautiful and moves with such sure grace. I can't help remembering the way fire flashed in her eyes when we sparred upstairs earlier.

As if feeling my eyes on her, she suddenly looks my way. "Oh," she says with a surprised little puff of air. "You."

I swallow hard, trying to get my wits about me as I stride into the room. "Me," I say, glad when my voice comes out normal.

"So I've informed my eldest brother of Remus's latest catastrophe, and you'll be happy to know that they're all heading back from vacation early."

She surprises me again when her eyes light up. "So I'll get to meet Hannah and the baby?"

I frown. "Uh. Yes. The whole family will be coming."

She smiles happily and drops her hands into the bowl, beginning to knead. "Excellent. Remus told me so much about them. I can't wait to meet them. I assume Kharon and Ksenia will be coming, too?"

"Just how much did my brother tell you about our family?" I ask, disconcerted as I walk closer.

Her eyes flash my way quickly. "Everything." She focuses her attention back on what's in the bowl. "Well, he didn't tell me very much about you. So now that you're here, you might as well fill in the gaps."

My mouth drops open a little. And then I get my wits about me again. "I think it better if you tell me about you. Where are you from?"

Her eyes narrow as she pulls a yeasty dough from the bowl and slaps it on the counter. "I'm not going to tell you that. You'll just try to take me back there."

Clever girl. "It doesn't matter if you tell me or not. Layden said the humans have video of Remus descending on your town. He will be able to tell me the location."

She hisses in a breath as her eyes flash up my way. Then she glares back at the dough and begins to knead it furiously. "It doesn't matter. Remus will come for me again."

Though by the uncertain look that enters her eyes after she says it, I can see doubt has been planted in her head. It's my job to water that seed.

"Whatever my brother told you," I say, making my voice softer, "was a lie. He is not who he presented himself as."

She scoffs at me as she shakes her head. "What do you know about it? You weren't there. You were asleep."

My jaw tenses, and for a moment, I worry Remus is threatening to take back our body. But no, I'm still in control. "I know my twin. Don't you think I know him better than anybody?"

She slams the dough against the counter one last time before not only looking at me but taking several steps toward me, planting her flour-dusted hands on her hips. "Oh yeah? Are the two of you ever awake at the same time? Do you ever actually *talk*?"

"Well, no." I blink a couple times. "But that doesn't matter. We share a memory—usually anyway, apart from whatever he's managed to do these last few days. . ." I frown, then regret having said it out loud when she looks curious. I shake my head. "It doesn't matter. He makes a mess, then I wake up and have to straighten it out. That's how it's always been between us."

She just shrugs. "Sounds to me like you're just normal brothers with a serious communication problem."

I huff out an incredulous laugh. "You have no idea what you're talking about."

"Maybe. But I've met him, and now I've met you. So yeah, I get it. You and him are caught in a seriously inconvenient situation." She gestures toward my body.

Then she lets out a long, deep breath. "Okay, that's not fair of me to say. I don't understand. I'm sure no one can really understand it except you two. I'm sure it sucks a lot of the time to have to share a body. It's gotta drive you both crazy."

"He's definitely crazy," I mutter.

She cracks a smile at that, and I'm so completely dazzled by her that I lose the thread of whatever I was saying. "Who's not a little nuts these days?" she says. "We're all living in a late-stage capitalist dystopia. Besides, sanity's overrated."

Then she turns around, attention back on the bread as she starts kneading it again.

Wait, how am I losing this argument? What point was I trying to make? Is she intentionally using her femininity as a weapon against me? Because it's an excellent tactical tool.

I stride toward her but make sure to stop on the other side of the counter. Probably best to keep a hunk of stainless steel between me and her delectable curves if I'm going to keep my head.

"What I'm trying to say is that there's no way Remus showed you who he really is. He's dangerous."

"So dangerous your brother locked him in a dungeon for two hundred years?" She looks angry as she says it. "Yeah, he told me. Who does that to their own *family*?"

"So he didn't tell you *why*?"

She bites her bottom lip, and I think *ah*, finally, I've landed a point.

"Fine. Why?" she asks without looking up.

"Because he's a psychopath who couldn't be trusted not to continue rampaging the countryside."

"What does that mean?"

"It means my brothers and I had just finished sacking Moscow on Napolean's behalf after one of the bloodiest campaigns the world had ever seen. The rest of my brothers and I were exhausted by all the bloodshed, but Remus only felt energized by the war. It was the last time the Horsemen would ride before rebelling against our father and retiring for good."

I see her brow furrowing. Good. She's listening. So, I press my advantage. "My other brothers and I had blindly followed our father's orders for so long, but Remus did it because he loved it. As the French finally left Moscow in defeat, he roused the peasants to attack in guerilla warfare, decimating the very army he was supposedly fighting for because he craved war so much. Nearly a *million* humans died in just six months, soldiers and civilians. Yet Remus only hungered for more."

Her hands have withdrawn from the bowl, and she stares past me at the wall. "He said he was a soldier..."

I laugh harshly at that description, and she looks up at me.

"I knew he hadn't told you everything. Did he mention the part where my brothers and I are the Four Horsemen of the Apocalypse?"

She swallows hard, and her eyes go wide. "He might have left that part out." Then she shakes her head and laughs a little. "Horsemen of the Apocalypse? I mean, are you even being serious right now?"

I look her in the eye. "Deadly. Remus and I are War. My eldest brother Abaddon is Pestilence, Kharon is Death, and the youngest, Layden, is Famine."

She just blinks. "But, but," she sputters, "I thought—" She waves a hand uselessly in the air, obviously confused. "Doesn't Abaddon have a wife and a baby? And isn't Kharon's, *Death*, according to you, wife or consort or whatever *pregnant*?"

"Yes," I say shortly, not wanting her to miss my point. "Like I said, we retired. And it was different for them. They were just trying to be good sons to our father. Obediently following his orders because they didn't realize there was another way. They were just roles we played, not *who we were*. Except for Remus."

She scoffs at this. "Are you kidding? You can't have it both ways. He told me you're all thousands of years old. Are you really going to blame everything you did on your *dad*? I'm pretty sure you're considered a grown man after the first hundred years, let alone, *thousand*."

I breathe out hard. No one has challenged me so equally in. . . well, a long time. "It's true, what you say. It's just a story we've told ourselves over the years. But you're right. We had full responsibility for everything we did. We simply considered human life to be. . ." I breathe out again. "Of little consequence."

Her eyebrows shoot up. "Wow. You just said that out loud."

I stand up straighter. "Unlike Remus, I will never lie to you about who I am. We thought ourselves gods. Humans were merely the fodder in our father's games to gain power. He manipulated human leaders like pieces in a chess game and cared nothing at all for the pieces knocked off the board, especially pawns. His only concern was for gaining advantage and winning."

"And Remus?" she asks. "What did he care about?"

"Nothing! He cared for nothing at all. He just delighted in chaos. He was a constant thorn in our father's side because he didn't care about winning or losing. He just wanted war, discord, and madness."

She crosses her flour-dusted arms over her chest. "And you? What did you care about?"

I want to disseminate. But I've just promised not to lie to her. Besides, it's not like I should want her to think well of me. The sooner we drive her away from here, the better.

So I look her straight in the eye as I tell her the truth. "I, too, am War. As much as I might hate my twin at times, I can't deny we're two sides of the same coin. He can stir the chaos and mad bloodlust of war, but I brought the order and genius tactical planning that allowed for true, effective, and total destruction."

I put my hands on the counter and lean in so she really hears me. "Remus and I have decimated everything we ever touched, and my brothers knew it. Far more than even my brother Death, who is kind-hearted and gave peace to those in the worst suffering imaginable, Remus and I were the most destructive Horseman to your world. And I believe with my whole being that we should still be chained to the dungeon wall downstairs. Because I fear Remus will tear a hole through the heart of this realm with his rage and selfishness if he continues to remain free."

Chapter Fourteen

LAUREN

Okay, so that's a little intense. Nothing like hearing that the man of your dreams whom you've had the most amazing connection with is. . . well, one of the Four Horsemen of the *Apocalypse*.

My forehead feels hot with the overwhelm of information and for lack of anything better to do, I grab the dough and put it back in the bowl to rise. I turn away from Romulus to search for a towel to lay over the top of the bowl. I see one on a rack by the wall and am glad for the breathing space while I walk over and snatch it up.

"So, are you ready for me to take you home now?" Romulus asks.

The breath I hadn't realized I had trapped in my chest expels out in a huge blast. "You just laid a lot on me. Give a girl a minute."

I keep my eyes averted as I drape the towel over the rounded dough ball. Finally, I give him my eyes. And really take in the face in front of me for the first time.

There are similarities between Remus's and Romulus's features. Romulus's are less exaggerated than his twin's: his jaw isn't quite as wide, his forehead isn't as broad, and his lips are just as full but somehow not as widespread.

I blink a couple times and understand what I couldn't quite put my finger on when I first looked at him. Aha. He's the more classically handsome version of Remus.

The thing is, I've always thought that perfectly symmetrical, so-called *perfect* faces were boring. I *like* Remus's stretched, slightly mad-looking features. I think he's wildly handsome, and I love the puckish glint in his eye and never knowing what's going to come out of his mouth next.

But was he just playing with me? Doing what his brother says and making chaos by stealing me away?

Then I frown, remembering the way he tenderly promised never to hurt me. Were those the words of a man who had no value for human life? Because, uh, *I'm* a human, and he's been so careful with me. Was it all a manipulation? It felt so... real.

"How does your magic or power or whatever it is you're talking about work? How did you influence these armies and *stir bloodlust*?"

Romulus blinks at me. "I think you're missing the point here. My brother is a very bad—"

I wave a hand. "Yeah, yeah, blah, blah. He's the worst. Would tear a hole in the fabric of all that's good and holy, whatever. I'm asking *how*. Like, what do you even *do*? How does your magic work?"

"It's not magic," he snaps, sounding a little appalled.

I roll my eyes and give another hand wave. "Okay, then what is it? How does it work?"

He looks a little put-off, and I think he thought I would run screaming after he told me all the boogeyman stories about his brother. "What does it matter?"

I cock my head. "You're expecting me to take off just because of what you're telling me about Remus. It matters." It matters because if Remus has been somehow using magic on me to make me feel all the things I've been feeling for him, just to use me for his own reasons and then toss me away, that's one thing. If not, then this gets complicated.

Romulus shrugs. "It's a power not of this world, imbued by the godhood of the Great Hall. When the Horsemen ride, our aura spreads across the land. Each curse works differently. Remus and I influence events by lassoing existing energy and pouring in our own will to amplify it."

"So, can you change people's minds to do what they don't want to do?"

He breathes out, and I think he's begun to see why I'm asking. "No. We can't affect free will. But we can drive men to madness with their own existing desires by amplifying and feeding off them."

"Feeding off them? Like some sort of energy vampire?"

He shakes his head, then pauses. "No and yes. My brothers and I never *fed* to use such a coarse term. But our father. . . sometimes I wonder."

"What?" I'm curious every time I make Romulus pause. He seems so brash and confident, and yet sometimes, it seems like my questions take him off-guard. He doesn't seem used to it. Either that, or he's far, far more covert at manipulation than even his brother. Because he, too, seems really genuine even though he's obviously trying to be off-putting. I guess that's maybe why I believe everything he says.

I know his objective is to get me to leave. Something he seems to forget as he looks reflective while answering my question as if he's lost himself in conversation with me.

"It was the question that used to drive me to distraction. *Why* did Father do it all? War after war, each different but essentially the same. Backing some human leader who would conquer, sometimes whole empires, but only for a time. Eventually, they would fail and be overtaken, everything they'd built falling to ruin.

"My father would then start all over again, whispering promises in the ear of another upcoming warlord. What was the point of it all?

And Father remained so robust and determined. I thought for a time he was waiting for the perfect empire. And then I realized he hated peace and longed only for the thrill and madness of the *conquering*. He was like Layden, always hungry but never satiated."

His eyes had gone distant as he spoke, but he blinks, coming back to me. "So I don't know if destruction and devouring somehow fed him or if he just..."

"Could never be satisfied with the good things he had," I finish for him. I've known people like that. My ex, for example.

His eyes lock with mine, and he nods. To my shock, I feel a sizzle of connection.

And then, upstairs, there's suddenly loud noises and commotion. Romulus's eyes jerk away from mine. He shakes himself and pulls back from me, and it's like a solid wall falls down between us as he jerks to attention, ramrod straight again.

"Good," he says curtly. "Everyone's back."

Chapter Fifteen

ROMULUS

I lead the way up the stairs and try not to hyper-focus on her lighter footsteps behind me. Abaddon is home, and he'll side with me about the necessity of sending her away. This is a good thing.

I ignore the clenching of my chest at the thought and focus any emotion I feel into fury at Remus for ever bringing her here in the first place.

I reach the first floor and, across the space of the large open room, see my brothers and their families spilling through the front door. Baby Raven escapes her mother's arms and starts flying in spiraling loops toward the high ceilings.

Ksenia, heavily pregnant, waddles over to one of the stuffed chairs near the fireplace and plops herself down while my three brothers head directly toward me.

I stride confidently over to them.

But apparently, I'm not fast enough. Because from behind my back, Lo-Ren scurries forwards.

"I'm so excited to meet you!" she exclaims. "I've heard so much about you. You must be Abaddon," she says and holds out her arms. "I'm a hugger. Are you a hugger?"

Abaddon looks a little dumbfounded at the reception, which is a comical look on my lion-man brother's face. The movement does look a little like a nod, and Lo-Ren must take it as such because she throws her arms around his middle and squeezes.

Hannah pops up behind her husband. "Did I hear you're a hugger?" she asks enthusiastically. "I'm Hannah!"

"Hi! I'm Lauren," Lo-Ren says, barely getting the words out before Hannah has consumed her in a hug.

"Welcome to our home," Hannah says. "We're so glad to have you."

I'm already shaking my head no as Hannah introduces her to Kharon and Layden.

"No," I finally make out. "Not welcome to our home. She has no business being here. Remus captured her. We need to return her to where she belongs immediately."

But Lo-Ren just waves a hand at me. "Isn't he so dramatic? No one captured me."

Abaddon's head swings my way, eyes questioning.

"You said there's video," I defend myself. "He flew down in a human city and took a woman. How is that anything but capturing?"

"Oh," Lo-Ren says breezily. "I volunteered. No capturing. Girl Scout's honor. I mean, I was never a Girl Scout, but I was always their best customer every year during cookie season."

Abaddon's eyes meet mine again. Every word out of her mouth is obviously nonsense. We need to talk man to man.

"Come, let's speak," I say, gesturing him away from the women.

But Lo-Ren puts a hand between us. "Hey, no. What, are you two big men gonna go and decide the fate of the little woman without any input from me? That's bullshit. If you're gonna talk about me, do it in front of me. I deserve to be part of this conversation."

"I like her," Hannah declares. "I say we keep her."

Abaddon rolls his eyes but also crosses his arms, staying put. "She has a point. Why discuss her fate apart from her presence?"

I shoot a glare Lo-Ren's way. She wants to hear what I have to say? Fine. But I won't hold back.

"Remus is a loose cannon. He lied to you, waiting for the family to leave so he could pull this stunt."

Abaddon grunts, and I know I've scored a point.

"Plus, he's found some way to manipulate our connection. He made me sleep for three *days* while he. . ." I wave a hand as I search for the right word, "*wooed* her."

Kharon's eyebrows go up at that. They've all circled around us.

"What's the longest you've slept before?"

"You know us. It's usually hours at a time. Twelve at the extremes. One time, during an arduous battle, I slept for twenty-two while he had one of his especially manic, blood-thirsty episodes. But that was five hundred years ago."

Abaddon taps his bottom lip with his finger, and then his eyes zero in on something past my shoulder. I turn and see Layden looking down at his hand-held device, absorbed as ever.

"Did you have something to do with this?"

Layden doesn't even look up at Abaddon's question.

"Lay," Abaddon snaps and Layden finally looks up.

"Huh?"

"Remus's sudden ability to stay awake?"

"And our blocked memory? Did you do something?" I turn on my little brother. Of course, it makes sense. He and all the new magic he's brought with him. I should have suspected him sooner.

He just shrugs, eyes back on his device. "Are you gonna accuse me of everything that goes wrong? Did I or did I not bring you the potion that unlocked the potential within so you could finally put on a glamour and travel amongst the humans as one of them? That allowed you to take your whole family on vacation safely? And what do I get in return? All I've done since I've been back is nice things."

"You mean apart from the time when you were trying to separate me from my family by sending me back to a realm apart from them forever?" Abaddon growls.

Layden's eyes snap up from his device, and I see the fire in them. "No forgiving and forgetting from you, huh, big brother? Guess I'm not the only one who can hold a grudge. I thought that was just me getting even for you letting our father cut off my wings and stab me right in front of you. And that before *you* buried me alive. My bad if that doesn't make the slate between us clean. You're still gonna suspect me of every little thing."

"Abaddon," Hannah hisses, obviously furious at him.

But Layden's already turned and is stomping away.

I toss my hands in the air. "Great. We didn't get any answers."

Hannah spins on me. "You're just as bad as him." She throws a thumb at Abaddon. "Always treating Layden so suspiciously. How is he ever going to feel like this is home? You're going to drive him away again if you aren't careful. And he's right. The glamours were so helpful. Abaddon and Kharon were able to walk around the city just like anyone else. Even Raven."

She looks up at her daughter flying around the ceiling with a warm, maternal gaze. "She'll have so many more opportunities if she can walk in the human world, too. She can go anywhere she wants when she grows up. *Be* anything she wants to be."

Abaddon's gaze immediately softens, and I know he'll give Layden anything he wants as long as it makes his wife happy.

But I just narrow my eyes after my retreating brother's back. I'd bet anything he had something to do with Remus's sudden new abilities.

Time to get this little talk back on track. "We've lost the point. Remus is being Remus, and we all know how dangerous that can be. He's taken this woman in under false pretenses."

"I don't know about that," Lo-Ren pipes up. "I think I knew what

I was getting into. Like you said, he did fly down from the sky. I saw the tail and everything."

I turn on her. "But you didn't know he shared a body with me. And you didn't know he was one of the Four Horsemen of the Apocalypse."

She waves a hand breezily. "You know, I was thinking about that. Really, how much pressure should I put on the guy to disclose *everything* in the first few days of knowing someone? I think he wanted me to get to know him for *him* without all his baggage. And I really liked what I got to know. I want to get to know him better."

I cough out a scoff. Baggage? Did she just call me baggage?

"Seems reasonable," Hannah says. "Besides, what's the harm of her staying a little longer?"

"There's lots of harm!" I explode, and all their heads swing my way at my outburst. Dammit, I'm losing tactical ground because of my emotions. Something that usually only happens to my opponents. I'm always the cool, calm, and collected one. I try to gather myself, stand up straighter, and use reason.

"The humans will be looking for her. You said the video of Remus's reckless actions was all over the human's networks."

"It's not that bad, actually," Layden pipes up from behind us. Apparently, he didn't storm off to his room after all. He meandered to the fireplace couches, but he's heading back in our direction, having been listening to our conversation the whole time. Again, my eyes narrow at him.

"Look," he says, holding out his phone.

A video plays on it, a serious man in a suit speaking while sitting at a desk. "The incident that took the Internet by storm has officially been debunked as a hoax. In Miami this week, a winged man appeared to descend from the sky to the shock of everyone in the plaza."

"Many took amateur video of the incident, "In the corner of the screen, a shaky video shows a shadow descending into the center of the plaza and people running all directions away from it, "and the world has been ablaze with conspiracy theories about the man, who some on the scene heard claim to be a god. But today, the Florida man has been arrested, along with his illegal jet pack."

The video changes to police pulling a tall, drunk-looking man out of a trailer while another policeman holds up a large jet-pack, and still another drags out a pair of large, synthetic wings.

"In other news, yet another federal bank has been hacked—"

Layden turns off the video. "See? No long-term ramifications. The humans have already moved on to the next story. They have no attention span."

"That's that," Abaddon says with a smile, clapping me on the shoulder. "Problem solved."

"Wha—"

"What's for dinner?" he asks, turning to Hannah. "Should I sear some steak?"

"What do you mean, problem solved?" I demand. "She can't stay!"

Abaddon turns to her. "Do you want to leave?"

She shakes her head. "No, if it's not too much to impose on your hospitality. I'd really love to stay and get to know Remus better."

Abaddon claps his hands. "Sounds like it's solved to me."

"What about the little problem of he and I sharing a body!" I demand.

Hannah looks sympathetic as she reaches out to put a hand on my bicep. "I can't imagine how difficult this is for you. It's not like you could really discuss what it would be like if one of you started dating."

Dating?! What alternate universe have I stepped into?

"This is Remus we're talking about!" I pull away from her touch. "Psychopathic murderer? Does no one remember?"

But Kharon only steps forward, brows furrowed. "We all have a past, brother. Even you."

"Exactly," I say heatedly. "Which is why we need to keep *her*," I wrench my head so fervently in Lo-Ren's direction that it almost snaps, "away from *us*."

Kharon's eyes are full of compassion, and I want to let loose and punch him. Especially when he says, "We are no longer the monsters we once were."

Instead, I just laugh, a cackle that I know only from my memories. My brother's manic cackle. "You think people *change*?" I say accusingly, pulling back from all of them. "You think you've all become so civilized because you put on these stiff clothes and play happy family?"

Baby Raven has flown down to perch on the back of Ksenia's chair. All of them are watching me like *I'm* the crazy one. I'm the only one speaking any *sense*.

"We're monsters!" I shout. "We were born cursed, and we'll die cursed."

My words ring out, echoing off the stone floor and walls.

And then Lo-Ren steps forward. "You know, I used a quick-rise yeast for the bread I started downstairs, and I bet it's the perfect time to pop it in the oven." She smiles winningly at Abaddon. "Some fresh-baked bread would go fabulously with steak."

"I can make some rosemary potatoes and salad that will round out the perfect meal," Hannah says. She puts an arm around Lo-Ren, and together, they start toward the stairs. Everyone joins them.

I'm left alone in my righteous indignation.

The last one to go is the baby, who flies in my direction, shakes her head at me like she's disappointed, sticks her thumb in her mouth, and flies away to follow her parents.

Chapter Sixteen

LAUREN

I take a long nap for most of the day and excitedly rejoin the family for dinner. It's delicious, and it's easy enough to ignore Romulus, who's still sulking. He sits quietly like a stone statue at the other end of the table, barely eating.

Meanwhile, the rest of the family is so fun and engaging. I understand why Remus spoke so warmly about them. Each one of them is such a character.

Abaddon is the gruff head of the family. But then he absolutely melts and becomes a teddy bear whenever it comes to his wife or daughter. Like right now. Baby Raven is perched on his shoulders, grabbing his horns like she's riding him.

Hannah keeps trying to get her to eat bites of food, but Abaddon is more intent on swinging his head around to make Raven giggle as she rides him. The baby is the size of a toddler, even though they said she's not even one year old and seems to have the dexterity of a toddler, too. She doesn't speak yet, but she seems wickedly intelligent.

Kharon is constantly doting on his partner, the very pregnant Ksenia, whom I shared some pleasant words with earlier on the way down the stairs. She seems understandably tired. They said she's only six months pregnant, but apparently, that's when Hannah popped. These special hybrid pregnancies work differently.

Which makes me frown. Uh. . . I'm usually so good about using protection, but I didn't think about it this time, things getting so hot and heavy so quickly between me and Remus. But I'm not exactly ready to be a mommy as cute as Raven is.

Layden spends most of the dinner looking at his phone. He's the most—I cringe away from the word *normal* even when I think it—and try to replace it with *human*-looking of the brothers. It seems that that's due to some horrific trauma of his wings getting cut off by their father? Jesus. I don't know the whole story, but I guess after the whole buried-alive thing, he went off and lived among humans for a long time, too?

Anyway, while Hannah bustles off to get dessert from downstairs, I sidle up to Layden. I try to speak low because I can feel Romulus's eyes on us. "Hey, can I talk to you for a minute?"

Layden's blue eyes look up at me, startled. "Uh. Sure."

I nod my head toward the fireplace sitting area, feeling Romulus's eyes but not wanting to acknowledge him.

"Now?" Layden asks, and I nod.

We leave the table and head toward the couches. "What's up?" he asks.

"Well, you seem like the guy who knows stuff. And you've been around humans more. So you know both worlds."

He nods, and I feel my cheeks go a little pink. "I noticed there's a lot of babies around here, and uh—" I wave a hand, feeling embarrassed but also determined to power through. "That's not really my thing. I don't suppose there's some sort of. . . like. . . supernatural birth control?" I whisper the last part.

To his credit, his eyes only widen the smallest bit before he nods. "Yeah. I know something. Come on. My bag's in my room."

I feel muscles I hadn't even realized I'd tensed suddenly relax. "Oh my gosh, that'd be great."

I start to follow him when all of a sudden, a hand on my shoulder is stopping me. "Where are you going?"

I turn in surprise to see Romulus.

"None of your business," both Layden and I say at the same time. I smile at him, then glare at Romulus.

I can feel Romulus seething as I follow his brother toward the stairs. He's only one floor up, and his rooms are nothing like the posh spaces I've seen everywhere else. Instead, they're just stuffed with monitors and computer equipment, along with stacks of dirty dishes.

"Wow, are you a computer genius or something?"

"Oh, nah," he says, shoving a pile of clothes—I'm not sure if they're clean or dirty—out of the way so he can pull a bag out of a corner. "I just like to keep a watch on things."

I nod.

"Okaaaaay," he says, sitting on the chair in front of what looks like his central monitor and plopping the canvas duffle bag on his lap. He sorts through it, and I hear metallic and glass bottles clanking around inside. His brow furrows as he grabs and then discards things to the other end of the bag. "No, not that. Not that. Where are you?"

He hums to himself under his breath. "Here we are," he says triumphantly, pulling out a small pink plastic disc. He hands it to me.

I frown at the familiar object, popping it open and looking down at the normal-looking birth control pills. "Um. Am I missing something?"

"Nope. These are—" He winces but then waves a hand and says, "*Magic*. I hate to use that word, but essentially, yeah. Let's just say I know some folks who are familiar with beings from other realms. Different realms from the ones my family is from. But you aren't the first to be concerned about not creating inter-realm offspring."

Okay, he's seriously blowing my mind. "How many are there out there? Realms? *Beings*?" I've just been walking around my whole life, not knowing there was a whole other world of creatures out there?

He waves a hand. "Fewer than you'd think, honestly. It's actually really hard to move between realms. My family makes it look easy, but that's just because the angels were the most successful at it, and most of them had the good sense to stop fucking around in a place they had no business being."

I think of the mosaic in the top tower and bite my bottom lip. "So who else is out there besides the," I gulp, "angels?"

But Layden just shrugs me off. "Don't worry about it. My brothers are the biggest bad around. And I've got plenty of tricks up my sleeve, too. You're safe here."

I frown. That was a nice non-answer. I have a feeling Layden's a tough nut to crack and get any real answers out of. But he is helping me when I ask. I hold up the birth control. "So how does this work? You said it's magic?"

"Just take them like normal. My friend's a really talented witch, and she made it look human so it wouldn't draw any attention. The pills will automatically refill after twenty-eight days and stop any supernatural pregnancy from taking hold. But it won't work for normal human guys."

I nod. "That's not a problem."

He pauses. "So you and Remus. . .?"

I blush and look down.

"Sorry, none of my business."

Quickly I pop one of the little pills into my mouth, then slide the compact into my pocket. Layden slings the bag underneath his computer desk before standing.

Before he can leave the room, I ask, "Did you give Remus something so he could stay around longer and keep his brother asleep?"

He pauses but doesn't turn around.

"Maybe something in that little flask he's always drinking from?" Still, he doesn't speak. "I won't say anything. I just want to know what I'm getting into here."

He turns around at that. "I did give him a little help. But you should know, you really have no clue what you're getting into. With either of them."

He's talking about Remus and Romulus.

"What do you mean? Are they. . . *bad*?" I feel silly at the simplification, yet I wait anxiously to hear his answer.

Layden sighs. "Aren't we all? Bad and good and everything in between? I mean, we like to think in those black-and-white terms. But the things our father forced us to do for so long. . ."

He breaks off, looking toward the wall. "Or maybe we weren't forced. Maybe it is who we are. Maybe the hunger inside me was always so large I was never going to be satisfied until I inflicted it on everyone around me. Maybe Romulus and Remus will always be at war with one another, locked in the same body."

I suck in a breath, blinking hard at his words like they're a physical blow.

"But then again, my brother Death put a child in the belly of the woman he loves, about to give birth to life. And my brother Pestilence has the power to heal. Hannah believes we've always had the opposite capacities inside us and that our Father just fed the destructive side. So maybe Remus and Romulus are capable of great peace."

"And you," I say, putting a hand on his forearm, "are capable of feeding the many, not just starving them."

He frowns at that, and I sense a lot of complex feelings coming from him. "I don't know. I think it might be too late to expect much of anything from me."

"Romulus thinks the same of Remus, but I see so much in him."

Layden's eyes pop up from the floor and meet mine. He looks wary, and I see confusion waging inside him. "I hope so," he finally says. "For your sake."

Chapter Seventeen

ROMULUS

Every moment Lo-Ren is away in Layden's room, my foot taps.

I don't notice until Ksenia snaps at me to stop. "We had to come back in the helicopter early for this little *emergency* only to find that the woman hadn't been kidnapped after all, and there *was* no emergency. I'm about to burst with the pregnancy, and I *hate* flying in that tiny thing. So do. Not. Test me."

The helicopter is a new addition to our toys. Kharon insisted we get it in case there was a difficulty with Ksenia's labor. Considering the increasing size of our family and the fact that only two of us have wings, I bought us a military-style one with lots of space in the back. If it was anyone else, I'd think they were calling it tiny to push my buttons. But Ksenia just hates flying in general.

I give her a wounded look, but she doesn't look the least bit impressed by me. Usually, Ksenia favors me. Perhaps it is more fair to say that she does not like Remus and always welcomes my waking. It's not really a high bar to be more preferable company to a madman.

My eyes creep toward the stairs again. At least I'm the more preferable company when it comes to everyone except Lo-Ren. And now she's spending more time with Layden than anyone else has since he's been back.

Apart from Remus. Back when our shared memory still worked, I did notice that he and Layden were spending a lot of time together of late. Mostly, it was just Remus inquiring about the technology and other magic Layden brought back with him.

Abaddon has grilled Layden on the same subjects plenty, but Layden is always pretty tight-lipped. Even the information about the glamours that allow my brothers to walk about looking like normal humans wasn't offered up freely. He only told us about it when Kharon became anxious about the baby's birth. Yes, Hannah's birthing had been fairly seamless, but should there be any complications with another hybrid birth, considering Kharon's very different physiology, he wanted to be ready. What if the baby had extra limbs and they got caught in the birth canal?

Remus's solution was to kidnap a human doctor, naturally, but Layden offered up the possibility of glamours. When Abaddon demanded to know why he hadn't offered the magic remedy earlier, Layden demurred, saying he'd been working on perfecting the potion.

Abaddon hadn't looked like he believed it, and all things considered, now I wasn't sure if I did either. It was around then that Remus suddenly became *very* pliable about not joining them on their vacation venture to try out the magic potion.

Every time any of us called it that, Layden got a strained look on his face and said tightly it was not *"magic."*

But "inter-realm ingredient potion" was too much of a mouthful. As to *how* he'd gotten matter from other realms into this one and *where* exactly those other realms were, he refused to say a thing. He'd rolled his eyes when I said that and corrected me, "No, it's *essence* from other realms, not matter."

I stare harder at the stairs. Was he telling *her*?

Had he given Remus a different potion to keep me sleeping and separate our memories? As soon as I thought about it, in spite of my frustration at my attached twin, I couldn't say I didn't feel a burn of curiosity. Because I wondered if it worked both ways. Everything I did now, would my twin be blind to it?

I breathed out long and hard and stretched my neck, blinking at the thought of the first true privacy I might have in... well... *ever*.

It made for a certain kind of life, knowing that while in the moment, I might have my mind and body to myself, the second I fell asleep, every corner of my memories could be excavated while my body was inhabited by someone else. A completely different mind and perhaps even a different soul. If we had souls, which, over the millennia, I'd begun to doubt.

I remember when Kharon once confessed to me, horrified and weeping in a rare moment of lucidity while we were locked together in the dungeons, that there was no afterlife for our kind. He'd searched every inch of the deathly planes for our brother Layden. Back then, we thought Layden long dead, and while the news devastated Kharon, selfishly, I'd felt such wild relief. At least in death, I'd be free of Remus. At least I wouldn't continue to be chained to him for eternity.

But now Layden is alive, and our father, too, who survived being burned down to an *ember*. Now that we know these bodies are truly indestructible, that though we may appear to die, no death is truly possible...

My stare drifts bleakly to the wall. There will never be any escape for me.

Did Remus realize the same thing? Is that why he made this rash move now? Or has he simply been biding his time since he's been free of the dungeon chains to steal himself a consort of his very own?

If we were burned in a great fire like we did our father and came back from embers, would we grow back to this same shape, still so tightly bound to one another? What would it be like to each have our own bodies?

It's a foolish thought and one I imagined I'd outgrown. Usually, I have more of an iron grip over my own mind because I know Remus can see it all. And he is the last being I will appear weak in front of. I stand straighter and clear my mind of foolishness.

There is only strength in me and determination to see to my task: protecting the woman and getting her as far away from him as possible before he wakes up again. I'll only allow my twin to ruin one life— mine.

I might not know her well, but I know she deserves so much better than him. She's smart, and beautiful and— And she's coming back down the stairs, Layden at her heels.

What did they talk about? Hannah and the others have finished dessert by the time she's back.

"I saved you two some pie." Hannah bounces up as soon as they're back to the table. "We were thinking of heading out to the lake in a bit here. Raven loves to swim."

"Oh." Lo-Ren's eyes glance my way, lingering for just a moment before she looks back to Hannah and smiles. "An afternoon swim sounds really fun. Remus got me a swimsuit when he ordered me a bunch of clothes. I'll save the pie for afterward."

"Let's get in the lake then," Ksenia groans. "I'd give anything to feel weightless right now." She stands up and rubs her back with one hand, the other holding her protruding belly.

"Of course." Kharon pops up immediately behind her, one of his three pairs of arms wrapping protectively around her stomach while another set massages her shoulders. "I'll go up and get your suit."

"I don't care about a suit," she says irritably. "I'll just go in this and you can bring me a change of clothes later."

"Excellent idea." Kharon nods over and over.

Hannah beams at him for his attentiveness.

"I'll get towels," Abaddon says.

Lo-Ren looks to me. "You coming?" It sounds like a challenge.

I stand up stiffly. "I usually join the family on lake outings."

"Perfect!" Hannah snatches Raven out of the air where she's been fluttering near everyone. Raven giggles, and her wings flap harder like she's trying to get away from her mom until Hannah says, "Honey, we're going to the *lake*."

The toddler's eyes widen with delight and she scoots out of her mom's arms anyway, flying toward the stairs. Apparently, she knows the order of things because we're only halfway to the stairs by the time she's back down with her little polka-dot swimsuit in her hands, thrusting it toward her mom.

"Yes," Hannah laughs. "But the rest of us have to change, too."

Raven starts to whine a little as Hannah tromps toward the stairs, especially when she sees Ksenia and Kharon immediately heading outside.

"Wait for your mother," Abaddon chides, and Raven flies in circles around his head but calms down a little as they trudge up the stairs to change. Even Abaddon has adopted some swim trunks that Hannah sewed him, which I secretly find hilarious considering he went through most of his long, long life in little more than a loincloth if that.

We have truly been tamed by these women. And then I frown. Could even Remus be tamed?

I immediately reject the thought. He's not like the rest of my brothers.

War and chaos are in his soul.

Lo-Ren is the last to emerge from her room, and I glance away quickly after seeing her. But it's too late. The image of her perfect, shapely curves is seared into my mind. I blink hard, yet there it still is, taking my breath away.

I lead the way back downstairs. It takes every inch of my iron self-discipline not to look over my shoulder so I might steal another look at her.

All for naught because when we reach the bottom of the stairs, she and Hannah pass me, easily chatting. If I thought the sight of the front of her was enough to take my breath away, I was truly not prepared for—

Her generous backside and hips sway alluringly back and forth as she walks.

I'd never given much thought to how ridiculously little cloth is involved in the outfits these females call a "bathing suit" before, but suddenly, I'm appalled and entranced. It barely covers her nakedness. And yet, I also want to rip the rest off to reveal everything.

Then I realize my thoughts and am appalled at *myself*.

Was I not just thinking that Abaddon has spent most of his existence naked? And I know that in ancient times, plenty of women went about barely draped in clothing. Yet none of them ever affected me as much as this female strutting before me.

I only realize I've been standing still, dumbfounded, when Hannah looks back at me and laughs. "Close your mouth, dear. You'll catch a fly."

Lo-Ren looks back then, too, and I jerk my eyes guiltily up to hers. There's a moment of searing connection before they head out the door into the sunshine, leaving me feeling like I've just been kicked in the chest.

I let out a huge breath I hadn't realized I'd been holding and sprint across the hall to catch up with them all.

I get to the door just in time to see Abaddon and his daughter launch into the air. Raven lets out a squeal of delight like she's finally been set free to *really* fly. Kharon and Ksenia are already in the lake, his arms protectively around her as she lays back against him with her face to the sun.

Hannah has her arm linked through Lo-Ren's as they walk to the edge of the lake, so comfortable as if they're already sisters-in-law.

The sight squeezes my chest tight in something like terror. And not for fear of my family becoming too attached, like I ought to be thinking, either. I'm terrified because of how much I want it. Of how much I want *her*.

For *myself*.

Because if there's one thing in this life I've learned, it's that I can never, ever want anything. Remus will always make sure of that. I could never want my father's affection or to succeed at anything I put my focus into. And I could certainly never want to gain the love of a good woman.

Remus chose her for exactly this reason, and damn him to hell, he always chooses his torments exquisitely well. She is perfect. And she can never, ever be mine.

Chapter Eighteen

LAUREN

I hold tight to Hannah's arm as we get near the edge of the lake and pretend I can't feel Romulus's eyes on my back. He about took my breath away when I caught him checking me out earlier in the castle. The heat that man was looking at me with was indecent. My cheeks are still flushed. Something I have a feeling Hannah doesn't miss as she looks over at me.

"Ready?" she asks as we navigate the smooth rocks at the lake's edge.

I'm about to say yes when the water laps toward us and hits my ankles. "Holy shit, that's cold!" I yelp.

Hannah laughs. "Yep, you can never quite be ready for it the first time. It's like swimming in Lake Michigan. Even in the summer, it's freezing. But it gets better once you're all the way in."

"If you say so."

I can't help glancing over my shoulder. And yep, Romulus is right there, watching us with a now-stern expression on his face. Somehow, that gives me the courage to wade forward. This at least gives me a reason to not mind the cold as much because heat is bursting in my cheeks and more embarrassingly, my belly.

When the water gets to my thighs, I decide to take the plunge and dive forward. The shock of cold takes my breath away, and I pop back up to the surface, gasping for breath. "Oh my god!"

"It gets better the more you swim," Hannah says laughingly.

"I fucking hope so!" There's nothing else to do at this point except trust her because now even the air feels cold. So I start to swim vigorously away from shore.

Hannah's a little bit right. The more I move, the less absolutely frozen I feel. After maybe another ten minutes, I begin to feel all my body parts again, and Hannah and I are having fun as we race each other around.

The lake is an absolutely gorgeous, deep, dark blue. It extends so far, and it feels wild to have so much natural beauty all to ourselves.

Eventually, Hannah and I turn around and head back the way we came. I try not to look at Romulus standing right at the shore, arms crossed like a forbidding figure against the backdrop of the castle, but it's hard not to.

Overhead, Abaddon and Raven fly in circles, and I'm glad when we get closer that Hannah diverges away from the shore to swim on her back toward Kharon and Ksenia.

"How are you feeling, honey?" Hannah asks Ksenia.

For the first time since meeting the very pregnant woman, she has a peaceful smile on her face, and her large belly is bobbing just out of the water.

"Amaaaaaazing," Ksenia says, extending the word. Her partner lounges in the water behind her, one set of arms looped lazily under her breasts. She leans her head back against his chest. "I'm never leaving."

Kharon chuckles and kisses the top of her head.

My chest clenches from seeing how sweet they are together and how devoted he obviously is to her.

In the distance, Raven dives straight toward the lake. I gasp a little when she shoots into the water but Hannah just laughs and shakes her head. Especially when Abaddon follows right after his daughter.

They both pop up a moment later, right back up into the air, hovering for a moment as their wings shake off the water like a wet dog might.

Then Raven takes off straight toward her Uncle Romulus at the shoreline, skimming a hand along the surface as she goes.

His stance finally changes, and he holds up a hand to stop, which doesn't stop Raven in the least from splashing him as soon as she gets close, her tiny, bell-like giggles ringing out as she flies in circles around him, droplets flinging as she goes.

Romulus doesn't laugh, but he spins around, snatching in the air for her, which makes her giggle more. She keeps diving for him, and he jumps, reaching for her again and again. It's clearly a regular game they play.

"She loves her uncle," Hannah comments from where she's treading water beside me.

"Oh," I say, glancing away. "She's so cute."

I backstroke a little away from Ksenia and her man, and Hannah follows me. I look over at her, squinting in the bright summer sun. "Do you think it's possible what I'm attempting?"

Hannah's eyebrow lifts, and she glances back toward Romulus, quiet for a moment before responding. "Hmm. To tell the truth, I think the twins are more entwined than either of them wants to admit. And I think hating each other was probably the easiest way to deal with the life their father thrust them into."

I lay on my back, floating, as I contemplate her words. "How so?" It's amazing to be able to get insights from their family on the situation. It helps me feel more grounded when I've felt so swept away by emotions I barely understand.

"Remus is a rebel by nature, making situations worse, and Romulus always took it upon himself to 'fix him,'" she lifts her hands out of the water to make air quotes, "I think Romulus craves stability, something he'll never have with Remus."

"Not necessarily," I say in frustration. "If they could just work *together* instead of *against* each other."

Hannah nods, though she doesn't look particularly convinced. But then she looks at me, really looks at me. "If anyone could give them a reason to work together, it's you."

I frown at that, not sure how it makes me feel.

"If they could just *talk*."

Hannah snorts. "Wouldn't that be something? But they're never awake at the same time. Something I think is frankly for the best. Sharing a body has got to be hard enough."

"Hmm," I say again. "Maybe."

"Come on," Hannah says. "Wanna swim to the rock?" She points to a rock really far out in the center of the lake. "Everyone else is always flying around, and Ksenia's been hugely pregnant all summer since the lake melted enough to swim in."

"Sure." I smile, glad to get my mind off Remus and his troublesome twin again as we take off through the water.

*　*　*

I'm even more glad for the long afternoon swimming by nighttime because it feels like I'll sleep like a rock. I don't want to toss and turn thinking about my absurd boy problems.

Except as I change into the silk nightgown Remus ordered for me before he disappeared into his brother, I find my mind spinning with thoughts of him.

What am I really even doing here? I've started wondering if what I thought I shared with him was even real. I felt so invested in it, in *him*, that I've fought to stay. But after not being able to talk to him all day, each hour feeling like a week, it's easy to question, well, all of it.

And as lovely as his family is...

Maybe I don't belong here. This has been a fairytale dream. Maybe I've fought to stay because I don't want to go back to my *real* life. That's not very lovely if it's true. I don't want to be the person who runs from her problems.

I always want to be the person who runs *toward* life, not away from it. I thought that was what I was doing here.

A knock on my door startles me from my thoughts. I wonder if it's Hannah stopping by to say goodnight. The sumptuous rug is soft underfoot as I head to the door, the brass doorknob cool in my hand as I turn it and pull the door open.

"Oh," I gasp a little in surprise when I see Romulus's hulking form in the dimly lit hallway instead. "It's you."

"Who were you expecting?" Then he waves a hand, his eyes seeming to darken. "Never mind. I just wanted to check that you have everything you need before I go to my rooms."

I can't help leaning against the doorjam and arching an eyebrow at him. "I thought I was in your rooms."

He swallows, his eyes traveling down to my neck before he jerks them upwards as if forcing himself not to check me out in my slinky silk nightgown.

I feel confused by my disappointment that he didn't look. I'm here for Remus... Aren't I?

"I don't sleep. I spend the nights reading in the den." He gestures with his head further down the hall.

Ah. Of course. He only sleeps when Remus is awake. Which, again, makes me suddenly long for the wild, reckless man I first met.

While Romulus stands there in front of me, I rush around to the back of him. When he starts to turn around to ask, "What are you—?" I put out a hand on his shoulder to still him.

Instead, I lift a hand up to Remus's sleeping face. I breathe in, feeling a dart of pain in my chest right along my sternum as I caress down his cheek, running a thumb along his bottom lip.

"I miss you," I whisper.

There are only a few sconces lit along the wall at uneven intervals, so when Remus's eyelids flutter, at first, I'm not sure if it's just a trick of the lights.

And then their tail comes and wraps firmly around my waist several times.

"What's happening?" Romulus asks. "That wasn't me."

"Remus?" I ask, reaching up on tiptoes to excitedly kiss his sleeping lips. "Remus?"

But when I pull back, he sleeps on. The tail around my waist goes slack, and my heart drops to my feet. I sigh and walk back toward my door. Which is when I happen to glance down and see that, whoa, damn.

Romulus is wearing thin pajama bottoms and has a *massive* hard-on jutting out.

"Is *that* you?" I ask with a little gasp.

Romulus reaches for my waist and pulls me to him, right up against his hardness. I think we both groan a little. I'm not quite sure because suddenly, our faces are close to one another, just inches apart. His body feels so familiar, and mine instantly reacts.

Romulus's eyes are dark and wild, and both of us breathe heavily for several charged moments.

Is he about to—? Do I want him to—? My eyes dart down to his lips, full but not as wide as his brothers, and my tongue darts out to wet my bottom lip in anticipation before I can think better of it.

But then I jerk away, turning away with a strangled, "Wait."

"Good night." He's gone, and the door to the den slams shut before I've quite gotten my bearings on what the hell just happened.

I watch his closed door for probably longer than I should, waiting. For what, I'm not sure. And when I finally head to bed, I toss and turn, my mind on overload.

Just when my eyelids finally start to feel heavy, and I think I might be able to fall asleep, I hear the creak of my door opening.

With a start, I sit up in bed.

And there he is, the shadow of Romulus headed toward me in the darkness.

My hand fumbles for the lamp on the nightstand, and he's nearly by the bed before I find the switch and turn it on. When I do, my heart leaps to my throat when I see the face of the man who's come into my room.

"Remus!" I cry, throwing my arms around him. Thank god.

"Shh," he says urgently as he embraces me roughly in return. "I don't want to wake him. I've only just gotten myself back. How long have I been gone?"

But before I can answer, he shakes his head. "It doesn't matter." And then he's kissing me, and I'm kissing him back. I've missed him so desperately, and it was so easy to question everything while he was gone, but now that he's back in my arms—

Half of me is sure that I fell asleep and this is a dream. I don't want to question anything too much in case I wake up, even though I want to ask him a thousand things. But he's holding me in his arms again in the way that is so distinctly *Remus*. Holding me like he knows me and my body, possessively like this was the way we were always together and always meant to be.

"I've missed you," I breathe out, and then his lips cover mine. We kiss each other with more passion than I knew a body could possibly hold.

I groan low when his hands wander down my body, the flat end of his soft, leathery tail whipping around to slide up the inside of my thigh underneath the nightgown, lifting it.

When he starts kissing down my neck to my breasts, I grab his shoulders, loving the strength in them and knowing I should make him pause.

"There's so much we need to talk about," I whisper, half whimpering from the rising excitement of his body pressing against mine as he crawls on the bed between my legs. God, even just the weight of him there against me almost has me coming.

"So much has happened. I've met your family, and Romu—"

"I don't want to talk about him," Remus growls. "It's just you and me here," he says, lifting his face toward me, expression serious for a moment before he extends his wicked tongue to lick my nipple through the thin silk of my nightgown. The next second, he tugs down the fabric, exposing my puckered nipple to the night air.

"Fuck," he hisses. "You're so beautiful. I dreamed of you the entire time I was asleep. You drive me mad." He dips his head, and the screwed up thing is that I can just glimpse Romulus's face when he does, and I wonder. . . is he dreaming of me, too?

"Remus, I'm serious." I try to sit up, but he holds me in place with his hands, kneading my hips.

"I am, too," he growls sexily. "You want to talk, we'll talk. But first, let me pleasure and taste you. Please." He looks up, eyes heavy with a longing that seems deeper than just lust. He wants to reconnect with me in this most basic of ways, body to body.

And if I'm honest, I want it, too. *Desperately*. My body's been warring with my head since I saw his shadow in my bedroom. Because I want him desperately.

The only thing is, I wasn't sure when I saw him come in if it would turn out to be Remus or Romulus. Either way, I knew I wanted them like this. Hands on me, bodies thrusting together, sweat mingling. That feels. . . wrong somehow? Or maybe it's the fact that it *doesn't* feel wrong that feels wrong. You're only supposed to want one man at a time unless you're on *The Bachelorette* or something.

And even then, they still have to pick in the end.

"Don't think," Remus says. "Just feel."

I breathe out in a long hiss as he grips my inner thighs, his thumbs massaging as he draws my legs open. His hands are underneath my silk nightgown now, and the sharp inhale of his breath tells me he's just discovered I'm not wearing any underwear.

"Was this for me?" he asks, a heavy rasp in his voice that immediately gets a harsher edge as he finishes, "or for *him*?"

"Don't do that," I warn. "Don't pit me against you two." I start to pull away from him. "Because that is not a game I'm interested in playing." This is all way more confusing than I ever could have anticipated.

"I'm sorry, I'm sorry. Please stay."

He rolls us so that I'm lying on top and he's underneath me.

"I'll crush you," I say as my legs slide on either side of his hips. I prop myself up with one hand and start to lift off him but he just chuckles softly and pulls me back into place.

"Immortal god here." His hands glide up the side of my hips to my waist and squeeze. "And you feel amazing. You have no fucking idea."

He shifts slightly so that I feel his shaft against my wet sex. I hiss in surprise. When did he pull himself out? Does that mean he trusts that I want *him*? Even though it's in fact more complicated than that? And is that a conversation that we need to have before we do this?

"Remus," I start to say.

"Do you want this?" he interrupts me to ask. "Do you still want me?"

"God, yes," I say honestly.

Just the tip of him slides inside. We both groan. He doesn't push for more, though. With me on top like this, I know he's giving me the space to guide everything.

Don't think he said. More like *don't overthink*. Because yes, I want him. I want him like this. And it's so easy and right to shift my hips so that he settles in an inch and then another inch. My arms slide against the mattress underneath his arms and then back up to clasp around his shoulders. He wraps his around my back.

"I could spend eternity like this," he hisses in my ear.

I press my face against his neck and breathe him in. "Me too."

He moves his hands down my back and then slowly, ever so slowly, massages my full ass cheeks, guiding me as we begin fucking.

Oh god, he's so thick. It's so satisfying feeling him fill me like this.

I don't know how to describe it. It's both fucking and making love at the same time. Dirty and sweet. The way he clutches me feels obscene. Yet the *need* I feel from him as he drags me down his huge cock and back up against his body in a way that hits my clit so perfectly—

He grips my neck to lift my face to his and then kisses me passionately, his tongue tangling with mine, his other hand still on my ass as our motion continues. So in sync, him so hard and perfect inside me.

He breaks from my mouth just long enough to say, "Everything makes sense when we're like this."

I couldn't agree more. Even though he's lighting up every pleasure nerve inside me, I don't want to come. I just want to stay connected. I need this with him.

My hands on his chest curl, nails scratching as I bear down on him.

"Yes, honey," he growls. "Just like that."

Our hips move together sinuously, bodies dancing. God, I only ever dreamed of it being like this. My whole body clenches on him, his shaft inside me growing thicker. My fingernails dig into his chest. I try to hold back my orgasm because I'm not ready to lose this moment with him yet.

But it's like he can see it in my eyes. "Give it to me, honey," and then his lips are on mine again.

"Don't go away again," I say through my kisses. "I need you here."

I see the pain hit in the way his eyebrows crumple.

"I want to be with you more than anything. Leaving you last time tore me apart."

I feel guilty for bringing it up in this moment. Of course, he didn't want to leave. I clench around his cock, making him leap inside me. I stop moving even though it kills me a little, as close to climax as I am.

He tries to shift my hips, but I shake my head.

"I don't want you to leave again." I start to climb off him, shuddering as I do from the way it makes his cock shift inside me.

But he merely rolls with me, pinning me to the bed and thrusting deep inside. We both groan with how good it feels.

"If I go, I promise I'll come back." In the light from the moon streaming in the window, I can see fierceness flash in his eyes.

"This is messed up to be having this conversation with you hard inside me."

His cock leaps in response, and he rotates his groin to rub against my clit. "I think it's the perfect place to be having this conversation." He grins, bright teeth flashing.

I laugh, relaxing back, legs open wide to him. "Of course you do."

He reaches down and lifts my knee so he can settle in even deeper, lazily thrusting in and out several times in a way that has my eyelids fluttering. I bite my bottom lip to keep from crying out.

"Fuck, I love the way your body responds to me."

I try to open my eyes but only succeed in clenching and unclenching my pussy muscles around him, luxuriating in the feel of the position as he slides in and out again. Finally, blearily, I manage to look up at him looming sexily above me.

"Well, I guess it's not the worst way to talk," I finally manage to gasp out. "But I can hardly think clearly. What are we going to do about your brother?"

"Which one?" he asks with another lazy thrust. He reaches the hilt—well, as far as he can reach inside me anyway, when I look down I see there's still a few inches of his cock sticking out of me. Then he rolls his hips so that I feel at the start of my cervix. And it makes me spasm with pleasure as if he's found another G-spot when he hits one of those sides.

He reaches down and strums my clit with his thumb until I'm writhing beneath him. I'm a millisecond from climax when he pulls his hips back and removes his thumb so that I'm left gasping from want. It takes several more moments for my head to clear enough to remember what we were talking about. There was something important I was trying to ask. I blink blearily, finally lighting on it.

"R-R-Romulus!" I manage to stutter triumphantly. "What are we going to do about R-Romulus?"

Remus's face sours. "I don't see that we need to do anything at all."

I suck in a breath and attempt some fortitude. "When you're not here, he is. I'm getting to know him, and I wish there was some way for the two of you to just talk it out so we could find a way to all work together—"

"You know what?" Remus says, bending down low so that his voice is raspy in my ear. "I think that's enough talking for now."

And then his thumb moves back to my swollen clit and starts strumming.

"But don't you think—"

That's as far as I get before he does that thing with his cock again, hitting all my buttons and thrusting upward while he really works my clit, pressing downward. Until I'm consumed with sensation and pleasure and the man on top of me.

He kisses my lips and then down my neck, where he begins to suckle my pulse point in a way that, along with all the other sensations—

I scream out my release into the night. It pulses on and on, the most endless, deep pleasure that wracks my body.

Remus pulls out of me with a groan but keeps working my clit with his hand, hugging me against his body. I grasp him back to me desperately, reaching for his shaft. I want him inside me, climaxing with me. Now that I have the birth control, I'm not worried. Layden said that, unlike human birth control, it starts working instantly. I want to feel him come and see the release on his face.

When my fingers glance against his cock, it's still stiff as a board, yet he pulls away from me.

I'm still shuddering with release when he rolls to the other side of the bed from me.

"Remus," I reach for him.

"I can't," he says, voice choked. "Last time it took me from you." He slants his face down but lifts it back up so I can see his pleasure-strained eyes as he tucks his hard, veined shaft back into his pants. "And I'll do anything to stay."

"Baby, come here," I say, opening my arms. He did all that and isn't even going to come? Is he holding his pleasure at bay so he can stay? Oh my god. So many emotions choke my chest. I want to hold him tight all night long. And longer. Maybe even forever. A thought that should scare me more than it does. But he was right. Everything makes sense when we're like this.

He pulls me into his arms instead, and I think about what he said about doing anything to stay. I should ask him if he has anything left in the flask he got from Layden. I should leap out of bed right now to get it in case he disappears this very moment.

But. . . won't that just make it like when I first met him? Yes, I'd get him for an extended period, only to lose him again for God knows how long? Isn't it better to get to know the usual rhythm of his and Romulus's switches so we can all learn how to live together for *real*? If we actually want this to last.

Remus might not want to talk about his brother, but after the heights of pleasure he just sent me to, all my thoughts and worries are suddenly rushing back in like an unstoppable tidal wave. I'd rather get to sorting how we might actually make this work.

"You'll always come back," I say as he strokes his hands through my hair.

"You know," I try, biting my bottom lip before going on, "I could be a sort of go-between if there are things you want to talk to Romulus about. I think if the two of you tried to communicate a little, then maybe we could all—"

But Remus just lets out a great scoff and hugs me closer to him. "I just got much-needed privacy from that bastard by separating our memories. The last thing I want is to *communicate* with him."

I huff out a disappointed breath, but Remus doesn't seem to notice as he squeezes me tighter. "It's just you and me here."

I relax against him and try to fight my eyes fluttering closed at how good it feels in his arms. I want to stay awake and horde every moment with him, but suddenly, the weight of all the day's events and how long I've been up slams me. My eyes pop open only to blink slower and slower, closing several moments later as Remus keeps strumming his hands through my hair, lulling me to sleep.

"Just you and me," he murmurs again, the last thing I hear before I drift off.

Chapter Nineteen

ROMULUS

I spring awake and blink in shock at the feel of the warm, naked woman curled in my arms. At least I have my pants on this time.

I should disentangle myself from her immediately. It's wrong for me to stay here and steal this moment enjoying the thick curves of her leg thrown over my hip, my hand wrapped around her soft waist. Reflexively, my hands squeezes a little, and she responds, nestling her face in further against my naked chest.

For a moment, I can't breathe.

And it strikes me that I—

Dear god I never knew what it was to want before this moment.

Because I want *her*. Not just sexually, though, yes, my rod is stiffening with wakefulness. But it's so much more than that. I want to wake with her curled around me like this every morning. I want her to look at me with those laughing, teasing eyes of hers. I want to protect her and care for her so she is safe and never has a want or need that is not immediately met.

My chest lightens with this amazing discovery. But then I'm struck with the deep blow of loss the next.

Because the only reason she's curled around me so intimately at this moment is because she was with *him*.

Remus.

My eternal nemesis who's finally gone too far. If I could carve him out of the back of my head, I would. He picked the one woman in the world who was perfect for me but also had a big enough heart to care for *him* in spite of all his bullshit.

She's impossible, and yet here she is.

The question is, what the hell am I going to do with her now? What are his plans for her? Because he's somehow managed to block his mind and memories from me, so for once, I can't see his schemes. I'm playing chess, blindfolded, with a maniac. And it's not just a battle in the name of some faceless warlord I care nothing about.

This is for *her*.

I won't let anything harm her. Especially not my twin.

Selfishly, I stay perfectly still, holding her for hours until sunlight begins to spill through the windows. Her face is so perfect and serene in sleep. Her beauty makes my chest ache.

I feel her begin to stir and know it's time to depart, but still, I don't. If I'm to have stolen these moments with her, I won't flee without her knowing about it. Unlike my brother, I'm no liar.

So I stay there as her eyes blink awake, sleep-encrusted and bleary in the morning light. She starts a little, a slight gasp at her lips when she sees my face hovering above hers.

"You," she whispers.

But she doesn't immediately yank away, and it gives my foolish heart hope.

"Me," I say, my voice coming out more gruff than I mean it to.

She blinks and then swallows, her arms and legs still entangled with mine. "How long have you... been awake?"

I'm tempted to say I just awoke, but I remind myself, no. No lies. "Many hours."

She blinks rapidly, looking confused.

"You were sleeping so peacefully. It seemed wrong to wake you."

Her eyes search mine as if waiting for me to say more. When I don't, she reaches for the sheet, disentangling from me as she covers herself and rolls away. "Oh."

Heart-hammering, I rush to say, "And it felt so good to hold you. Selfishly, I didn't want to wake you."

I hear her sharp inhale as she turns around to look at me, her bare back exposed as the rest of the sheet is drawn tight around her front. Her eyes are full of questions. "But I thought you hated me and wanted rid of me."

"I never said that," I say heatedly and dare to reach out and place a hand on her sheet-covered thigh. It feels cruel to have the fabric between us after hours of holding onto her soft, bared flesh. "I've only been afraid my brother was using you for some purpose that would harm you."

"Remus wouldn't." She pulls away.

"Perhaps not," I say, only to humor her. I have no faith in my brother, but the tactician in me knows that playing along may get me further toward my goal, considering where Remus has positioned me.

"I've been thinking about a lot of things during the night while I had the privilege of holding you as you slept."

She blushes and looks away.

"I was wondering if maybe there's a way we could all work together. You want my brother, and"—*I want you*, I leave unspoken, no need to put all of my cards so blatantly on the table—"and I don't want to stay in the way of your happiness. But there remains a reality I hope you won't find too inconvenient."

She looks back at me as I reach for her hand.

"I share this body with my brother."

She blinks again in confusion. "What are you proposing?"

Again, I keep my cards close to my chest. "Just that if we communicate, maybe it doesn't have to be uncomfortable, you falling asleep with him and waking up to me. It's an unusual situation, but we could all find some happiness and comfort here."

"Really? You'd be open to something like that?" she breathes out, and I can't help but rub her palm with my thumb. I don't miss the hitch of her breath.

She blinks, looking excited. "Remus and I could finally have a chance."

I try to ignore the stab of pain and her eyes suddenly search mine. "But wait, is that fair... to *you*?"

I smile. Oh, my precious one. Give a tactician an inch, and he will take a mile. "I will be more than content." Continuing to rub her hand with mine in low, massaging circles, I say, "Because even a moment of intimacy with you in my arms makes up for a lifetime of not having anything. I'm not a greedy man."

All right, so perhaps I have told one lie after all. While no, I have not been a greedy man in the past, I have a feeling I might become very, very greedy when it comes to Lo-Ren.

She smiles at me then and throws her arms around my neck, filling my chest with happiness like light bursting through after the darkest storm.

She pulls away far too quickly, but I hold on to the feeling. "I knew there was a way to make this work. Just wait until I tell Remus!"

I hide my smile. Unlike me, Remus has always been greedy. And selfish. And self-serving. But him showing his true colors will only drive Lo-Ren more into my arms. Together, we will deal with Remus the way I always have, and I will trust in my family to help me contain him when that time comes.

Chapter Twenty

LAUREN

Two hours later, we're all around the large dining table, digging into the fresh cinnamon rolls I helped Hannah bake. Well, the humans are digging into the rolls. Romulus and his brothers are tearing into barely cooked steak. I have to look away from where Abaddon devours his meal, holding it between his claws, bloody juice dripping down his forearms.

Hannah seems oblivious to her husband's lack of interest in utensils, perhaps having given up at this point, and baby Raven just flits in the air around her father, picking up little pieces of meat he tears off and discards on his plate for her.

Kharon and Ksenia finally come downstairs. "It's happening again," Kharon says, one of his three sets of arms holding tightly to his wife as she walks.

Ksenia looks exhausted and she pauses to hold her stomach. My eyes widen when she winces, and another set of Kharon's hands shoot to surround her stomach as the ghostly specter of runes like I've seen the family use several times erupt from Ksenia's stomach—barely formed like smoke—before dissipating.

"Whoa," I whisper, turning to Romulus. "What does that mean?"

"We don't know," he says quietly back, obviously not wanting to disturb Ksenia and Kharon, who've started walking toward the table again. "It didn't happen in Hannah's pregnancy. So it's worrying."

I gulp, even happier that I got the birth control from Layden yesterday. After last night with Remus. . . yes, he pulled out, but still, I'm not sure I'm ready for babies. And it's looking like we could actually make this work between all of us after all. Remus might not see it yet, but talking with Romulus this morning gave me real hope.

I frown a little, confused about some of my feelings in that regard. Because it didn't feel wrong or weird to wake up like that in Romulus's arms. It felt. . . natural. In a way, I felt so much hope that, of course, this was how it should work. Of course, the three of us could make it work together.

Romulus is so different from Remus and I feel drawn to him differently. And if I'm honest with myself, I don't *only* have strong feelings for Remus. Not that I have the same kinds of feelings for Romulus that I do for Remus! I feel a tight little knot of anxiety even having the thought. No of course not! But was that just because I met Remus first? The thought feels disloyal, and I've never felt so confused.

Would it really be so *bad*, anyway, considering the situation we're in? Romulus is right. They share one body. And considering how complex everything is, if I'm going to love one of them. . . my tummy tightens as I think the L word. . .

I can't finish the terrifying thought, though, because Layden's voice comes shouting down the stairs. "Evac! We've got to evac! NOW!"

Abaddon immediately leaps to his feet, looking to the stairs just as Layden jumps down them two at a time, a huge backpack and several other heavy bags slung over his shoulder.

"What? Why?" Abaddon demands.

"They've found us. They're coming en masse. We've got to go," Layden shouts. "Now!"

"Who?" Kharon demands.

"The government. Russian military," Layden barely stops his motion to explain, clearly annoyed that he even has to. "The wards that kept the castle invisible broke somehow."

"But they were set a thousand years ago and have never so much as—" Kharon starts.

"Well, something happened!" Layden shouts, obviously out of patience. "Because we're visible and on their radar, and they're sending all their firepower at us! We have five minutes, if that. So get your asses to the 'copter!"

Ksenia just sat down, but she grabs the table, readying to heft herself to her feet, a stern expression on her face. "I'll get my guns. We will fight."

But right as she does, she bends forward, a hand on her belly as she squats over, and a rush of water hits the floor. Her water breaking would have been shocking enough.

Except that a second after the first splat of water comes a second rush, this time of blinding white-blue runes that hit the stone floor and turn it into a pearly white pool.

Which Ksenia's left foot then touches and starts disappearing into. It's as if the floor, which was solid only moments ago, is now a deep pool. She slips calf-deep into it before Kharon grasps her with all his arms and yanks her backward out.

I'm frozen, staring at the, what? Multidimensional pool of amniotic fluid? Suddenly, I'm being lifted into Romulus's arms as he sprints with me toward the door.

Kharon has done the same thing with his very pregnant—and I assume *in labor*—wife. Normally, I might have something to say about being carried around like a damsel in distress. But considering the fact that I am officially *way* out of my comfort zone and the entire might of the Russian military is about to descend on us, not to mention the whole woman in labor with a magic baby thing—

So, yeah, I'm happy to be a passenger in Romulus's arms at the moment. I'm capable of a lot of things. Cinnamon rolls, for instance. Office work. I can make a mean spreadsheet.

Battling an oncoming army? Officially beyond my pay grade.

When we get outside, I'm still clinging to Romulus's neck like a monkey. Oh god, what if we're all about to die? Yes, these guys might be like, ancient gods or whatever, but missiles are missiles!

I asked for adventure, but I don't think I meant the scary parts!!

I squeeze my eyes shut, only opening them again when the wind whipping my hair around me stops and I look around, realizing that Romulus is depositing and strapping me into one of the bench seats at the back of the huge military-size helicopter.

I blink, stunned, as I watch Kharon do the same with Ksenia. Her face is knotted in pain as she holds onto her belly. "Just give me a gun, and I'll shoot the fuckers," she yells after breathing through a contraction.

Holy crap, who *is* this woman?

Hannah's in the seat beside her, one arm clutching her daughter and the other reaching out to grasp Ksenia's hand. "How about we focus on keeping this baby inside you 'til we get to safety?"

Ksenia looks up, shooting daggers at Hannah. "But I have to kill anyone who threatens my baby."

Hannah just nods like this is a completely reasonable argument. "What if the contractions disrupt your aim? We can't afford friendly fire right now."

Ksenia frowns as if she's reluctantly forced to acknowledge this logic, only moments before her face is screwed up again in pain from the next contraction hitting.

Kharon stays standing, hovering near Ksenia while also looking out the windows at the top of the helicopter as the back ramp closes up behind us. I look toward the front, where Layden is at the controls, quickly flipping buttons and, moments later, lifting us off the ground.

"I still don't understand what changed," Kharon says, eyes flipping back and forth all around, on guard for incoming threats. "Hundreds and hundreds of years, those runes held."

"Come on, connect the dots," Romulus spits from where he's crouched beside Kharon, similarly on guard and looking out all the windows. "Days after Remus pulls his public stunt, they find us? He exposed us, and they were obviously able to trace him back to our location somehow."

Kharon growls, glancing toward the back of Romulus's head.

My stomach flips with guilt, wondering if Romulus is right. Is this really all because Remus came for me? If that's true. . . My eyes land on Ksenia's pained face as she clutches her stomach through another contraction. Then, dear god, this is all my fault.

"Where are you taking us?" Abaddon demands as we lift further into the air.

"I know somewhere we can go."

"Is it safe for us?" Abaddon asks.

"Safer than here," Layden mutters. Then, "Shit. They're here. On our six. Incoming. Eight fighter jets, and they're firing missiles. Abaddon, Romulus, get the fuck out there and deal with it, or this 'copter and anyone not immortal will be wiped out in about fifteen seconds."

The back ramp of the helicopter lowers again, and before it's even halfway down, Abaddon and Romulus run, wings flared, and dive out.

I scream, then cover my mouth with my hand. Screw it, we're mostly stable. I unbuckle because I have to see what's happening with Romulus. He just flung himself out of a helicopter!

The ramp is now fully open, and my hair whips around my head as I hang on to grips along the roof. I gasp at Romulus and Abaddon, flying with their black wings outspread straight toward the missiles. The twin speeding projectiles are moving so fast I can barely see them, only knowing where they are because of the white trails they leave in the sky. But each brother dives in *front* of them, causing mid-air explosions.

I scream.

But when the smoke clears, the brothers remain, apparently undamaged. They streak toward two other missiles that have gotten even closer to us.

They reach them, and these explosions are even louder, creating turbulence that has me unsteady on my feet. The guys are close enough that I can hear Abaddon's roar as he shoots back toward the jet fighters who launched the missiles, white runes pouring from his hands toward the approaching planes. Almost immediately, they duck off course, one beginning to spiral.

"Unmanned drones coming at our three o'clock!" Layden yells. I'm not sure if Abaddon and Romulus have super-hearing and can hear Layden's call or if they also catch sight of the incoming drone-piloted planes. And it's not just from the right. They're also coming in from the opposite direction.

Abaddon starts tearing into the planes coming from the west, and, midair, I see Romulus's head spin so that Remus's grinning face greets the drone planes from the east. He tears them from the air with such joy and abandon, sling-shotting one into another so that the metal shears another apart.

More and more planes come, but Remus and Abaddon destroy them before they can come near or get a shot off. Kharon, too, watches the skies.

I only happened to look down because Layden swung us south to make our escape, and I have to grab for the wall. Through the window, I see tanks lined up on the ground. Tanks with their long firing tubes pointed straight at the air we're about to fly toward.

"Guys? Guys! There're tanks!" I scream at the same time that Ksenia screams really, really loud.

Layden swings his head back to look at us. "What?" he yells.

I'm about to scream *tanks* again when Ksenia unhooks herself from the bench chair, drops to the floor, hikes her legs up, and screams so loud it's clear she's ready to push out her baby before Kharon can even get there to catch it.

But none of us expect the baby to emerge from between her legs, along with a rush of bright white-blue light runes that burst straight through to the front window, shattering it. The runes continue on fifty feet outside of the helicopter, creating a pearlescent pool like earlier when Ksenia's water broke.

"What the fuck?" Layden shrieks as I finally yell again, "Tanks!"

Layden looks down, finally seeing that the tanks have launched their missiles during the explosive birth. He has just enough time to move the stick of the controls full speed ahead right toward the hovering pearlescent mirror still hanging in the air in front of us.

And just like that—

We head straight into darkness. It's like going from day to night, and it's so pitch dark that the lights of the helicopter barely penetrate, the sky somehow thick and inky.

Then we all hear it, and our heads swing around. That sound. It's already loud in the helicopter with the wind rushing in through the front broken window, the rear ramp still open, and the blades overhead, but this is something far louder. It's a horrible, deep, squawkish scream from some sort of beast. First one and then another.

Raven begins to cry, and Hannah holds her tightly. All of our heads twist back and forth, trying to locate the sources of the sounds. Or to try to discern how close the ungodly creatures might be because they sound like they're in the sky with us.

And they don't sound happy that we're here.

But exactly where the hell *are we*? Is this some sort of—

"Get buckled in," Kharon demands as he grabs his wife and new baby, still wet with afterbirth, off the floor to buckle them on the bench wall. Before he can even get the buckle cinched, something bumps against the helicopter, sending me flying into the opposite wall.

"Thing!" Layden shrieks from the cockpit. "Get us the *hell* out of here."

"I don't know where *here* is."

"Your kid brought us here, and you're the only other realm-jumper I know. So get us all out of here before whatever the fuck is out there decides to eat us for dinner. *You* spend a thousand years boiling in its intestines."

"Fuck," Kharon says, clutching his freshly born daughter tight with his center pair of arms. With the rest, he grabs hold of the helicopter wherever he can, spewing runes that start to cover the helicopter both inside and out.

I watch on in awe, finally managing to buckle myself in right as we jerk roughly again. I look toward the back ramp, where a gigantic, reptile-like claw has gotten hold of us.

"Faster!" I cry, clinging to the belt straps.

"I'm going as fast as I can," Kharon shouts.

The baby in his arms starts crying, and runes begin to pour from her waving fists in a bright stream out the back until another bright pearlescent mirror looms again in the night. The light is enough to illuminate huge beasts with giant flapping wings and clawed feet. Holy shit! I can barely breathe. Are those—? Are those *dragons?*

"Turn it around; we have our way out!" Ksenia yells, one hand clinging to Kharon.

Layden doesn't wait. He swings the 'copter around, backend heavy from our extra passenger still clinging to the entrance, and we wobble as another claw lodges into the side right above my head.

Oh god, we're not going to make it! Those things are going to drag us down out of the air before we can get to the portal—

We tilt wildly back as the snout of the beast holding onto the ramp comes into view. His head is huge, but it's clear he's still much smaller than some of the other shadows we saw silhouetted in the distance.

The entire copter tips backward. Hannah, Ksenia, and I would have fallen out the open back if not for the straps holding us in while Kharon held onto the walls and his newborn daughter with his many hands to keep himself still.

"Get the fuck off my bird!" Layden shouts, and a fire of runes shoots from his fingertips down the center of the aisle past where Kharon is barely holding on.

The runes strike the dragon in the face, and the helicopter drunkenly rights itself just as we tip forward into the shimmering white portal.

Hannah and I scream as the helicopter continues bobbing and then spins wildly once we're back in the sunlight. Hopefully, we at least left behind our passenger when we came back through.

Layden continues spitting out curses as he tries to get the helicopter back under control.

My stomach roils as I try to glance at the ground to see if the tanks are still there, my stuttering mind remembering the threat we were running from when we teetered into that outlandish place, but I only catch a glimpse of smoke rising before we tilt wildly in another direction.

I throw a hand over my mouth. Puking is about to be the least of my worries because we're going down.

Oh god, we're going down. I don't think Layden's going to be able to right us in time!

Suddenly, Abaddon's there in the space visible by the open ramp, grabbing one end of the helicopter from behind. His wings flap furiously as he begins steadying us.

Remus appears at the front windshield.

Together, they straighten us out, and the terrible noise of the churning blades from only moments before suddenly calms down to the normal, easy rhythm.

I breathe out and then laugh, a quick sob escaping before I swallow it down and gulp in a breath. Maybe this is just another day in their lives, but hello? Human here. My life is usually boring, so I'm definitely not used to multiple near-death experiences within minutes of each other.

Remus flies around to join Abaddon at the back and they enter through the open ramp. Remus eyes the claw marks cut into the side of the metal chassis. "What'd we miss?"

He sits down beside me after Abaddon pours a coat of shining blue-white runes around the copter. "There," he says gruffly. "At least the bastards won't be able to track us while we fly."

Everyone seems so calm, like we almost didn't just die in multiple disastrous ways. My heart is still in my throat, and I swipe tears from my eyes.

"Dragons from another realm, I think." My voice is barely a high-pitched peep, and I'm still white-knuckling my seat.

Remus rubs his hands together and looks at Kharon holding his newborn daughter. "Ahhh. *Excellent.* That'll certainly make the vampires happy."

All the heads in the back of the helicopter turn toward Remus, eyes wide. I think I choke a little.

"Vampires?" Abaddon says, sounding anything but amused.

Layden glares back from where he's flying. "Dammit, Remus, I told you that in confidence."

Abaddon glares as he stalks up the narrow aisle to the cockpit. "You're taking us to the vampires?"

Wait. I sit up in my seat straighter. Are they serious? I want nothing more than to hurl myself into Remus's chest and cry for hours until the adrenaline coursing through my body calms down, but his eyes are bright from battle, and now he's talking excitedly about vampires.

So I sit back in my seat, a numb sort of calm descending as Abaddon demands, "Are you an idiot? Did you learn nothing from our little escapades during the Ottoman Empire?"

"They've become more interesting since then," Layden says, never looking away from his beeping instrument panels or acknowledging Abaddon's glare. "Plus, they've gone and gotten themselves a god along with some very powerful witches. Who I happen to be friends with."

"The god or the witches?" Abaddon asks.

"Both." Layden waves a hand over his shoulder. "It'll be a safe place to land." Finally, he does look at Abaddon. "As long as you trust no one and keep your glamours on at all times. I spent some time with them while I was... away. They'll know we're magical but can never know *just* how magical we are."

"We aren't magic, we're gods," Remus grouses.

"That's a matter of contention and certainly not how you should introduce yourself if you don't want trouble," Layden says, shooting Remus a smile. "Or if you'd like your lovely consort to be able to leave."

Immediately, Remus looks my way. It's not the first time he's looked at me since he landed back inside, but it feels like the first time he's actually *seeing* me. "I'd kill them first." He moves toward me. "No one will harm you, I swear it."

"Vampires, remember," Layden mutters. "They're just as immortal as you."

Remus turns his head toward the front, his voice angry. "Then why the fuck are we taking our vulnerable women there?" His entire body hardens in a protective stance.

Another day, another time, I might have argued against the whole *his vulnerable woman* descriptor, but considering I was almost just eaten by a dragon, and they're talking about going to visit some vampires, I'm not going to squabble about semantics. Especially when his arm comes around me, squeezing my shoulder when he feels me shaking.

"Because they're the only place that's truly guarded from the outside world. Which, I'll remind you, is currently trying to kill and or capture all of us right now."

"That was just Russia. And they only found us because Remus is an idiot," Abaddon groused.

Layden ignores us, pulling his headset back on and pushing several buttons.

He makes a motion for quiet that no one pays attention to until he starts talking, his voice suddenly much softer as he connects to whoever's on the other end of the line. Almost intimate.

"Hey, it's me. I know we haven't talked in a while. Okay, longer than a while. Do you still live at your grandpas? Can you meet me there?" Even not being able to see his face, I can feel his wince at whatever response he gets. "I know, I know. But I'm with my family, and it's an emergency."

He pauses. "Yes. All my family. The protection around the castle was breached. You know that thing we talked about? I think it's happening."

"What does that mean?" Abaddon demands, clearly making no pretense of not listening in.

Layden holds up a hand and shoots a glare over his shoulder at his brother before his voice turns soft again. "Okay. We're headed there now. If you could call ahead so they know to expect us, it'd be appreciated. Call Sabra, too." If possible, his voice gets even gentler when he says, "See you soon."

Abaddon's arms are crossed over his chest by the time Layden pushes several more buttons and then stands up, turning toward us.

"Shouldn't you be flying?" Kharon demands.

"It's on autopilot."

"Explain yourself," Abaddon barks.

"Autopilot is—"

"Not that," Abaddon growls impatiently. "Who were you speaking to? Why the hell do you think going to a nest of vampires is a good idea? And what is this *thing* you anticipated that is finally happening?"

"I've been seeing some weird stuff online." Layden sighs. "Not just me. Some of my hacker friends have noticed, too. It's why I don't think it will be just Russia after us."

At his brothers' blank stares, Layden hefts out a breath. It's calming to just observe the brothers through what I absently realize is some sort of shock. "On my computers. There's weird shit going on in the code. I only got a glimpse of it in the Russian government security site I was hacking before I realized they were coming after us—"

Abaddon waves a hand impatiently. "What do we care about the humans' little technologies?"

"We care," Layden says emphatically, "because I saw angelic runes amidst the code."

This has everyone shutting up.

"What does that mean?" I ask.

Layden shakes his head. "I don't know. I've never seen anything like it before. I mean, I've been tempted to use runework with my algorithms before but never dared."

"Why?" This from Hannah.

Layden laughs. "Are you kidding? Human AI has enough dangerous capability to outlearn the humans who engineered it. How fast would the singularity happen if the technology could learn and feed off of angel tech?"

"Our runes are not tech," Kharon says.

Layden rolls his eyes. "Sure they are. Runes are an advanced form of energy and mathematical code far beyond the understanding of this plane of existence. But if they could *learn* it, or their machines could. . ."

"So wait," Hannah says. She's obviously been around all this craziness more because she's taking it in much more stride than me. "You're saying that some other angel did what you didn't and fed runes into the AI, and now we've got an angelic AI about to take over the world?"

"Oh no," Layden laughs. "I doubt we've gotten that far yet. That's just a worst possible scenario."

"Then what the hell are you even talking about?" Abaddon explodes. "And remind me again why we are heading to the *vampires*?"

"Because there *are* angel runes in *some* of the code, mostly government code so far. And not just the Russians, either. I didn't have much time to look, but it's out there. I don't think it's the AI on its own. I'm telling you, there's an angel out there trying to fuck with us. And it's savvy and using every available modern warfare method to find and track us. It's not all cannons and swords anymore, big brother."

Abaddon rocks back on his feet, looking dumbfounded.

Sitting beside me, I can't help but notice Remus's eyes glittering. Is he... excited by these developments? My stomach knots. They *are* talking about war. And from what everyone always says, that's kind of his whole deal, isn't it? Maybe his past isn't as much in the past as I want to pretend.

"Who?" Kharon demands. He's finally handed his daughter to Ksenia since the helicopter has righted, and she's nursing her.

Layden throws his hands up in the air. "Your guess is as good as mine. I didn't think there were any more of our kind left on this plane. Got any more siblings you've pissed off and buried alive while I was away?"

"Are you ever going to let that go?" Abaddon growls. "You know we are the last of our kind."

"Unlesssss," Remus says slowly, drawing out the last word, something like a smile on his face, "Unless Father did something when he got dropped back into the Great Hall by brother dearest." He nods toward Layden. That silences everyone. "Surely you don't think Daddy would have gone down without a fight? He could have sent back something or someone as a present for his misbehaving sons."

Everyone looks at everyone else for several moments while the helicopter flies on in silence. And then Abaddon lets out a single, abrupt "*Fuck.*"

Chapter Twenty-One

REMUS

I stare at Lo-Ren seated beside me on the helicopter, which is finally flying calmly now. Layden even managed to get the back ramp up, though it squealed something awful on the way.

My chest hums with the buzzing adrenaline of the recent conflict and from whatever waits ahead of us. But on the other. . . I frown.

For the first time in my life, I actually want to run in the *opposite* direction of the fight. I want to grab Lo-Ren and flee whatever dangers lay behind these startling developments that have chased us out of our fortress home.

I'm disturbed by the impulse even as I have it.

I'm War. I meet fury with fury and fire with fire.

I do not have pacifist thoughts and have never fled a fight in my life. I should be delighted that we're flying toward a nest of vampires.

I should be planning on how fun it will be to fight an unkillable foe should they get out of line.

Father briefly took an interest in the Ottoman Sultan Mehmed II as he fought to retake Constantinople, a pet city of our father's. He enjoyed backing leaders over the centuries as one after another wrestled the city from each other's control. He once told me that the humans were toddlers fighting over cities like toys.

I'd wondered only very briefly what that made him, whispering in warlords' ears and dispatching his sons to do his deadly bidding on behalf of his whims. He played with the humans like pawns in a game, relishing their destruction over and over again. And when a game piece was crushed, he felt nothing. Certainly not remorse.

I didn't question too deeply, though, for I knew it was in his nature, as it was in mine. We couldn't help ourselves. And heaven pity the poor humans caught in our endless bloody 'game,' for we certainly did not. Allowing cities to be built up, knowing that a hundred or two years later, we'd be back to raze them again.

Mehmed II was conquering the world, for Father had not yet turned on him and soured things as he inevitably always did.

But at the Battle of Vaslui in what is now known as Romania, we met a surprise. We had far superior numbers, one hundred and twenty thousand to their forty thousand. With Romulus helming our strategy, we foresaw their planned ambushes. We were confident of our victory, and my brothers and I went in amongst the armies with the usual confidence, strengthening our number and weakening the opponents.

Then, our troops began falling at alarming speed. Romulus and I kept swapping back and forth—him trying to strategize our way out of the suddenly losing battle and me fighting with all the bloodlust in my heart.

It was Layden who first alerted us to an inhuman being fighting among their ranks—one with an unending thirst. It was no angel, though, and soon Thing was able to give us more detailed reports of those he was carrying to the plane of the dead. They'd all died the same way, not by crossbow, halberd, or sword. Instead, they'd been taken from this plane by brutal gashes at their necks. The neater ones showed two fang marks. Other times, throats were simply ripped out.

I had clenched my two scimitars, one in each hand, and raced into the fighting throng, eager to encounter the thirsty being. The battle was already lost, but I didn't care. I wanted to find it and capture its head. Finally, a battle worth fighting.

When I found it, though, I was surprised to discover it looked just like a man. It moved so quickly it was difficult to see at first, flying through the ranks and ripping out throats, occasionally pausing to gulp the bright red blood before dropping the body of its latest victim.

Then it whirled toward me, its face cocking sideways as if it had sniffed out something different.

Blood gushed like a fountain from its mouth down its neck and chest. It didn't wear the uniform of our opponents; instead, it was dressed like a peasant.

I lowered my scimitars. It looked directly at me, obviously seeing past my rune shield of invisibility. "What are you?" I asked.

I'd barely finished my words before it launched itself in attack.

I easily brought up my scimitars, but my blades clashed against flesh as hard as stone. Harder because I'd cracked stone before with my blows.

It flew at me, fangs bared, and I laughed. I felt the tickle of its fangs against my neck, but that was all. It roared in frustration, and I placed my hand on its chest, pouring runes at it to blast it back from me.

The white-blue light knocked it halfway across the battlefield, scattering troops from both armies as it landed. Then it stood up, shaking its head blearily. It took one last look at me and fled in the opposite direction.

I was about to give chase when Romulus stole my body back, his focus entirely back on the battle at hand instead of the fascinating prize that was slipping through our fingers.

It was little comfort that Father had later agreed with me, beating Romulus with hell-metal chains for not realizing that long-term gains were more important than short-term goals. Especially since we lost the battle anyway. And when I next woke, I had to pay with a body sore from the harsh beating.

But then, I was constantly paying for his bad decisions. I close my eyes as the helicopter blades whir overhead, trying to access our shared memory to see what had happened when Lo-Ren had awoken since *I* obviously wasn't there to see it. But still, there's nothing. I swallow a growl. I didn't intend for my gambit with the potions to work in both directions. I'd only wanted to hide my actions from him, not his from *me*.

My eyes pop back open, and I look at Lo-Ren, whose eyes have dropped closed as if napping or perhaps just trying to regain some equilibrium after the insanity of the escape. I did not mind the chaos of battle—I even enjoyed it a little, if I'm being honest—but these humans have more fragile constitutions.

Did the potion Layden gave me allow me to permanently sever that connection to our shared memory, or like the long bout of wakefulness, will it too wear off?

We haven't had any more run-ins with the vampires since that battlefield more than five hundred years ago, and Romulus always thought the encounter with my angel runes had sent it scurrying underground like a cockroach.

We only heard tales of pale bloodsuckers over the years from the same region of eastern Europe. Yes, I have to say my interest is piqued to meet them again.

If only these were different circumstances. I frown deeper and feel my eyebrow furrowing as I continue to look at Lo-Ren. Fuck, she's so young and perfect and... *innocent*. That word whispers like a curse through my mind. And now we're taking her from one den of monsters into another.

All for what? Because I wanted a consort? I press a hand to my chest and swallow.

"What is it?" Kharon asks. "Are you well?"

I drop my hand. "I'm fine," I bark gruffly. Lo-Ren's eyes pop open, and she looks at me, which makes me feel even—

Dammit, that's the problem. She's making me *feel* things. Things other than want and lust and bloodlust, the only emotions I thought myself capable of. But this...

Again, my chest squeezes uncomfortably, and I want to press my palm against it until the sensation goes away again.

For the first time in my whole life, I worry I've done the wrong thing.

If I end up putting her in harm's way, I'll never forgive myself. She is not just another human. I knew she was a prize above all others, but I did not anticipate how...

Yes, my dumb brothers were capable of falling for *their* humans, but I thought getting a consort of my own would just be like any other thing I conquered. She is not just some prize, though. She is more. She is—

"Okay," Layden says from the front. "We're about to land. Glamours on."

Chapter Twenty-Two

LAUREN

"Be calm," Remus says from beside me as the chopper begins to descend. It's strange to see him and his brother without wings, hidden under the guise of whatever a glamour is. I want to ask a thousand questions as I look up into his face, which is even more slightly altered, as if the proportions have been pulled back into a less exaggerated shape. He doesn't exactly look like his twin, but it's nearer. Speaking of—the glamour made Romulus disappear completely, cloaking him with a natural-looking head of hair.

Even Kharon looks fully human, with only two arms, like a large wrestler with tan skin instead of blue. In one arm, he holds his swaddled newborn, and in the other, he cradles Ksenia, who looks exhausted from the mid-flight birth.

"I'm calm," I say in a whisper.

Remus arches an eyebrow down at me. "Your muscles are tense

as stone, and I'm sure your heart is racing. Our new guests will be able to hear it."

I feel my eyes pop wide. "That doesn't help!" I squeak.

He shrugs and reaches over, intertwining his fingers with mine. "I suppose it's better to be more on guard than less in this situation. But you should know better than to worry when you have me at your side."

I look up at him, still a little weirded out by how, well, *normal* he looks. "Are they really—you know—" I gesture with the hand he's not holding, not quite able to bring myself to say the word 'vampires.' Because, seriously?

"I've only met one, and he was very," Remus wiggles his eyebrows, "*you know*." What? No, I do not know? But then he looks away, not offering any more explanation. "Let's hope they've become a little more civilized since the last one I encountered."

Well, now my heart is *really* racing. But I guess I should have known better than to turn to Remus, of all people, for assurance. I know what everybody says about him, but surely he's not *looking* for a fight, is he? Is it bad that I'm kinda sorta wishing it was Romulus in charge of the body right now instead of him? Immediately, I feel bad for the thought and squeeze his hand tighter. Maybe I'm just letting everyone else's voices get in my head. Remus squeezes my hand back. I try to take it as reassurance.

And then we touch down.

Moments later, the back ramp is lowering. It screeches before making it past a certain point and continuing, I assume, because of the damage incurred when we were in that terrifying other place when the creature attacked us. My eyes immediately zoom in on the claw marks.

That is, until the ramp lowers more to see a tight grouping of about twenty men, all dressed in sleek black and standing in the courtyard where we've touched down. They stand ramrod straight, hands behind their backs, identical black hair and dark eyes watching us.

My nails dig into Remus's hand, but he doesn't so much as flinch. Indeed, when I look over at him, he's smiling.

Layden immediately walks up the aisle and down the ramp before it's all the way lowered, easily hopping off to the ground. The rest of us stand up, Abaddon taking the lead and pushing his wife, who's holding his daughter, behind his large, bulky, glamoured shape. Even disguised as a human, he's still intimidating, especially with the scowl permanently plastered to his face as he waits to see how Layden will be received.

Layden walks right up to the group and instead of holding out a hand, tugs down his collar and bares his neck. I hear a little growl from Remus in front of me and immediately know there's no way he'll be offering the same in greeting.

The man at the front of the pack tilts his head slightly in acknowledgment, and they begin to speak. I'm too far away to hear what's being said, though I suspect Remus and his brothers, with their superior hearing, catch every word. The suspicion is reinforced when Remus, Kharon, and Abaddon all tense and lean forward at the same time like they're getting ready to attack.

Ksenia must sense the same because she places a hand on Kharon's shoulder from behind. "We need a place to rest," she reminds him.

He only lets out a small, growled murmur in response, eyes still tensely on the exchange happening between Layden and the man at the head of the group.

But then the brothers' heads swing toward the right. It takes several more moments before I hear what they obviously already did —a loud motor of some kind speeding towards us.

I frown, wanting to bend over and look through the chopper window but not wanting to draw any attention from the men below. They, too, are looking the same direction, but they don't seem perturbed by whatever they're seeing. Layden, also looking that way, smiles like he's relieved. What on earth?

And then the motorcycle comes into view, louder than ever,

circling right behind the gathered men in the courtyard and stopping dramatically. The slight figure pulls her helmet off to reveal a shock of curly dirty blonde hair and a beautiful face.

"Grandpa," the woman sing-songs, "I'm ho-oooome." Then she kicks out a stand, leans the bike over and hops off it at the same time, sauntering up to where Layden and the scowling man he was having a glare match with are standing.

She kisses the scowling man on both sides of his cheeks. I frown. *Grandpa?* The guy looks to be in his early thirties. Then I remember... *vampires.* And gulp. Holy crap. Am I really looking at a group of vampires? So how on earth is he her grandpa? How do vampires... make more vampires?

Which is when I realize that I am so in over my head and have been for a while now. I thought I could handle being a consort or whatever to a god. And then the rest of his god or supernatural angel family comes home. And oh yeah they're all the Horsemen of the Apocalypse. Then we're attacked and now seeking refuge with freaking *vampires...*

A smarter girl would have gotten off this ride about five stops ago.

And maybe I would have. I don't like danger. I can't even handle scary movies.

But I do actually know why I keep hanging around, and it's not even a morbid curiosity that, like the cat, might just get me killed if I'm not careful.

Dammit, this man who's hand I'm holding has bewitched me. Though I know, or think I know, that in spite of all the supernatural crap swirling around me, it's the one thing that feels... well, *real.* Grounded.

So when Layden seems to relax after the woman has a quick conversation with her 'Grandpa' and then Layden's waving a confident hand for us all to depart the helicopter, I'm able to follow confidently. Well, I can pretend confidence with the best of them. I can only pray and trust its not one of the most foolish decisions I'm making in my life.

Chapter Twenty-Three

REMUS

I'm constantly aware of Lo-Ren's presence as we walk down the ramp and into enemy territory. My nose takes in every scent. My brother's and their women and children. The summer air and the forest beyond the mountain fortress.

And of course the group of cold, deathless creatures standing in front of us, faces grave in anything but warm greeting. I search the faces of each of them. Granted the one I met so long ago was covered in blood, but I have an excellent scent memory, and I don't think he is here.

"Hi, I'm Phoenix," says the woman who rode in on the motorcycle, stepping up and holding out a hand to Abaddon, a welcoming smile on her face as if she is not standing in front of a host of vampires. I frown and tilt my head. This one's scent is quite different. Like nothing I've ever encountered before, and I've traveled everywhere there is to travel on this small globe. She certainly does not smell undead.

My eyes flick to Layden, who's eyes bounce back and forth between her and the men behind her. We wasted time on the plane. We should have been grilling little brother more about the dynamics of the tenuous situation we were walking into.

Abaddon introduces himself and his little family, then the rest of us. We all nod when he says our name.

The man Layden first approached steps forward—Phoenix's *Grandpa Vlad*. "Layden never told us of his extensive family when he last visited us."

The man is tall by human standards, six feet at least, and he has perfectly smooth skin. He watches everyone with his dark eyes.

"I would think one such as you would understand the need to be... circumspect in matters of family."

Vlad's eyebrow lifts ever so slightly. "One such as me. And what might one such as *you* be called?"

"I've already told you my name is Abaddon."

"I was not referring to your name."

I know my brother well enough to sense the danger in his smile when he responds, "I'm sure I don't know what you mean."

"I mean," Vlad bends forwards at the waist, inhaling deeply, "that I can *smell* the power emanating off of you. But you are not witches, nor dybbuks, nor any other wielder of magic I've ever met before."

"Yet my brother spent time amongst you."

"We thought he was an anomaly."

Abaddon shrugs. "Everyone comes from somewhere."

"You dance around my question."

"I was informed my family and I might have sanctuary here." Abaddon's voice and stance becomes harder. "Is that the truth, or should we leave now?"

"Of course, we'll provide sanctuary," Phoenix says, butting into the conversation, her grandfather shooting her a look that would shrivel the soul of most. Phoenix ignores it—fascinating. Even more fascinating, her grandfather allows the interruption. He seems like the beheading rather than the benevolent kind.

"We appreciate powerful allies in these tumultuous times," Phoenix says smoothly. "And we don't have to tell all of our secrets. We barely know each other." She shoots her grandfather a significant look. He glares back silently for so long I don't think he ever will.

Finally, though, he turns back toward us, putting on a clearly disingenuous smile. "I am Vlad Dracul. Welcome to our home. We are glad to offer sanctuary to your family. One of my sons will show you to your rooms." He makes a quick gesture, and a man from behind him scurries forward.

"I'm happy to take them," Phoenix gestures her arm towards the building behind her.

"You will stay here," Vlad says, voice gruff but clearly authoritative. I don't miss the twitch of Phoenix's mouth at being ordered around, but she nods, tilting her face toward the ground. There's some sort of fascinating play for power between these two. Usually, it would be the sort of thing that would fascinate, nay even delight me.

Right now, though, I only frown seeing it, because I don't like my consort and I being caught in the middle of a vampire family power struggle.

My family is usually raucous and loud no matter where we are, but we're all quiet and on guard as we follow Vlad's 'son' out of the courtyard and into a corridor that finally leads into the wood and stone fortress. Are all the other twenty or so men in the courtyard really his sons? I can tell they're vampires, but we have so little information on the creatures, we do not even know how they are created.

"We will send someone to the local town for food," says the man leading us. A chilling reminder that our hosts don't need to eat. Which makes me curious about how they meet the needs of their peculiar dietary requirements.

"Here is our guest wing," the man says once we get to an inner corridor, gesturing ahead. "You have your pick of five guest suites.

Father suggests you rest for the evening. He and Phoenix will meet you, Layden, to discuss security concerns in an hour."

"And me," Abaddon adds. "I am the patriarch of this family."

The man looks like he wants to argue but finally nods. "And you, then. But the rest of you," he looks us all over briefly, "can rest until we meet again in the morning to talk over more details of your stay."

Kharon nods, putting a large glamoured arm around Ksenia and heading toward the closest room, obviously only wanting to get his wife and daughter to a place to rest. It's understandable, considering the woman just gave *birth*. I don't know much about human females, but I understand that birthing another being is generally quite an ordeal.

Normally, I would be feeling a flutter inside to get up to some mischief or other considering all the possibilities of this place. . . but I find myself also experiencing some strangely mundane protective feelings. I decide to be annoyed about that another time. At the moment, all I want is to put a thick door between Lo-Ren and anything with fangs.

I put an arm around her shoulder and start to direct her to the door beside Kharon's, at the last moment detouring one room further down. Babies cry, and I don't want us to be disturbed tonight.

Chapter Twenty-Four

LAUREN

As soon as Remus closes the door behind us, I grab his arm. "Oh my gosh, this is officially the creepiest place I've ever been," I whisper, looking around a room that looks like a fine hotel suite, if the interior decorator had a fetish for black. At least it wasn't black and red—that would have been a little too on the nose.

Instead, there's a black accent wall behind the large king-sized bed, with textured wallpaper on the other three walls. There are no windows. *Naturally*, I think, a moment later. Is this where visiting vampires sleep? Just how many of them were out there, anyway? How has a whole world been hiding right within the one I knew?

Then again, from what Remus said, he'd only seen one vampire before, and he and his brothers have been around forever. But I shudder as I remember the other things the head honcho guy had talked about. "And what the hell is a dybbuk?"

Remus just waves a hand. "I wouldn't worry about that. They're probably just a myth."

"Like vampires?" I ask with a hand on my hip. "And the Four Horsemen of the Apocalypse?"

He shrugs and comes closer. "All that matters now is that we're safe."

"For the moment."

With another shrug, he wraps his arms around my waist and draws me close. "This moment is all we need."

I let out a little huff, staring up at his strange, glamoured face. "It's weird not being able to see you."

"I'm still here. And what, I thought you'd like this more handsome me?"

I frown at him. "I like you just the way you are. And I miss your tail and wings."

He cracks a grin at that. "For once, I'm trying to be a good boy and follow Abaddon's rules. He says to keep the glamour on at all times here. But I still have these two hands."

He drops them down my waist, curving around to my backside and squeezing. "Even when I was plucking planes out of the air today, I could still taste remnants of your essence on my tongue. You drive me wild, beautiful one." Then he quirks an eyebrow, far less dramatically than usual in his glamoured state. "Or perhaps I should say, you drive me tame."

"I don't ever want to tame you." I frown.

He chuckles. "It might not be the worst thing in the world. Even I can admit sometimes I get a little. . ." his head goes side to side, ". . . unpredictable at times."

Which makes me laugh. How on earth can he make me comfortable enough to laugh here? Maybe because when I'm with him, even in what feels like a dangerous place, I feel at home. That's a wild thought, and it feels risky to think. Also far too soon. It's probably just the leftovers from the multiple rushes of adrenaline today.

At the same time, I don't care if it's that same adrenaline that has me throwing my arms around his neck. So strange. The glamour even makes his hair *feel* like hair instead of when my fingers brush against his brother's face. I want to get lost in him completely and wash away all the terrors and uncertainties that lie outside that door.

He drops his lips to mine so I can kiss him, but before I've gotten a taste of his lips, he's pulling back again. He frames my face with his large, strong hands and searches my eyes, his face serious.

"How are you really, though, my beautiful one? Everything has been happening so fast. I want nothing more than to fall into bed with you—"

"So let's," I interrupt, reaching up on tiptoes to kiss him again.

But he pulls away just before I can make contact, and I let out a little discontented whine.

"I want to connect to you in every way," he says, smoothing my hair back from my face. "There were many shocks today. I have seen humans after battle before. It can take hours for the effects to be felt."

Even as he says the words, I start to tremble.

"Come," he says gently, reaching down for my hand to draw me toward the attached room where there's both a bath and a large, separate shower. Large enough that there's a bench along one wall and multiple showerheads.

"Big enough for two," he says, sliding his hand down my curves. "After the day you've had, you deserve to relax." He leans in to whisper. "Let me wash it all away."

I shiver this time from good feelings, not remembered terror. I've almost forgotten this side of Remus. But this is how he was when I first got to know him. Before any of the craziness. Before I met Romulus or his family or we had to run for our lives.

He shifts me and tugs my shirt over my head, and I relax back against his chest. The room is cold, so I shiver a little.

"Don't be sweet and gentle now," I whisper, crossing my arms to cover my tummy. "I can't bear it." Tears cluster in my eyes.

"Would you rather I was a beast?" he murmurs, turning me

around to face him after peeling off the rest of my outer clothes. He's undressed, too, and I blink, struggling not to look down.

I'm still wearing my bra and underwear, but somehow, I've never been so bared and naked before him. I don't know if it's just because I'm so exhausted by everything that's happened today, but I feel terribly vulnerable.

"Today must have been terrifying for you," he says as if reading my mind.

I nod, my throat clogged. "I was so worried—" I cut off, almost hiccupping. "Ksenia, I mean, she had a baby right in front of me on a helicopter that was about to go down. And then we were in this whole other—" My brain scrambles for the words to even describe it. "*Place* where these huge flying things were attacking us, and you weren't there—"

His arms close around me and shut off my increasingly frantic words. I guess even I hadn't realized just how freaked out I'd been by it all. Everything happened so fast, and then it was over, and I was so thankful we were all okay, but—

Suddenly, I'm crying. Tears I can't control.

"I should never have left your side," he says. I'm all but shuddering in his arms now.

"Yes, you should have," I cry into his chest. "Or else we would have been blasted out of the air by missiles! But yeah." I turn my teary face into his warmth as he rubs my back. "It was a lot."

"Let me make it up to you." The words are a whisper against my ear as he nestles his head down against mine. "Let me take it all away."

I nod fervently against his chest, and he walks us toward the shower, only pulling away long enough to turn on the shower spray. He unhooks my bra and slowly, eyes never losing contact with mine, peels it off me. Then his hands are at my hips, and when he bends over to tug my panties down my thighs, I swear I can feel the heat of breath as he inhales and exhales quickly before my panties are at my ankles.

He leads me inside the marble and glass, and it's the perfect amount of hot and steamy.

He positions me right underneath the main spray, and my muscles immediately relax a little. He's standing behind me and must feel whatever tension is left, though, and begins to massage my shoulders.

"I want you to give yourself over to me completely now," he murmurs.

I nod, still hiccupping from tears. Yes, please. I still feel so overwhelmed by everything. I feel so secure in his arms, in his care, and it sounds like heaven to give it over to him. To give up control.

I've been fighting for so long to keep my head above water. Long before I met him. In my last relationship, I always felt like I had to walk on eggshells because I never felt secure with Michael. Then, at home with Mom, I felt like I had to have a hard shield up all the time so her little barbs wouldn't skewer me.

But from the beginning with Remus, it's never been like that. In spite of all the unusual circumstances of meeting him, he's always made me feel safe and secure. So it's the easiest thing in the world for me to say, "Yes. Please take care of me for a little while."

He gives a corresponding growl of appreciation from low in his throat that almost sounds animalistic.

One arm wraps possessively around my thick waist as the other reaches in front of me for the shampoo. The most heavenly scent fills the steamy air, and moments later, I sigh in pleasure as his lathered fingers sink into my hair.

He washes my hair slowly, massaging my scalp as he goes. I sink back against him, trusting him to hold my weight. It almost feels like some sort of sacred religious act as he tips me forward to wash the soap out of my hair. I keep my eyes closed, breathing out of my mouth as the hot, soapy water falls around my face, his fingers continuing to massage my hair clean.

"So, so soft," he murmurs in his deep voice, and I feel the reverberations of his deep timbre all throughout my body.

But turns out I've only begun to feel the holiness of his ministrations. He conditions my hair with just as much gentleness and provides a second scalp massage.

Next, he draws one arm up, placing my hand high on the still-cool marble, and he washes from under my arm to the tips of my fingers, paying attention to each one. He does the same with the other hand, pressing it against the glass, both arms still raised as he comes back to my breasts, which swing free. After pouring more soap into his hands, he cups my breasts.

Stepping close into me from behind so that his chest is against my back, I shudder, my pussy clenching in need as he soaps and massages my breasts, pinching ever so slightly at my nipples before washing down my belly.

I shudder again, and my hands start to drop, but his soapy hands massage up my biceps, pressing them back against the marble and glass. I sigh in pleasure at the reminder that he's in control and I don't have to think or worry about a single thing. For once, I'm not the one making any decisions, and it's so freeing.

His hands come back to my breasts, and again, his thumb and forefinger pinch at my nipples. A hiss of pleasure escapes my lips. I feel his lips against the back of my neck, and then he's rubbing down my belly.

Unlike most men who barely want to acknowledge I have a belly, much less ever glancingly touch it on accident, he massages deep with purpose down the center of it as he gets lower and lower. My eyes blink open in the steamy shower as I feel—Oh god, that feels so good. The pressure there, I can feel it in my—

When he makes his way to my fupa, both of his hands get involved, massaging me in a way that is so teasing that I'm panting and want to turn around and climb him.

But no. I've given over control to him.

I just didn't think it would be so hard, especially when he keeps teasing me, skimming his fingertips across my pussy in the barest touch before moving around to massage my ass. I'm not sure if there's even the pretense of washing me anymore, and I'm not mad about it.

His hands are so strong as he grasps my ass cheeks, rubbing them firmly. I begin to tip forwards from the pressure, but before my hands move to right myself, his tail suddenly whips out to wrap itself around my waist.

I gasp. "But you're not supposed to—" He's supposed to stay glamoured.

His hands tug my ass cheeks wide apart, and then suddenly, I feel his hardness there and shudder with want. "I never was good at following the rules," he growls in my ear.

I nod vigorously. "Rules are overrated," I gasp.

"Move your hands to the front wall of the shower," he says, his voice low and gruff in that way it gets when he's turned on. God, I love it when he gets like this. Like a barely controlled storm.

He moves with me, his body all but cemented against my back as we step forward into the multiple sprays so that I can press both palms against the front marble wall.

"That's my good girl," he whispers in my ear before leaning forward to tug my earlobe between his teeth. His hands are still on my ass, tugging me wide, and I can feel water rushing down between my ass cheeks.

He reaches for a squirt of soap, and then he's washing me there. I gasp in excitement at the intimacy as his fingers probe me.

"You said you'd give me all of yourself. Would you even surrender this?" he asks, one of his thick fingers probing my anus.

"Yes," I barely manage to gasp, wiggling my ass a little further toward his searching fingers. "*Everything.* I'm yours."

He does that satisfied growl thing that he did earlier, and his tail unwraps from my waist, instead looping around my upper thigh and squeezing. The very tip of it swipes back and forth against my swollen, sensitive pussy. I gulp, my fingertips scrabbling for purchase against the smooth marble.

"Relax," he hisses as his finger continues exploring me. Guys have wanted to fuck my ass before, but I've never let anyone. This is why, I think. I've never trusted anyone this much to be able to relax. I've played with myself back there. Used some beads with a lot of lube and all the lights off a couple times.

But I feel safe with Remus. I suck in a breath of air and do as he says, relaxing for him.

His strong hands pry me open, and I'm even more excited at the forbidden heights he always pushes me to. Especially when his finger searches unashamedly against my back hole, feeling out the contours. The constantly rushing water isn't exactly the same as lube, but he's got me so relaxed...

His finger pops inside me, and we both groan.

"That's right." His voice is in my ear as he leans down, cuddling his face against mine from behind. "Let me inside your secret places. Relax and let all of me in." His finger slides in and out just the tiniest bit, and my eyelids flutter at the unusual sensual sensation. It was nothing like this when I played with myself furtively in the dark.

I don't know what it is about being with him, but every sexual act feels ten thousand times more intense when it's at his hands.

"I'm here with you," he murmurs just loud enough to be heard above the spray. I relax back against him, knowing this is what makes the difference. Trust, yes, but also the intimacy of being totally *with* him, present in each of these moments. I've never known anything like it.

My whole life has been so combative with the people around me. This kind of intimacy is almost beyond understanding.

And with his finger probing me back there, I feel even more wild. Like he's stripped me down beyond skin to the being I am within. Human, angel, none of that matters here. We're two creatures who managed to find one another against all odds, and I need more; I've never felt so hungry for *more*.

So I wiggle my ample backside against him, and with one hand, he holds my cheeks open wide while he wiggles his finger deeper. I gasp as he stretches me, slipping a different finger inside my sex for lubrication before joining the first.

He's stretching me with purpose.

I groan my pleasured assent and wiggle even harder against him, pushing back as his second fingertip massages around the entrance of my anus where the first is already inserted.

The flat, leathery tip of his tail has begun massaging my wet, swollen clit and I let out a high-pitched whine, so on edge even as there's a small bite of pain as his second finger finally pops past the ring of muscle to make its way into my ass. I know how thick his fingers are and the thought of two of them in my ass makes my head thrash back and forth in the spraying water. Because I know his cock is even thicker. His fingers hook inside me and he massages me, opening me up as he steps closer so I can feel his hardness between my legs.

"Will you let me take you completely?" he asks in my ear. I'm already nodding before the question is out. God yes. I feel so crazy turned on at the very thought.

"Let me hear you say it," he rasps, his fingers working me even more fervently. "Beg for what only your dark god can give you."

"P-p-please," I finally manage words. "Please let me feel you there."

"Where? Where do you want me?"

He spanks me with the hand not inside me.

"I want you to fuck my ass," I holler, my voice echoing back in the small, enclosed chamber of the shower.

"That's right," he growls. "You are mine."

Then I feel his cock drag along my pussy lips between my legs before it's there where his fingers are. At the same time I feel his hardness nudging while his fingers pull out, his tail moves from my clit to probe at my pussy's entrance.

I gasp, my fingers again scrabbling against the wet marble.

The next moment, he's penetrating me. Both from behind, and oh, god—

I reach a hand down from the marble and clench it around the thick tail that has just slid inside my pussy, urging it deeper. Fuck, that's so dirty. And so right. I feel completely claimed.

"Yes," Remus says, "You are mine. Finally. Completely. Mine."

"How much control do you have over your tail?" I whimper as I grasp the thick appendage even harder. It swivels around in my pussy while the intense fullness of him at my backside has my eyes rolling back in my head.

"Not much, why?" Remus says, at the same time that a nearly but not quite identical voice says, "Complete. And I can feel everything."

"What the—" Remus starts to tug away, but I hold tighter to his —*their*—tail.

"Don't go," I beg, wild with lust and on the edge of the headiest orgasm I've ever had. Are Remus *and* Romulus really both there? Both awake and penetrating me at the same time? I clench all my muscles on their cock and tail, and almost simultaneously, both of their voices groan in deep pleasure.

"Feel her brother," comes Romulus's voice. "She wants this."

"How are you awake?" Remus growls but doesn't pull away this time. Instead, he only grips my hips and begins to move his cock in my ass, plunging slightly in and out in a way that has me barely able to separate one thought from another. Especially while the tail in my pussy has found an especially sensitive spot that has my eyes flying open.

"I don't know, and I don't care," Romulus says. "Let's take care of her. Together, brother."

I gasp, my fingernails squeezing the tail as pleasure bites through me. *G-spot*. I think Romulus found it and is massaging my G-spot with such intensity that I—

At the same time, Remus's cock presses forward between the thin layer of flesh between their two appendages, making it feel sooooo—

I scream and thrash, their hands keeping me up as I give over to the pleasure spiking from my pelvis outward. It feels like a miracle, and my entire body seizes and clenches on both of them.

Chapter Twenty-Five

ROMULUS

I don't know if this is some once-in-a-lifetime magic. I can't see her, only the steam and the back wall of the shower.

But oh, gods that I'm suddenly tempted to believe in, I can *feel* her. It's so intimate with her grasping my tail like that with such need. I never imagined a tail could feel like a—

I'd swear I was fucking her, except with the most dexterous cock, and when I close my eyes, I can feel every bit inside her, especially the tiny bulbous, bubble-like spot deep in her center. When I rub and press on it, she clenches her inner muscles at the same time, and her nails dig into the outer length of my tail.

Feeling her go wild, losing herself to pleasure while impaled between us, is the single most glorious moment of my life. Beyond battle glory, beyond any successful scheme, waking to find her grasping my tail and tugging me into her sacred place is the single most cherished memory I'll ever care about. This alone I want to hold on to. Forever.

I feel my shared spine with Remus go stiff, and then pleasure rocks us both. It is both my body and not. I can control nothing except our tail, but I don't care. I'm awake, and I feel the echoes of my brother's pleasure as his cock releases its gush.

The adrenaline of pleasure lights up my own brain centers, and together, the three of us quake and drip and clench around one another. The shower spray continues as if it will wash away all our secrets.

And then, when I blink next, I realize I am now looking at the back of my beloved Lo-Ren's head, and *my* cock is still stiff, though spent and dripping, embedded in her dark anus. I shudder, one last small gush of pleasure spurting out as Lo-Ren clenches again around my cock. *My* cock now.

I can't feel my tail anymore, and I look behind me as if I could see if Remus is awake. But, of course, it's impossible to see the back of one's own head.

"Brother?" I call, but there's only silence.

I close my eyes and bow my forehead against Lo-Ren's back. With a grunt of disappointment, I carefully withdraw my cock from her precious ass.

"Who's there?" Lo-Ren asks, voice uncertain.

My chest clenches. Will she be displeased to hear it is me? "Romulus," I say, hoping my voice is not as weak as my legs suddenly feel. "Just Romulus now."

It feels both wrong and right to have this stolen pleasure with her. But I can still remember her hand clutching the tail and guiding me into her. I can remember her holding both of us, *knowing* it was both of us. When I feel her body stiffen slightly, I fear for the worst.

Still, I dare to ask, "May I wash you clean?"

She's still facing forward, and I hear her small inhale of breath before her quiet, furtive voice comes. "Yes. Please."

My hand trembles as I reach forward to touch the flesh I was just so intimate with. Looking around, I find the soap. I rub my hands together to create suds, then dare to touch the sweet globes of her ass. She trembles at my touch, and I know it's not from cold. It's far too steamy for that.

"Is this too much?" I ask, my open palms paused on her wide, sumptuous ass cheeks.

"N-no," comes her stuttered voice. "P-please."

Maybe it's wrong to steal this moment when Remus isn't here. But she needs to be cleaned after our release. It's what I tell myself anyway as I slide my hand down between the seam of her ass, working my soapy fingers toward the anus we were just buried inside.

She hisses when I come in contact with her sensitive back entrance. My cock surges with blood again, but I ignore it. I instead focus on her, reaching up and detaching the shower head so I can direct the spray toward where I've just been washing. I spray with one hand and wash thoroughly with the other as soap and the remnants of our cum drip down her inner thighs.

"So beautiful," I can't help hissing. She's slightly bent over so I can aim the spray better, her gorgeous ass pushed back. From this angle, her pussy winks at me, and so badly I want to give it attention under the guise of 'washing it,' too.

"Is this wrong?" she whispers, suddenly standing up and spinning around to look up at me with innocent doe eyes. It takes everything within me not to stare down at her gorgeous, dripping breasts. "I mean," she frowns, looking so confused. "I'm with Remus. And I know he seemed okay with what just happened." She shakes her head, frowning harder. "But this. . ." She waves a hand between us.

"Don't worry," I say, ignoring every instinct that tells me to swoop down and press my advantage. I want to take her lips. I want to press her against the marble and work that sweet pussy of hers some more. I want to drop to my knees and taste her with my tongue until she forgets she ever knew my brother's name.

Instead, I merely place a tender kiss on her forehead. "We can get out and dry off now." I reach behind her and turn off the shower. I can't help noticing her gasped breath as I do so, though, because my cock is still hard and long. But I won't push.

She's been so brave, so unafraid to open herself to us. Yes, I might wish I could kiss and taste her, but I will not beg heaven for the whole kingdom when I have been given a day pass to the palace.

She doesn't say anything as we step out of the shower into the steamy bathroom. I hand her a large, sumptuous bath towel and stay mute as I tie a towel around my waist and then take another to gently wrap around her hair.

I lead the way back into the other room, where clothing has been discretely laid out for us on a cart just inside the door. Did Remus not lock the door when they came in? Oh well, some servant or other likely got an earful because we were not quiet in the bathroom.

Lo-Ren turns her back to me as she dresses, so I do the same to give her privacy. Not that I will ever forget the sight or feel of her wet, naked body in my arms or how she clenched around me while I was inside her. No, that is not something a man gets over quickly or ever.

I've gotten so used to her silence that I'm a little startled when she suddenly speaks. "Are you okay with what just happened? Because god, to wake up to that, and not to have any say in what's happening— We're barely even friends, and then you wake up to Remus being *intimate* with me with your own body. I can't even imagine what any of this has been like for you or how weird—"

"Not weird at all," I say, turning back to her as I yank a well-fitted sweater over my head. She's dressed in a similar dark sweater and shapely, fitted jeans. "I know I haven't always expressed myself well. But I find you very attractive."

She frowns and I am frustrated with myself. For famously being a tactician, now that it is my moment with the woman that I've begun to long for, I am not finding the words well. "I mean that I like you very much."

"I know last time we talked, you said you would be content if

Remus and I could find a way to make it work. That's one thing. But this is—" She breaks off, eyes wide. "It feels unfair to you."

She's expressed this sentiment before and I shake my head, frustrated she misunderstood me back then because of all I didn't say. "If there had been any way for me to pursue you myself. . ." I trail off. "I recognized that you were with my brother, but at the same time, I didn't trust his motives."

But she's caught up only on the first part of what I've said. "You would have wanted to pursue me?" She sounds shocked.

"I—" I start, then break off, scrubbing a hand down my face. "Were I not attached to a—" I stop myself before saying *madman*. We're too far past the name-calling stage now. "Were I not in this unique situation, of course I would."

I take another step closer and clasp her hands. She looks up at me searchingly, her eyes so deep and glossed with a sheen of tears. All I want to do is swoop down and kiss her. "If I weren't in this impossible situation."

She nods, then looks down at our hands. I see her head shake. "The truth is, normally, I wouldn't even be looking at another man if I was with someone. But this—" She lifts her face to me again. "Neither of you wants to admit it, but you *are* stuck with each other. And today, for the first time, you were able to *communicate*. What if this is an amazing opportunity we're all being presented with?" she asks, her eyes suddenly so full and bright.

I blink at her, a hope I can't even name taking flame in my chest even as I tell myself I'm the world's biggest fool to allow it.

But she just continues, unaware of how she could crush me. "What if we could make this work?" She squeezes my hands so tight that I'm tempted to believe anything that comes out of her beautiful mouth. "The three of us? What if that's why Remus found me after all this time of you two being alone?"

Her sweet hope and optimism are so beautiful and tempting to believe. I want to believe there's a small possibility she's right and that the brother I think I know will surprise me with a maturity and depth

I never suspected him capable of. Maybe she *has* been seeing things in him I've refused to my whole life out of some kind of jealous spite. Maybe if we *could* just communicate rather than mutely battling one another for dominance and space in this body. . .

Even as I think about it, I remember my brother is the angel of War. My conscience pricks the next second because that's not exactly true, either. We *both* are. And maybe we can never change so long as both of us keep such a combative stance. Surely, if one of us were to give before the other, I'm the logical choice.

Still, I'm not sure I completely believe in the possibility of peace between Remus and me as I pull Lo-Ren to my chest and stroke her wet hair with my fingers. "Maybe so. Maybe so."

With my other arm, I hold her fiercely. "I just know that any bit of yourself you'd share with me would feel like a miracle."

Her arms wrap around my waist in return. "We should get some rest," she says against my chest. "Will you hold me tonight?"

I want to growl in satisfaction at her request, and for a brief rebellious moment, I wish I could meet my brother face to face on a field of battle so I might fight him for her favor like the knights of old. Then I remember, *peace, peace,* yes, we're trying out the wild idea of peace.

As I climb into bed and Lo-Ren tucks her warm body against mine, I wonder to what lengths I might go in order to keep her by my side now that I've discovered this feeling. It is not a thought that feels especially peaceful.

Chapter Twenty-Six

ROMULUS

As I wake, I realize I'm still me and in charge of our body. I hear a gentle knock at the door and, hurriedly so Lo-Ren won't wake, unwind her body from mine and lay her on the pillow beside me. She stirs slightly, but then her gentle snores continue. I smile, then hurry toward the door before whoever's there can knock again.

I quickly glamour myself, then open it to find Abaddon hulking beyond the door. It's strange to see his usual lion's face shaped into that of a bearded man's. At the same time, it's still recognizably Abaddon.

"Romulus?" Abaddon inquires, eyes narrowed.

I nod.

"Good," he says. "The gathering's about to start, and I need my strategist."

I tug on my shoes, take one last glance over my shoulder at Lo-

Ren sleeping peacefully, and follow him out the door. Layden hovers behind him, tapping his foot. "We need to get going. *Now*." Hopefully, if the meeting goes quickly enough, I can be back before Lo-Ren even knows I'm gone.

"Kharon's staying behind to watch over the women," Abaddon whispers, obviously sensing my anxiety about leaving Lo-Ren alone. I breathe a little easier as I shut the door behind me and follow my brothers down the darkened hallways.

Layden takes the lead, obviously knowing where he's going. Abaddon and I exchange glances. Our little brother has some explaining to do, and soon. He's spent time here, that's clear, but also managed not to reveal the secret of who and what he is? Grandpa Vlad doesn't seem like the most welcoming sort of fellow.

Finally, Layden pushes through two double doors to a large, vaulted room that has no windows and, like our bedrooms, a suffocating black décor broken up occasionally by gold accents. Several dark, lush couches are arranged in a circle. Grandpa Vlad sits in a golden wing-backed chair in the center of the room, on a small rise as if it were a throne. He's obviously used to being the presiding power in any negotiation.

"Have a seat, gentleman," he says cooly, a noticeable lack of welcome in his voice. To his right sits his granddaughter, Phoenix, whose eyes immediately warm when they meet Layden's. I clock that and the position of all the other players in the room.

Several of Vlad's apparent "sons" are positioned around the room, their hands held loosely by their sides and within easy reach of the bulges of what I can tell are firearms at their belts. Which tells me they are used to dealing with human rather than supernatural threats. Interesting, and likely good for us. I prefer to be underestimated in any potential conflict.

"Tell us the situation," Vlad instructs his granddaughter, looking at her pointedly after we've all taken our seats. "Leave nothing out."

"We're still waiting for—"

"I said to begin," Vlad snaps, but then the door opens, and

another young woman scurries inside, looking around at both the room and the people inside with wide, alarmed eyes. She only calms down slightly once her gaze catches on Phoenix, who half-rises out of her seat as if to welcome the woman before her grandfather places a hand at her elbow to stop her.

"Sabra," Phoenix breathes out, obviously relieved, and I wonder again at the dynamics between everyone involved here. It's clear Phoenix's grandfather has some kind of hold on her, and yet she, amongst all of his kin, is the only one seated. Clearly, she is a favorite or holds some sort of other sway.

"Sit," Vlad's voice cuts through the room like ice.

Sabra sits nervously at the end of the couch nearest Layden, the two of them briefly exchanging a glance. Ah, so she, too, knows our secretive little brother.

"Now, as I was saying," Vlad sounds irritated, looking back to Phoenix, "begin."

Phoenix takes a deep breath and sits up straighter in her chair, which, I notice, not-coincidentally inches her closer to Layden and Sabra, who are seated on the couch beside her. "Sabra's mother was a powerful mage who worked with my grandfather," she says, looking back toward Vlad. I do not show the surprise on my face, though Abaddon's eyes register his.

Vlad's mouth tightens. "She was a mad-woman."

"Maybe," Sabra speaks up, eyes suddenly hard as she looks at Vlad, her earlier nervousness apparently gone. "Or maybe you just didn't like what she was telling you anymore."

A noise like a hiss comes from Vlad, and Phoenix jumps in. "She sometimes saw visions from other planes when they intersected with this one. Visions of the future."

"And what her mental state was like at the end of her life isn't the point," she hurries to say, leaning forward in her seat as if to block her grandfather's view of Sabra and get his attention. "The point is that you know she saw true things at times. And one of the visions we suspect might have been true was when she foresaw that all life on Earth as we know it would be threatened by spirits from the other realm."

Vlad makes a spitting noise. "Nonsense. Spirits cannot traverse realms."

I force myself not to look at my brothers, but I feel Abaddon shift beside me, something Vlad immediately takes notice of.

"Do you know different?" Vlad questions us.

Layden speaks up, though I register he does so cautiously. "We have some experience with spirits who can cross realms. Usually, it's only a one-way journey, though, to a very specific realm."

It's a half-truth. He's talking about Kharon, who carries human souls to the death realm when they die. But we all witnessed what his newborn daughter did on the plane. Lo-Ren shook with real terror as she described the place they'd crossed over to, and I saw the damage to the plane myself from whatever they'd encountered there.

"But it proves that realm-crossing is possible."

Phoenix looks her grandfather boldly in the eye. "And my mother told me she'd witnessed it before, too."

"We do not speak of that," Vlad swipes a hand harshly, face angry.

"I'm just saying we know realm-crossing is possible. So Sabra's grandmother's vision *is* possible if something unforeseen changes."

"Nothing ever has," Vlad says stubbornly, glaring back at Phoenix. "Short-term possession is not true crossing."

"Until now," Layden interjects.

"What?" Vlad demands, looking at all of us. "What does your family know?"

Again, Layden speaks for us. "I know that I've been watching the world's computer systems, and something alien has been infiltrating government AI. Soon, the humans will lose control of their own technology, and they won't even see it coming."

"How do you know if they don't?" Vlad demands. "What makes you so special?"

"I have a certain connection to the spirit realm," is all Layden says. "I recognize the runes in the AI algorithms as a language of spirits from another realm. It's invisibly interlaced on top of the humans' code, driving and directing it toward the spirit's end."

"Which is? What do they want?"

"We don't know," Phoenix says, "but they knew enough to realize Layden was watching them. They could sense him and his family and used the human military to attack them. Whatever they're trying to do, they don't want to be stopped."

"Even if I were to believe any of this nonsense," Vlad waves a hand, "why should I care about what computers in some other country are doing?"

Phoenix's mouth drops open. "They're infiltrating Russia and China, Grandpapa, and you know enough of the world to realize anyone who starts with those powers won't stop there. You have a good life here. You have control and power." Her last words are said through her teeth as if it's not something she's entirely happy about.

Vlad shrugs his shoulders, but Phoenix presses her point. "Think about how long you've been building this city—this country. Your wealth isn't in gold bars anymore. It's in Swiss banks. That's all numbers and digitized currency that's secure so long as the government is stable. You think it stays secure when an AI run by a rogue element has control of that government? Any force seeking power will go after the world's banks right after it gets control of the most volatile governments' militaries."

Vlad finally shifts in his chair, visibly moved by this argument at last. "Chase down this spirit with your computers, and then Phoenix and I will go to defeat it!"

"My family and I will stand beside you," Abaddon says confidently.

But Phoenix only sighs as Layden jumps in. "It's a different world than we have known in the past," he says to both Abaddon and

Vlad. "We can't fight whatever this is with cannons or muskets. It's about server farms and AI."

"What is this AI?" Abaddon barks, obviously frustrated by the conversation.

"Artificial intelligence," Phoenix says when Layden looks frustrated by our brother's lack of knowledge. "Computer programs the humans build to do tasks that can think for themselves."

"But the runework I've seen overlaying the human programming is allowing the AI to advance far beyond what the humans ever dreamed," Layden says. "It's speeding up what the AI is capable of by centuries, and from what Phoenix and I were looking at last night, it's only days away from completely wresting control away from the humans."

"Even if we could track it down, which we can't because the AI or the entity programming the runes is smart enough to bounce the source code off server farms all over the world," Phoenix says, "we still don't know what we're dealing with or how to fight it."

"So what are we to do?" Vlad asks, rising out of his seat and throwing his hands in the air. "Did you bring us all here to warn us of a coming apocalypse we can do nothing to stave off? I tell you, Granddaughter, that I have seen kingdoms rise and fall, and I fear *nothing*! I have always risen to greatness, and this shall be no different. Let these human armies come for me. I shall decimate them and put their heads on pikes as far as the eye can see, like my honored great-grandfather Vlad Dracul the First before me! Blood will rain down on the fields near and far!"

"Dad would have loved this guy," I mutter.

Vlad's face snaps my way, but Phoenix obviously has many years of managing her grandfather's tirades because she stands up, hands in a defensive posture. "Layden and I are monitoring the situation. And now that Sabra's here, we'll cast a circle to see if we can learn more."

"Bah! What has witchcraft ever done except make things worse?" Vlad says, throwing a hand toward Sabra.

But Phoenix's eyes narrow. "You *know* what gifts the witches have given us through contact with the spirits," she says, her voice low. "Even if they came in unexpected ways."

Vlad turned away from her. "You call betrayal a gift?" he snorts.

"You would not have *me* but for the witches," Phoenix says, standing her ground.

"And what have you been but a thorn in my side?" her grandfather shoots back. "And now a canary to warn of a coming doom it sounds like you can do nothing to stop?"

Phoenix swallows hard, taking a step back. It's clear to anyone that her grandfather's words have wounded her, not that he seems to notice or care.

"And what can you do?" Vlad says, turning accusingly toward Abaddon and me. "You come here for safety, but it sounds like you've only painted a target on our backs if this spirit finds we've given safe haven to whoever's watching it."

Abaddon looks like he wants to stand toe to toe with Vlad, but I put a hand on his knee to stop him. Huffing in annoyance, he stays seated. "My family has many gifts," he says through gritted teeth. "We can help in the coming storm."

"How, exactly?" Vlad says, coming to stand over my brother in a way I know must set all Abaddon's predator instincts on edge. "What do you bring to the table? Tell me or leave the sanctuary I have offered immediately!"

I see Abaddon's face coloring with rage and quickly lift from my seat, stepping in between Vlad and Abaddon but making sure to stoop slightly so that Vlad retains the advantage of height. Time for the tactician to make an appearance.

"As Layden says, we have some experience with spirits from other realms. You'll forgive our reticence to expose any weaknesses we may have to one as strong as you. We've never met any beings of such might." I bow my head and hear Vlad huff slightly.

It's an old tactic. Bullies who are scared love to be mollified by praise, reassuring them they're the biggest and baddest in the room, regardless of the truth of it. Reason is of little use with them, only flattery.

"But I promise we are allies you may rely on."

"I rely on no one but myself," Vlad sneers.

"Whenever your wise granddaughter finds this spirit to target, will it not be better to send us out as soldiers to face the threat first, at least, before endangering your own far superior family members?"

When I glance up, I see that the idea of using us as cannon fodder, at least, appeals to him.

He huffs out his displeasure as he steps back, then glares at where Phoenix and Layden are standing together near his golden throne. "If you don't have something more concrete for me by the end of the day, I will expel every last one of them from the compound. Including the witch. Now," Vlad looks Phoenix's way, lifting his eyebrows significantly, "your uncles and I will do our part to siphon you strength for any coming conflict."

Phoenix sighs and looks toward the floor. "Moderate feeding should be enough."

I have to work to keep my eyebrows from lifting. So, she is not a vampire but still gets power from them when they *do* feed? How exactly does that work? Is "granddaughter" as loose a term as "son" is? How exactly are they all related to one another? Layden mentioned there was a god here. Did he mean Phoenix? As soon as we can get our hands on him, Layden has some explaining to do.

Vlad glares at Phoenix. "Now is not the time for moderation," he snaps. "And a better leader would know that."

As he turns and begins to walk toward the door, his "sons" immediately move in formation to flank his sides and back.

"Yes, Grandpapa," Phoenix says to his retreating figure, her posture deflating the second he turns the corner out of sight. "Fuck," she says as she looks between Layden and Sabra. "What are we going to do?"

Layden looks worried, but Sabra just rubs her hands together. "Blood magic, baby."

Phoenix winces but looks resigned.

"I'm going to check on my wife," Abaddon says, finally standing. "Keep me informed." He looks around, his mouth curling in disgust. "The sooner we're gone from this place, the better."

I keep my peace. I'm torn, both wanting to stay to find out what will be involved in this "blood magic" the mage speaks of and needing to get back to Lo-Ren to make sure she is unharmed in this dangerous vampire's nest.

"What did you mean with that last bit about feeding?" I ask. Phoenix and Layden both look my way, before Phoenix drops her face, turning away from me.

"Can I tell h—" Layden asks her, and she waves a hand. "Whatever."

"Phoenix isn't like. . . *them*." Layden scowls, looking toward the door.

Phoenix huffs out a mirthless laugh. "Aren't I? Just indirectly." She turns back toward me, then confirms my theory. "When my ancestors feed, it feeds me. Don't ask me why."

Ah. Part of the blood magic, I take it. Before I can ask more, though, I feel my head getting heavy and my sight going dim.

Dammit, not now, I think, as my vision starts to go. This is an incredibly delicate political situation we're all in, not to mention how things are with Lo-Ren. *Remus better not screw anything up—*

But then my vision goes black as I fall into deep, undreaming sleep.

Chapter Twenty-Seven

REMUS

I wake up to find myself standing in an unknown room. I quickly take inventory. Obviously, I'm still within the vampire compound. Layden and the head vampire's granddaughter are the only other ones in the room, but I can scent others were recently here. Abaddon and more of the bloodsuckers.

The granddaughter—Phoenix, I think was her name? She's watching me oddly. How much has Layden told her about us?

I start to head out the door without a word. If I follow Abaddon's scent, I'm sure it will take me back to our quarters and our women. It's only once I'm outside that I pause, fully thinking through the ramifications of my time lost to Romulus, considering where we were when I passed out.

The shower. I was inside my woman after my brother had just woken up. An impossibility, and yet there he was, awake and so suave and sure, suggesting we share her.

My hands clench into fists.

How long has the tactician been working against me? He not only woke when I was supposed to be in control of the body but then kicked me out. What did they do together after I was gone, their naked bodies slathered in soap in that shower?

Has he allowed me to play the fool, thinking that I have the upper hand when he's been plotting against me this whole time? My teeth clench, threatening to crack.

I am no fool.

When warriors come against me with tactical perfection and coordinated strikes, I meet them with overwhelming chaos and rage. After all this time, still, my brother does not know me.

I lift my nose to the air and ignore the scent that would take me back to Lo-Ren. What is the point of going back to enjoy her sweet embrace for short moments if they will soon be stolen by my brother, who seeks to oust me?

No. I will come out on top, once and for all, and put an end to this endless struggle. I head in the opposite direction, toward the smell of blood and death.

The eldest vampire does not look pleased to see me when I knock on the door where his scent trail has led me.

Not that he's the one to greet me at the door. I can barely see him past the shoulder of the two brutes in black who block the door.

"I would speak to Vlad," I say.

The two men in dark suits glare back at me, saying nothing.

I crack a smile and hold up my hands. "I come in peace. Ready to bargain."

"What do you have to bargain with?" Vlad asks from the room beyond where he's seated, a young, naked blonde woman in his lap. They appeared to be necking, but as her head lazily flops against his shoulder, I see two dripping red marks on her neck.

"I have information," I say. "Information you want."

Vlad's lips are red with blood that he lazily licks as he welcomes me in with a swipe of his hand.

The two men move to the side to allow me in. I take in the scene without a word. I've seen many dens of sin in my long life. My father loved to acquaint himself with the most powerful leaders in the world, and they usually enjoyed living as laws unto themselves, beyond the mores of society.

So, I'm not surprised to see the many naked women draped around the room. It's only new to see them being used more as feeding fountains than for their other pleasures, though I suspect this is only the morning routine and that at night, things may...

Well, it is none of my business. After a brief perusal to get my surroundings, I keep my eyes locked on Vlad. "Can we talk alone?"

His eyes narrow. "Do you think I am a fool to leave myself undefended?"

"Do you need defense?" I ask. "From what I understand, you are a great warrior."

"And you are an unknown enemy. For all I know, your family has come here with all your stories as an elaborate trap for me."

I chuckle at that. "I have known paranoid men like you." I bow my head the slightest bit. "You are wise. It is how you stay in power. But I will still bargain only with you. Would you have everyone in this room hear the information you are so hungry for? Because I'm ready to tell you exactly what type of creatures my brothers and I are. But I would prefer it to be for your eyes and ears only."

He stands from his chair, the woman in his lap sliding to the floor. I don't think she's dead, just dazed from either blood loss or something else the vampire has done to her.

Vlad's eyes blaze with something more than curiosity, and I look at the woman for longer than I ought. What exactly are the full powers of this creature in front of me? What sorts of magic might I gain from an exchange with him? Enough to be rid of my parasitic brother completely?

"You would betray your family?" Vlad asks, eyes still burning with intensity.

I shrug. "Betrayal is such a harsh word. Perhaps I just disagree with my brothers on the best way to work together. They've already decided to ally with you; I just think that means sharing all our information. I think together, our clans could become very, very powerful."

I see his nostrils flare at that. Ah. I have hit the nail on the head. Desire for power is this man's weakness.

He lifts his hand and snaps his fingers crisply. "Leave me, all of you."

"But Father!" One of his sons, who also has a woman seated on his lap, immediately objects. "You can't really—"

Vlad whips around and glares at the man. "Do you dare defy your father's order?"

For a moment, they scowl at one another, and it's difficult not to chuckle at the familiar power struggle between father and sons. Oh, I know it so well. In the end, like the obedient boys they are, they stand, abandoning their feedings and filing toward the door. Several shoot me killing glances, and I try to note their faces. Difficult when they all look so much alike. Romulus is the one who's better with detail, but when I care about something, I can still do all right. I think I'll remember which of these are the trouble-makers and who merely follow orders by rote.

Finally, Vlad and I are alone.

"Make it good. You've got three minutes before they come barging back in."

I merely arch an eyebrow. "It's in your best interest to keep them at bay," I say. Then I drop my glamour and allow my wings to unfurl behind me to the rafters, my tail to whip free, and the angel spark I rarely allow free reign to glow from within my chest.

"Behold," I say, "an angel of the Lord."

Vlad lifts a hand and stumbles back as if my light will sear him to a crisp. I chuckle and drop the light show.

Vlad growls, and the next thing I know, he's coming at me faster than I can track with my eyes. Instantaneously, he's got my wings and back crushed against the stone wall, his arm at my throat, fangs bared. "Why shouldn't I rip your throat out right here?"

I can only laugh. "Why? Because I revealed we're powerful creatures?"

"You are from Heaven, and I'm from Hell," he spat. "We're natural enemies."

I roll my eyes. "We're not from heaven, and I don't know where you're from. I was just kidding with the whole angel of the Lord shtick. Yeah, we're angels, but that's just what they call us on this plane. We're from a different realm and snuck our way onto this one. Probably like your ancestors somehow did. We're just a non-native species, that's all."

His eyes widen when I speak of his ancestors, and his arm loosens ever so slightly from my throat. "So it's true," he whispers. "Spirits from other realms can break through."

I shrug. "I'm not a spirit, but sure, pal. We figured out how to get here, and the humans sometimes worshipped us as gods."

Vlad's eyes light up at that. Ah, the thirst for power. He drops his arm completely. "Tell me more. Tell me everything."

I hold up my hands. "Ah ah ah. Tit for tat. I'll share when you do. I have a little problem I need your help with."

His eyes narrow again.

"I've got this little parasite I need help with subduing." I turn around and point to the back of my head.

Vlad makes a surprised, disturbed noise, and when I look back at him, he's taken several steps back. Not wanting to get Layden in trouble, I say, "I heard that vampire blood could help me with this problem." He told me it was an ingredient in some of his potions, but that he was only ever able to get blood from the youngest vampires. How powerful would blood from someone as old and ancient as Vlad be?

Vlad looks immediately pissed. "Our blood is sacrosanct! None of us would spill it for—"

I hold up my hands. "Then I guess our negotiations are over. It's the blood—five vials worth, to be exact—or no more information." I start to walk toward the door.

I can all but hear him going apoplectic behind me. "Wait," he finally snaps right as I'm about to reach for the doorknob.

He lifts his hands and snaps several more times, glaring up toward the ceiling. Ah, so perhaps we weren't as alone as I thought. It makes sense. No true leader would leave himself completely defenseless. And yet, for whatever is about to happen, he won't allow any eyes at all. I repress my grin.

I turn and walk back toward him. "We both have something the other wants," I say quietly, not wanting to press my advantage but still trying to appeal to his deepest desires. "My family and I are immensely powerful beings. And what I ask would not only make me more powerful still but put us further in your debt."

"I do not know that our blood would do what you seek," he says.

"But you are the oldest of your kind, so surely your blood is the most powerful."

A growl comes from his throat, and I know I've asked more than he's comfortable with. So, I decide to sweeten the pot.

"My brothers and I are known as the Four Horsemen of the Apocalypse. For millennia, we have been the power behind the powers that shape nations and empires. I am the angel of War, Layden is Famine, Abaddon is Pestilence, and Kharon is the angel of Death."

Vlad's eyes grow wider with each of my words, widest of all at Kharon's designation. "What does that mean? What are your powers?"

"All I ask is a small price for any question you might have for me," I say meekly.

Vlad looks frustrated, and at the same time, I see the moment he makes the decision. He yanks a small dagger from his waistcoat, then leans over to snatch a crystal goblet from a nearby table.

His movements are so quick even my superior senses struggle to follow as he slices a neat slit along his wrist. Dark red, almost black liquid gushes into the goblet. It fills halfway before he winces and lifts his wrist to his mouth, licking the slash there, after which it neatly closes.

I eye the goblet greedily, but he holds it away from me. "My father met one of your kind once. On the battlefield. He warned me, should I ever come upon your kind again, to run and never stop. He said you were the only thing on Heaven or Earth that could challenge us."

Ah ha. So it was his father I met that day. I decide not to inform him of this.

"How many of you are there? How many angels?" he demands.

"Only my brothers and I. And, once upon a time, our father. But we sent him back to the realm we came from."

"Only ever you and your brothers?"

"Before our time, long, long ago, others like my father roamed this plane. But they retired back to their home many millennia ago. My father alone stayed, stealing the spark from the realm we call the Great Hall in order to fashion us, his children, that he might rule this world."

"So what is this threat my granddaughter speaks of? Tell me true."

"That I do not know. But if it is any apocalypse, who better to meet it than with the Horsemen by your side?"

"And the world to reshape as I will it in the aftermath," Vlad grins, finally handing me the precious goblet of red.

I nod my head to him. "I care nothing for kingdoms," I say. "All I want is my parasite gone and a quiet corner to retire with my woman."

"Then we have an agreement, friend." The last word sounds dangerous on his tongue but I don't care. I've made plenty more dangerous alliances in my long life, and never with as much potential as this.

I take the glass and raise it in a toast. "To our glorious future, friend."

He smiles, blood from his previous meal still coating his teeth. "Now, tell me in detail what you and each of your brothers can do."

I close my eyes, tip my head back, and down the thick goblet of his blood. And then I begin telling him all he wants to know.

Chapter Twenty-Eight

LAUREN

I was sad to wake up alone this morning but decided that was selfish, considering where we are. I mean, there are issues of global significance going on. I do realize that even though I'm so wrapped up in my own personal relationship drama.

It's just so easy to get lost in it all when every time Remus or Romulus walks in the door, so entirely swoonworthy. And I'm not usually a girl who swoons. Seriously. But I've never been around a man who seems so intent on me, my feelings, my well-being, my— Well, I've never had anyone in a relationship actually pay me enough attention beyond how often they could get me compliant enough to use my body as a wet hole for their dick. Oh, and the last one really liked it when I cooked.

So, to have this kind of attention from not just one man but *two*—

I don't know if it's fair to ask what I want to ask of Remus. But I just see so many possibilities of all of us living together happily.

When I peeked my head out of my room earlier, Kharon was there to assure me that Romulus was in a meeting and would be back soon. When I asked after Ksenia and the baby, he said they were well, and that they'd named the baby Luna.

And now I'm sitting here unsure if I'm hoping it will be Romulus or Remus who walks in the door. Which feels majorly messed up and confusing. From everything everyone says of Remus, he can be stubborn. But the man I know seems completely reasonable, and I'm sure if I can just talk it through with him. . .

I bite my bottom lip and play with the powdered sugar banana on my plate leftover from my breakfast crepes. For a place where they theoretically don't eat food, the breakfast was really spectacular. Do they bring in human servants? Do they. . . uh. . . feed on the same servants? How does the whole vampire thing *actually* work, like in reality? I shake my head, barely able to believe I'm even contemplating the practicalities of a day in the life of a vampire.

Apparently, they don't sleep all day or burn in the sunlight. They welcomed us out in the open yesterday. What else has the common lore gotten wrong?

I startle and almost upend the plate on my lap when the door suddenly opens.

It's Remus's wide, mischievous grin that greets me as he steps inside, his wings brushing against the doorway as he comes in. I'm glad at the rush of relief I feel when I see him. I wasn't even sure who I was hoping for until right at this moment. I set the plate aside, jump off the bed, and run up to him, flinging my arms around his neck.

"Baby!" I say excitedly. "It's so good to see you! How did the meetings go?"

His strong arms come around my waist, lifting me off my feet a little, which makes me so warm with happiness that, in spite of our circumstances, I can't help giggling a little. God, this man makes me giddy.

"You glad it's me?" he whispers in my ear.

I pull out of his arms and bang him on the shoulder. "Of course I am." I roll my eyes.

His grin gets wider.

"How did everything go?" I ask again. "Is it all stable out there? The world's not coming to an end or anything?"

He waves a hand. "Nothing for you to worry about."

I frown a little, but then he pulls me back into his arms and kisses my neck sensuously. I melt against him. I guess if they needed him on some sort of mission or something, he wouldn't be in here necking me. I sigh, my whole body liquifying against his. God, how does he do this to me?

At the same time, the excitement zinging through my body makes other ideas start to pop up.

"Honey, what if we try to do it again?" I ask excitedly.

My hand roves down his body, landing on the front of his pants. He's hard, and my excitement amps up even higher.

"This is a welcome home I can get used to," he growls, hands framing my face as he kisses me hard.

In his arms, with him kissing me voraciously, it's easy to believe anything—everything—is possible.

I go up on my tiptoes and kiss him back just as vigorously, loving getting lost in his scent, his taste, and the feel of his strong body flush against mine.

"It was so amazing." I break away from his lips just long enough to say. "I was thinking that maybe if we make love like last night, both of you will wake up again, and maybe this time, the two of you could actually *talk*."

The words rush out of my mouth so fast, at first, I don't notice Remus yank back from me. "Like sexual healing!" I finish excitedly, my eyes searching his.

Remus completely pulls away from me at that, his arms dropping from my face and the light in his eyes dimming. "I don't want to talk about him," he says flatly.

My heart sinks a little. Dammit, I've probably gone about this all wrong, but I'm not ready to give up yet. "Oh, come on," I say, putting a hand on his arm. "The whole problem with the two of you is communication. It's the oldest one in the book. But now that we've found a way to spark a connection between the two of you with me as a conduit—"

"You are not a conduit!" Remus says harshly.

But I just shake my head. "Of course I am, silly. I really think this was meant to happen. You went looking for a consort, not realizing the whole time what you really needed was a way to finally connect with your brother, a consort for *both* of you—"

"I don't want to fuck you so I can connect to my fucking brother," Remus says loudly, stalking away from me.

I finally stop, catching up to what I've been missing this whole time in my enthusiasm to present him with the idea. I was so excited about my revelation I hadn't seen how tense he was.

"What's wrong?" I ask. "Is there something going on you're not telling me about?"

His gaze slides to the side. Then he steps forward again, eyes coming back to me even though his body stays tense. "I've been looking forward to getting home to *you*. And for once in my life, I don't want to think about my goddamned brother. Can't it just be you and me here? Like it was at the beginning?"

He kisses me, and for a moment, I want to get lost in him and say yes, of course. But even as my hands lift to twine around the back of his neck, they bump into Romulus's face, and it hits me.

I pull away from his lips. "You're not wearing your glamour." And he hasn't been since he came in. I didn't register it then because I was so used to them, but his wings brushed the door as he entered.

He closes his eyes, and his wings shimmer, then disappear, along with his tail.

But what was he doing that he hadn't had his glamour on before he came in? Was a glamour something you had to concentrate all the time on and he accidentally let it slip? Wasn't that really dangerous here?

And why do I get the feeling he's trying to distract me from something he doesn't want to tell me?

When he tries to kiss me again, I pull back this time, searching his eyes. He just closes them, again moving in for a kiss.

"Remus," I plead, shoving lightly against his chest. "I just want to talk."

He breathes out hard, not looking frustrated exactly, but when he turns away from me, I get a closed-off feeling from him when usually there are more open lines of communication between us.

"We don't have to talk about Romulus," I say but can't help adding, "even though we have to sometime." I hold up my hands when his dark eyes flash my way. "It doesn't have to be now, but your brother is a reality that's not going away any time soon. Maybe right now, while everything else is going on, isn't the time. But you're not the only one in this. He's a victim here too—"

"Is that what he's telling you?" Remus lights up, obviously furious. "And who's the other victim, *you*?"

"No," I say, impatient with his attitude. I meant *he* was the other victim of the circumstances they're caught in, but obviously, that's the wrong wording to use with someone as prideful as him. "He'd never say that. He's long-suffering about the whole thing, but he deserves a life and happiness, too, you know. We all do."

"And you'd be happier with him, is that it?"

I throw my hands up in frustration. "I never said that. If you would just *listen* to the words coming out of my mouth. I don't think anyone should suffer in loneliness when there's plenty of love to go around."

He scoffs. "Just say it with your full chest. You prefer him to me, and you're both trying to edge me out."

"What?" All the breath leaves my chest. I try to approach him, but he physically bars me from him with his hands.

"Don't," he says, his voice dangerous. "It's been the same story my whole life. From the day I was *born*."

I see all of the hurt in his eyes at his words, even though he pulls away from me at the same time. Not so much physically, but it's like I can feel a mountain of walls spring up between us.

I want to tell him no, that I understand his hurt—maybe I don't know how bad it was with his archaic father and the abuse his brothers and him endured or what that kind of prolonged trauma was like—but I do know what it's like to want the love of a parent and feel constant rejection instead. If he would just let me *in* instead of pushing me away and assuming the worst about my intentions—

"Is it so impossible to believe that I could love both of you?" I ask, my heart breaking at the hardness on his face. "Is there no world where you could believe that I'm the kind of person with enough love in my heart to finally give you the absolute, unconditional love you've always deserved? Because I do, Remus. I love you. And I see how you're hurting. I want to prove to you that you can be loved completely in a world where he exists, too. Let me prove to you how worthy I think you are."

He's only standing a few feet away from me, and I can see him shaking with emotion he doesn't know how to express.

An explosive knock at the door stops both of us before anything else can be said or thrown onto the gauntlet between us.

Remus stalks toward the door and yanks it open with an explosive, "What?"

"It's happening," Abaddon says, voice urgent.

"What's happening?" Remus is impatient.

"Goddammit, Remus, you and Romulus need to figure out whatever's off between you two because it's really fucking obnoxious to have to say everything twice. The end of the world meeting we had this morning? It's happening."

End of the world meeting? I sprint over to where they're huddled at the door.

"Stay here," Remus orders me gruffly, stepping through the door and trying to shove it closed in my face.

"Are you kidding?" I slip through the open slit in the door before he can shut it. "He just said end of the world! I'm not just staying huddled in a dark room."

I see the other women pushing out their doors, too, babies swaddled against their chests in makeshift cloth carriers.

"Where you go, we go," Ksenia says firmly.

"We don't have time," Abaddon says curtly, turning to Hannah standing beside Ksenia. "And I need to know you're safe."

"Are any of us safe?" Hannah grasps his arm. "Better not to be separated."

He looks reluctant but turns. "Follow me. And stay close."

We do, a huddle of monsters and consorts hurrying down the hallway. We head back into the large central courtyard where we first entered. Do they think we'll have to take off again in the helicopter? I don't suppose anyone's going to stop and explain the whole "end of the world" thing to me, are they? Uh, hello???

"Do you know what's going on?" I ask Hannah as we rush forward.

She clutches her toddler to her chest and shakes her head as we spill out into the cloudy light of the courtyard. "Something about rogue spirits and a prophecy or something? I don't know."

In the distance, in the very center of the courtyard, I see the chief vampire's granddaughter, Phoenix, bent over with chalk in her hand, along with a woman I don't recognize. Several fire pits are set up along four points to create a giant circle with lots of symbols chalked all over the ground inside it.

Layden runs around the circle, and I jump back a little when I see light spring out of his hands, illuminating the chalk runes on the ground.

"What's happening?" Abaddon demands.

Layden doesn't stop, light still pouring out of his hands into the circle as he yells, "We finally figured out what the AI's doing, and there's no time!"

"Well? What is it?" Vlad shouts from outside the circle near where Phoenix stands up, surveying her work. Her grandfather steps forward, almost into the circle, when Phoenix shoves him back at the last moment before his foot crosses the line.

"Don't!" she shouts.

Vlad looks furious at that. I look to Remus, wondering if he's in the mood to do something foolish after our fight, but he stays back, his eyes darting around as if he's soaking in all the information of the situation, just like me and the rest of his brothers.

"The circle's almost complete," Phoenix explains hurriedly, eyes still on Layden and the other woman chalking lines. "And we just saw the AI start the sequence to launch nuclear codes in Russia and China. It doesn't want to control the world. It wants to destroy it."

I stumble back, Remus's hand steadying me.

"That will never happen," Abaddon growls.

"We have an idea to stop it," Layden shouts. "But you have to trust us. Together."

Abaddon looks Kharon's way, then to Remus. Trusting their younger brother doesn't seem like anything either of them are keen to do. But considering they can't use their usual ways to combat this enemy, there's little to do except stomp around in futility while Phoenix, the other woman, and Layden scramble, taking positions around the circle.

Phoenix heads to the center, lifting her arms up toward the sky.

The other woman runs forward with a knife. She slices along Phoenix's palm and then, together, they drip the blood in a line at Phoenix's feet. Layden offers his hand, and she does the same, squeezing it out in a line behind Phoenix. Then, he and the woman take positions in front of and behind Phoenix.

The woman begins chanting, and Phoenix lifts her arms even higher.

"What is this?" I ask, bewildered. Yeah, everything I've encountered with the boys up until this point has been wild, but at least it was still helicopters and missiles—things of this earth that I understood. It finally sinks in that I'm looking at straight-up *magic* about to be done in front of me.

Thunder suddenly cracks overhead, and the chalk-marked runes around the circle light up with blue light just like they did when they were pouring out of Layden's hands earlier, but all on their own. Not only that, but they begin spinning—some interlocked circles move one way, and others spin in the opposite direction.

The wind picks up. Kharon and Abaddon hurry to get their women back to the safety of the courtyard walls, but thankfully, Remus is just as enthralled as I am with what's happening.

As the wind whips faster in a circle, I realize it's becoming a small twister. Yes, the wind stirs my hair, but it's nothing to the way the clothes of the three in the circle are being all but torn from their body.

I gasp when Phoenix lifts off the ground. She doesn't go high, but her heels lift first, and then the tips of her toes hover over the cobblestones as she begins to levitate. A foot. Five feet. Ten.

She stays there and begins to speak, eyes closed. "I call to you, spirits. I call to the hungry ones. Who can help us?"

"Does she even know what she's doing?" Abaddon asks loudly, having returned after getting his wife and child to relative safety.

"Leave her alone," Vlad snaps, and we all stand and watch as Phoenix floats in the middle of the large, lit-up circle amid the wind, hair whipping this way and that. She frowns, and even though her eyes are closed, it's like she's looking at something the rest of us can't see.

Moments later, the furrow in her brow disappears, and she looks excited, saying, "Yes! Yes, I see you! Come over, Devourer. Come near and devour all of it!"

"What the fuck?" Remus says. "What the hell is she calling?"

"I don't know," Abaddon says, "but it doesn't sound good."

I back up a few steps but don't run away. I'm oddly transfixed by what I'm seeing, and none of the others are running. Granted, they're immortal beings, and I'm not, but I still don't move as I watch Phoenix start to frown. Her eyes open suddenly, and she looks to Layden and the other woman.

"They can't get through!" she shouts. "The circle doesn't have enough power—either that or I don't."

Layden starts running along one of the inner circles, laying down more bright blue-lit runes, but Phoenix just keeps shaking her head. "They can't cross the plane from theirs to this one. We didn't have enough time to—"

She sounds frustrated, despairing even.

"I will give you the power to cross planes," Vlad hisses. He's standing nearest me, and I'm not sure anyone else hears him. But when Remus's head swings his way, I realize I'm wrong. It doesn't matter, though; it's too late. Vlad has already taken off. He's moving so fast that I barely see a streak of movement.

And then, maybe a blink later, he's standing beside Kharon and the other women. I'm so startled by the quick movement, I'm not sure what I'm seeing until it's all over.

Vlad all but *climbs* Kharon and sinks his fangs into the big man's neck. Remus is halfway across the courtyard before Kharon manages to fling the much smaller Vlad away from himself.

But by that point, the storm in the circle has suddenly turned from baby twister to cyclone.

"They're coming!" Phoenix shouts. "I've opened the portal!"

My head swings back and forth between Kharon grabbing at his neck and the increasingly wild tornado contained in the circle. Lightning crashes every other second, and the other woman is flung outward, landing on the cobblestones near me. Then Layden's body comes out next, toppling end over end. I hurry over to help her up. She clutches her head and stares wide-eyed back at the cyclone in dread.

"Are you okay?" I try to ask, but she just keeps shaking her head.

"That wasn't supposed to happen," she says.

"What wasn't supposed to happen?"

But she just keeps crab-walking back from the circle, her eyes wide as we watch Phoenix rise higher and higher in the sky as the dark funnel cloud lifts up with her.

Layden runs over to the both of us. "What happened?" he asks her.

"I don't know," she says. "One second, we were at a standstill, and then—" She gestures in front of us.

Layden looks around. Abaddon fled back to his wife and daughter at Vlad's attack, and Remus is still near them, hovering over Vlad where Kharon tossed them off.

"Vlad just went nuts." I put my hands on my head. "He said something about giving her the power she needed and went and attacked Kharon."

Layden and the woman on the ground exchange glances. "How did he find out?" Layden asks.

The woman finally starts getting to her feet, and Layden and I both help her up.

"Find out *what*?" I ask as I crane my head back to try to see Phoenix. She's a small speck up in the sky above us at this point.

"Kharon's a plane-crosser," Layden says as if that explains everything. "He's the Horseman of Death."

The woman's mouth drops open. "You're the Horsemen— Why didn't you tell me sooner?" She shoves Layden in the chest.

"Will someone please tell me what's going on?" I shout.

The woman looks at me. "Vlad must have figured out that feeding off a plane-crosser might give Phoenix the extra juice she needed." She gestures wildly behind her. "To help the spirit she contacted on the other side make its way across the barrier between worlds." She shades her eyes with her hands, looking up in horror and pointing, "Oh my god, she did it. Look!"

I blink against the otherwise white-gray sky, and just beside where I see Phoenix at the top of the funnel cloud, yes, I can make out something emerging. A very *big* something.

"Is that a *whale*?" I ask in absolute shock.

"I didn't think they were real," the woman gasps, reaching out and clasping onto Layden's arm as if for support. "What the hell did she think she was doing?"

"It's done now," Layden says grimly.

The huge gray whale emerges from the top of the funnel, and then I see another follow it, and another and another. But no, as they separate from the funnel cloud, I can see that "whale" isn't quite the right descriptor. It's just the closest thing I have to describe what I'm seeing. They're creatures of some kind, I think, because they're sort of swimming or wiggling, and they're *huge*.

But when sunlight hits them, they don't look quite solid. Instead, they're almost translucent, like jellyfish.

"What the hell is that?" Remus asks, finally rejoining us.

"Devourers," the woman whispers.

"Sabra," Layden chides her.

"What?" the woman I assume is called Sabra snaps back. "It's the truth. I never thought she'd be able to actually bring them through."

"Then why did you help her with the circle?"

Sabra tosses up her hands. "It sounded like the end of the world!"

"So what's different now?" Layden asks. "Maybe now we have a chance." He gestures toward the sky-whale-jellyfish creatures that are starting to move more quickly and taking off in many different directions.

"How does averting one apocalypse make sense if we invite another one?"

"What do you mean?" Remus demands.

"When it was just circle magic, we could contain them. As in, we could *call them back* after we were through with them and send them home. With what Vlad did by juicing Phoenix up by feeding on a plane-crosser, they just got transported permanently here. Get it? Now we're stuck with the Devourers on this plane."

"Fuck," Layden and Remus say together, staring up as the sky-whales scatter.

"I don't get it," I say. "Why would you invite anything called a Devourer here in the first place?"

Sabra puts her hands on her hips. "What else would you suggest doing in a pinch to stop a nuclear apocalypse? Those guys eat nuclear energy like it's candy."

"How exactly do we know this?" Abaddon asks.

Sabra waves a hand. "That's the theory anyway, from the information we've gathered. They eat every source of energy starting with radioactive material until a particular plane is bereft of life, then they lie dormant for ages until they find a new source."

"So, what's your great idea for getting rid of *them*?" Abaddon asks.

Sabra starts to open her mouth, but her and Layden's cell phones go off, along with all of the guys in black suits. I left mine back at the castle, so I join Remus at Layden and Sabra's side.

"What?" Remus asks.

"Time to see if our friends here work as advertised," Sabra says, turning her cell phone out toward us.

I can't read the text—what country are we in now anyway?—but the flashing red radioactive symbol with arrows pointing to a skull and a figure running away is pretty difficult to misinterpret. It's a nuclear fallout warning. Nuclear missiles have been launched somewhere nearby.

I clutch Remus's side in dread. "Oh my god."

Did he know this was coming? Obviously, Layden and Sabra did. Is this what they talked about in the meeting earlier?

He just lifts me and runs toward the shelter of the buildings where the other women are.

Abaddon lifts off in the air. To do what, I have no idea. Layden just sprints beside his brother, hefting Sabra in a fireman's carry when she doesn't move quickly enough.

We pass by Vlad, who's paused near the entryway with his hand shielding his eyes as he looks to the sky. I only now remember—Phoenix! Did she ever come back down? Or is Vlad watching for missiles?

I lift up and look back toward the courtyard just in time to see Phoenix land back in the center of the circle with the tornado completely dissipated. She looks so small for someone who just made something so *big* happen.

"How will we know if it worked?" I ask the hallway of people gathered anxiously once Remus sets me down.

"Online feeds," Layden says, his phone already out, thumbing through sites.

Vlad, Phoenix, and a cadre of dark-suited men are pushing in the doors the next moment. "Out of my way," Vlad demands. His arm is around Phoenix. She looks exhausted as her grandfather drags her past us, but she looks up, her eyes briefly connecting with Layden's. He looks like he wants to reach out to stop her grandfather. Maybe pull her into his arms.

But then she's gone, shuffled off to whatever underground bunker Vlad obviously has no interest in sharing with us.

"Phoenix," Sabra calls uselessly. "We're going to need you to contain them again."

Phoenix doesn't say anything, just lifts a hand in acknowledgment before she's yanked around the corner. My constricted chest can't quite loosen in relief. Does that mean they think it will actually work? Big inter-realm traveling energy-devourers will save us from a nuclear disaster?

"Layden," Kharon demands. "Update."

"There's nothing," Layden mutters, thumbs moving faster. "Just people freaking out about the warnings going off everywhere. Shit. Shit, shit, shit."

The two babies start crying, and Kharon paces down the hall. "We can't stay here."

"Wait a second," Layden says, dragging a hand through his hair. "Just wait a second."

"We might not have seconds!" Kharon yells. The two dots on his neck are still dripping blood. Then he looks at his wife. "Maybe Luna and I can open another portal where we can hide?"

"Wait!" Layden shouts. "Here!"

"Here, what?" Remus growls, so tense beside me his body feels like marble.

"It's happening!" he laughs.

"What?" Remus starts, but Layden shows us his phone.

I squint at the grainy footage, but the shape of the sky-whales is unmissable. It's just hard to make out—

"What is it doing?" I ask, turning my head sideways as if that will help me figure it out any better. It sort of looks like the whale creature is just *sitting* on top of a building. Except now, instead of being translucent, it's lit up from the inside like it's got a hundred thousand lightbulbs inside its belly.

"Eating," Layden laughs, sounding punch-drunk. He snatches the phone back, flips through something else, and turns it back to us, where another whale is doing something similar on a very different-looking building. And another, and another.

"They're everywhere," he says, still giddy.

"He's right," Sabra says. She sounds disbelieving. "The news is picking it up now. Unknown entities seen attacking nuclear sites in Russia, China, US, Europe," she reads off, her thumb scrolling constantly. "Some countries actually launched missiles, but they were swallowed by the creatures midair. I mean, no one realizes that's what's happening. They're just saying averted missile launches. Oh my god, I can't believe it actually worked." And then a few moments later, she breathes out, "Damn, they're fast, too. They must've been really hungry."

"Great," Hannah says, clutching her crying daughter to her chest. "So where is Abaddon, and why isn't he back yet?"

Kharon looks at her sympathetically. "He will want to ensure you are safe even if it means lingering in the sky and stopping any missiles headed your way himself."

Hannah stomps impatiently, then starts pacing down the hall, bouncing their daughter on her hip and hushing her. "Everything's going to be okay, baby. Daddy will be back any moment."

"Come on," Sabra calls, following after Hannah. "There's a TV in here. I'll put it on the BBC."

We all head after her. It feels strange to just be watching the news with my big monster beau, but I'm glad that he's by my side for once and not out in action.

Sabra turns on the gigantic TV and flicks through the channels until she finds one in English. I'm not sure if it's the BBC, but British newscasters sit behind a desk. "Reports continue to flood in from all corners of the globe of the strange creatures. Initial reports indicate they are not attacking but rather somehow *feeding* off of nuclear material. No attempts to speak with the creatures have yielded any response. One attempt to fire on the creature only resulted in an explosion of the nuclear facility that should have been catastrophic, but no injuries were reported. . . You have to see it to believe it."

The newscast desk is replaced with footage like we saw on Layden's phone of a creature surrounding what I assumed was some sort of nuclear facility. You can see the light of a missile fired at the creature, but instead of hitting it or any sort of explosion, it's just sort of. . . *absorbed* by the Devourer, who glows brighter and brighter.

"Governments are urging citizens to shelter in place at this time until we know more."

We sit glued to the TV for the next half hour, with Layden occasionally adding more commentary when the news starts repeating itself and showing the same clips over and over.

About ten minutes in, Sabra starts asking the questions no one wants to hear. "This is great and all, but what about when they've finished with the nuclear energy? These things go for the most nutrient-rich sources of power first, but then they move on. Fossil fuels will be next. We've got to figure out how the hell we're going to get rid of them."

"Get Phoenix," Kharon says. "She brought them. She can send them home."

Sabra looks back at him. "She can't, actually. We can't use the same kind of summoning circle to send them as we used to bring them."

"Why not?" Kharon asks stubbornly.

"Because it's not built for that. Well, it was, until Grandpa Vlad went off script and used your blood to supercharge her."

Kharon glowers at her. "What difference does that make?"

"All the difference, actually," Sabra says, standing up and getting in Kharon's face even though she's only literally half as tall as him. "You're the planes-crosser. Can't you take them back to where they came from?"

Kharon's mouth drops open like Sabra is from an alien planet. Maybe he's shocked that she knows what he is? I get it. I feel absolutely lost here with everything happening so quickly around me.

"It doesn't work like that," Kharon shouts. "I can only cross to the deathly plane."

But Sabra just shakes her head. "I doubt it. Have you even tried going to other planes?"

Kharon scoffs in disbelief and what sounds like anger, too. "Don't tell me what I can and cannot do. What do you know of me? My father explained my role to me—"

"So just because your dad said you could only go to the human death plane that's the only place you ever tried?" Sabra doesn't sound impressed. "I've never heard of a planes-crosser who can only cross to a single plane. It's far more likely that was just the *first* plane you crossed to, and then you stopped looking because you thought that was all there was."

Kharon opens his mouth to disagree, but Sabra holds up a hand. "The fact that Vlad drinking your blood helped boost Phoenix's power to bring the Devourers over is more proof. If your daughter has inherited any of your powers, I bet she'll be able to travel to more than just the one plane you regularly go to."

Kharon and Ksenia exchange a look. Uh, *yeah,* cause everyone on the helicopter when we escaped Russia saw that newborn baby Luna was definitely able to travel to other planes of existence. I try to control my shudder and don't quite manage it.

"Fine," Kharon says through gritted teeth. "But if I can't access that power, it still doesn't help us, does it?"

Sabra breathes out, looking around. "We need Phoenix. Since she's reached out there once with her mind at least to call the creatures here, maybe she'll be able to help you, I don't know, connect with it? Maybe together, the two of you can figure out how to cross to the plane to get them back once they're done eating up all the nuclear power on this planet and before they move on to all the other energy sources we have left on Earth."

"I don't think Earth is the immediate problem." Ksenia's voice comes from the couch where she's breastfeeding her daughter.

"What do you mean?" Sabra turns to her.

"Look at the screen," Ksenia says. Our heads all swivel in unison, and Layden turns it up.

"Everything that's happened in the past hour has been absolutely unprecedented," the newscaster says. "And this new unfolding situation continues in that vein. The creatures who have descended on many nuclear facilities across the globe appear now to be retreating. . . into *space*."

The feed switches to a wide-angled view of the sky with a long, never-ending line of the now-glowing sky-whales heading straight up. And up and up and up.

"Space?" Kharon asks, obviously confused.

"Oh my god," Layden breathes out.

"What?" I ask.

Ksenia, obviously the first to connect the dots, fills the rest of us in. "There's still one more excellent source of radioactive material on this plane of existence. The sun."

Chapter Twenty-Nine

REMUS

Well, shit.
 I see the terror on my Lo-Ren's face and feel it in her tense body. I swore to protect her and that she would never have anything to fear being at my side.

Now, the world as she knows it is about to end. For the second time today.

And at least part of it is my fault. Phoenix never would have gotten the power up from Grandpa-Dearest if I hadn't given him the intel on my family, including Kharon's plane-crossing abilities. Granted, I didn't know that was how Phoenix's family's power worked without the intel on the situation my brother may have gathered while I slept, but still. Not sure it's up to quibbling about the finer points when the sun that warms my beloved's skin is about to go dark.

It would be just my luck to finally find love and then watch her die cruelly along with all of her kind, only for my brothers and I to be left all alone on a cold, lifeless planet.

No.

Fuck no.

I squeeze Lo-Ren to me. She's warm and breathing and alive now. I twist her toward me and kiss her.

She tries to pull back. "What are you—"

"Just kiss me, my love."

Her eyes pop open wide.

"I love you," I say to her shocked expression. "You've made my pointless existence worth living, and all I want in this moment is to taste your lips."

She closes her eyes and breathes out, her body going limp against me. "One last time."

I kiss her and she throws herself into me, her body coming back to life as our lips press furiously together. I'm glad to feel some of the fight come back into her because it's what I live for.

I pull back, the fire inside me roaring. After all, I am the angel of War. Except now, for the first time in my life, I have something to fight *for*.

"I'll see you soon, my love." I grin at her, all glamours gone, wanting it to be my face she looks into just in case it really is for the last time.

She clings to me, but I pull back. "Wait, where are you going? Don't leave!"

"I'm always in your heart," I say, pressing my hand to her chest. "Some things are eternal."

And then I yank away from her clinging grasp, turn, and sprint out of the room and down the hallway. Running is an inefficient way of travel, though, especially for where I'm going.

As soon as I reach the courtyard, I flare my black wings wide, leap, and take off into the air. Time for the fight of my life.

* * *

For all the many places I've been to all over the globe, this is my first time flying through the outer atmosphere into space. It's very cold. Not to mention the whole lack of air thing.

It feels strange at first to not breathe and feel my feathers crystalize in the beyond freezing temperatures.

My flight slows as I struggle to adjust to the darkness lit only by a million stars. I can't imagine the warmth of the woman I just left behind. But just the thought of her is enough to spur me forward in spite of the discomfort.

I am a Horseman of the Apocalypse, and a little discomfort is nothing to me. Finally, I have a worthy opponent.

Not that I have any idea how to fight them. I don't have sword or spear, and I don't think they're capable of language, so I doubt I'll be able to persuade them to turn back. But I am rage, and I am chaos, and there is no turning back now. So, I press on.

Ten more minutes, and I cannot feel my legs, arms, or face. But my wings continue to propel me, and what is the point of feeling one's limbs anyway? My tail has curled around my legs as if that can stave off the sub-freezing temperatures, and I'm vaguely afraid it might snap and break off completely.

The thought doesn't deter me.

I am made of eternal material. My father grew back to full strength from a mere ember of ash. Granted, my brothers and I are not the same as him—he was merely our architect.

But surely being eternal means being able to survive a little interspace travel? Too late now, anyway. I'm closer to the sun now than I am to the Earth, and I can just see the tail end of the Devourers. I press myself to move with even more speed.

I hear the crack but don't look back. All feeling is secondary, but I *think* it's what I feared. I think I've just lost my tail. By the time I reach the back of the line of glowing Devourers, my mind has started to grow fuzzy.

I may be eternal but I'm starting to suspect that doesn't mean indestructible. Maybe there is something beyond hell-metal that can kill us. Huh. All this time, it was waiting in the deep sky above our heads, and we simply didn't realize it.

I mean, even I had heard the story of Icarus. The storytellers just got it wrong. He didn't die because his wings melted off. They froze, and then he fell from the sky. But there's no gravity here. I won't fall back to Earth, my body to be mourned by my beloved in the moments before her sky goes dark forever.

At least I will have finally killed Romulus. Which is what I wanted all this time, isn't it? Saying I wanted to get rid of the parasite and other euphemisms was a coward's way out. I wanted to kill him. Like Cain and Abel, I wanted to fight him to the death, standing over my brother as the sole owner of this body.

If I get the both of us killed, will that give half the satisfaction?

I'm too cold and exhausted to even laugh.

Chaos reigns to the end.

I can't flap my wings anymore; it's just the propulsion I began that continues me forward in the airless void of space.

My mind blinks in and out of consciousness, but at least the vampire's blood allows me to stay in the barest of control. I'm glad for that. It would feel even more cowardly to sleep now and give this final battle to the tactician. Even if he's better suited to coming up with some brilliant last-minute strategy. This will have to suffice as my final victory. Being in control and stealing the last moment with Lo-Ren that was mine and mine alone.

I reach the front of the line of Devourers, so bright from their internal lights, as we all approach the burning ball of the sun.

What will I do now that I am here and can barely move? I have no idea. They take no notice of me, their attention solely on the combustible sun in front of them.

They are strange creatures now that I see them up close. They are huge, obviously, with eight bulbous sections to their long torsos, covered with filaments propelling them forward at incredible speeds through space.

Here, at what feels like the end of all things, it seems as ridiculous as anything else in my chaotic life to pause and take in the strange beauty of these luminescent creatures. They aren't filled with the spark of life fire that my father first stole from the Great Hall. Instead, they've turned one of Earth's most destructive forces into nourishment, conquering without intent or greed. Just the simple fact of hunger.

The line of them glows as bright as the stars in the distance. For another moment, right before the creature at the head of the line gets to the sun, all its filaments reaching toward the bursting fire that leaps forth from its surface, I feel completely calm. Absent of rage. Absent of want. Absent of greed or jealousy or any other thing.

For one stretching, infinite-feeling moment, I feel peace within myself.

And then I blink and realize that the warmth of the sun has brought feeling back into my limbs and, with it, the memory of *her*. The woman waiting for me back on Earth, and what will happen to her if I let these Devourers eat this star.

My eyes widen, uncrystallized and regenerating as memories and fire and fury rush back into my blood.

No. I will not let this happen. I have come all this way to stop it.

Suddenly, everything sparks at once. Thought and purpose connect. The witch told Kharon he could do much more than he ever thought. He only ever traveled to one other plane because it was all he thought he could do. Because our *father* told him it was his only purpose.

We saw it with our glamours. We can do so much more than we ever thought. We were limited only by our own beliefs about ourselves, holding us in manageable leashes for our father.

But I'm done with leashes and cages.

I'm not just War. I am Chaos and Destruction and Division, both large and small.

So, with my wings warmed just enough to be able to use them again, I race to the front of the line, aim my body like an arrow, and fly straight at its head.

I pass straight through the creature, and at first, there's a spike of panic. Can I still accomplish my purpose if it's not even corporeal?

But as I feel the warmth of its inner fire, all that remains murky becomes clear. I don't just divide brother from brother in war. I divide cell from cell. Stem from stern. It doesn't matter if the substance is of this plane or any other.

I am not just the angel of War. I am a *god*.

I vibrate the innards of the creature, my own fury fueling my work as I fling my arms out when I'm in the blinding inner core amid the transformed energy it feasted upon earlier.

The creature explodes from the inside out, bits of it blowing outward into space.

I exalt in my power as I continue on to the next creature. It does not even run from me. One after the other, they absorb me and I destroy them.

It's only after several that I realize how easy it's become and that I myself have begun to glow. Not just the glow from my chest from the angel-spark that I rarely shine forth. No, I'm glowing from the tips of my fingers. I feel the heat bursting forth from my eyes, my belly, and the tips of my hair.

I'm being transformed by this, absorbing some of their digested energy as I destroy them. The Devourers are feeding me in a way I never anticipated. It makes me able to move faster and with even more deadly intensity.

When I'm done with the entire line of creatures, I'm far from the sun but feel no cold. I'm burning up, instead. I'm alight with power.

I am now truly a god.

More than any of my brothers. More than my Father-Creator. More than any beast or spirit from any realm.

I can rule and conquer them all!

I laugh into the emptiness of space.

And then I remember. Whatever power I have just gained for myself can never be mine alone. I do not own my body. I'm just a temporary passenger, forced forever to share.

It's not *fair*! No one would endure this!

Then I laugh again, a great, body-shaking chuckle. Because, of course, I *don't* have to endure it. I am a *god*, for the moment in control of this godly body.

I have the ability to divide cell from cell. My brother and I have been at war from the day of our birth, but now I know how to conquer him. I finally have the knowledge to simply *cut him from my body*.

I will destroy him and be left in blessed solitude, alone to my own thoughts and all I want, with no one threatening to take it from me the moment my eyes close in sleep!

I shut my eyes and fling my arms out once more. A buzzing starts in my ears, and I see it so perfectly, what I could not before. Perhaps it is the bursting energy inside me; perhaps I was willingly blind out of some misguided affection or reliance on the parasite who was only ever holding me back.

But I see him now, my body in golden outline projected perfectly in my mind and the exact lines demarcating where I can cauterize the neurons that are him so that only *I* remain. In my new godly state, what seemed impossible is now child's play. His outer face will be easy to slice off, then I can grow hair where he once was so that finally, I will be a whole man.

I breathe in satisfaction, imagining how her eyes will glow when she sees me flying down to her in a triumphant return. Just like the first moment I met her.

I remember the moment so well as it is burned in my memory. Eyes wide in shock and then interest, she all but glowed when I announced my intentions and raised her hand as a volunteer to be my consort. The only brave one as everyone else fled.

Her bravery has only continued to impress me, never once turning her face or embrace away from me, no matter what the circumstances of being with me have thrown at her. Not missiles or strange creatures from other planes of existence or...

Or *him*.

I frown, the first moment of doubt I've felt since I began destroying the Devourers.

What will she say when I return without Romulus? I could tell her he was lost in the battle with the creatures.

Immediately, I reject the thought. A god such as me does not need to resort to deceptions.

Also, it feels wrong to lie to her. It has never been that way between us. We have always laid bare our truths to one another. I frown again. Mostly anyway. It's true; I did not tell her how homicidal I've felt lately toward Romulus.

I wince at even thinking his name.

If I do not lie to her, what will she say when I reveal I have destroyed him with my newfound powers?

At first, my anger only sparks hotter. What should it matter what some mortal thinks of what I, a god, do? I do not bow to the whims of a mortal from this inferior plane!

But then, in my mind's eye, I can imagine the disappointment in her eyes. Already, though the deed has not even been done, I feel her withdrawing.

My arms fall, and the light inside me seems to go cold.

Reminding me how cold and lonely I have been these many, many millennia.

What use is it to have all the power of the most almighty god, ruling the whole world or all the realms, if one rules alone? Haven't I seen enough earthly despots make the same mistake?

I will be different!

But I'm already shaking my head.

I don't want to be alone.

The devil's voice in my head, which sounds very much like my Creator-Father's, whispers, *And when she chooses your brother like everyone else does and you're alone anyway?*

I roar into the silence of space and crash my fists against my head.

What if the Devourer's fire within me goes dormant, and I lose this one chance to excise Romulus from me? I'm a fool to give up the opportunity when it's finally within my grasp.

I lift my arms again, shaking my head as my fury rises. I cannot be weak now. Everyone knows who I am. I've been told often enough throughout my entire life how I'm an untrustworthy asshole. How I'll always fuck everything up. How destructive and selfish I am.

Is it really even my fault if I prove them all right in the end?

She'll still want me. It's *me*, after all. I'm a god, more powerful than ever, and she wanted me before when I was a far weaker version of myself. It is weakness that's even made me stall this long.

I lift my arms, close my eyes, grit my jaw, and allow my determination and fury to light the fire within me until I burn.

Goodbye, Brother. Forever.

Chapter Thirty

LAUREN

We can do nothing but wait, and I hate feeling so powerless. I pace back and forth in the vampire's den, taking turns with Hannah entertaining her daughter, Raven. The only way to quiet the girl was to allow her out of her glamour. She flies around the room, quieter if not exactly content.

We haven't seen any sign of the vampires since they fled to whatever saferoom or underground bunker we assume they headed to earlier.

The news plays endless footage of the Devourers flying toward space, and I've run out of nails to bite in nervousness. Hours pass, and still nothing.

Then the door bursts open. I shoot to my feet, but it's just Layden. He'd left for a room with a stash of computers, saying he needed to keep an eye out, whatever that meant.

"The runes are gone!" he declares dramatically.

I look around, confused. Is this supposed to mean something? But others in the room react as if it does. "How?" Kharon asks.

"I don't know," Layden says, "but they've disappeared as if they were never there. The angelic AI is completely gone, even though that shouldn't be possible. It was its own learning entity. There shouldn't have been a way to scrub it, but it's completely disappeared—"

"Look—" Hannah says, pointing to the screen. The news has just been repeating the same thing over and over, but now a banner reading "Breaking News" scrolls across the bottom. Hannah grabs the remote and turns it up.

The newscaster speaks again. "We're now receiving information from official sources that everything we've witnessed today was due to an incredible coordinated internet hoax, complete with deep-faked videos of the footage we've been showing all afternoon. Governments and militaries all over the world remain on high alert. The British Army Reserve and in America, the National Guard have been called up. Shelter-in-place notices remain in effect in countries across the world as everyone struggles to make sense of this unprecedented event that still has many citizens in a panic."

"Bullshit," Layden says, eyes on his phone. "I'm checking my sources to see if we can get eyes on the Devourers after they left the atmosphere."

"Are they just trying to cover it up to stop people from panicking?" Hannah asks, pacing up and down the room while keeping one eye on her daughter circling the ceiling.

The newscaster holds his ear as if receiving incoming updates. "From the reports we're getting, there's more and more confirmation this was indeed all an elaborate hoax. The Internet has gone wild with conspiracy theories to the contrary. Barbara?" he says, throwing to his fellow newscaster.

"That's right, James," she says, also putting a hand to her ear in a way that seems overly performative. "But both NASA and the United Kingdom Ministry of Defense satellites have no reports of the supposed creatures once they left Earth's atmosphere, leading more and more credence to the fact that this was a ruse. This just proves the danger of realistic hoaxes that can cause public panic in this era of deep-fake technology. Looting and rioting in response to the perceived threat, however, have been very real consequences. Police and even military in some instances around the world are struggling to maintain control over a panicking public."

"Did you see?" Everyone's head swings back toward the door when Phoenix bursts into the room. Hannah turns down the TV volume.

Layden rushes toward Phoenix, halting abruptly as if he barely stopped himself from embracing her. Vlad stands behind her, eying the both of them.

"See what?" Hannah asks. "Them denying all of it as a hoax? They're obviously covering it up to try to calm the public down."

But Phoenix is only looking at Layden. "The rune-code. It's all gone."

He nods emphatically. "As if it never existed."

"What does it mean?" Phoenix asks, brow furrowed. "The Devourers couldn't have done anything to the spirit who created and was controlling the AI. Them leaving shouldn't have had any impact on the AI."

"I know," Layden says. "It doesn't make any sense."

Hannah hurries over to join them. "Unless Abaddon stopped them!"

"I didn't."

Now it's Abaddon appearing at the door behind Vlad. Hannah pushes past Vlad to jump into her husband's arms. "Don't you dare run off like that ever again," she shouts, banging him on the back even as she clings to him.

"Daddy!" Raven cries, flying at her father like a little torpedo. She lands on his back, wrapping her legs around his neck and hugging his head fiercely, tiny hands attached to his horns.

"Did you hear that?" Hannah cries. "She said her first word."

I jump up and hurry over to where the little family is scrunched up at the door. With all these sudden returns, I can't help expecting Remus to pop up the next moment.

But when I grab the doorway and look down the hall in hopeful expectation—

There's no one.

Behind me, I hear Vlad start arguing with Layden and Abaddon about what happened to make the AI runes disappear. Theoretically, the nuclear attack was just a first strike. If the spirit driving it had control of the governments and really wanted to destroy the world, it could have just kept trying. Why then disappear, as if giving up?

"Well, something made it retreat," Kharon says. "Can't we just count that as a win? Maybe Remus was able to destroy the Devourers."

"Why the hell did you let *Remus* be the one to take care of them?" Abaddon shouts.

"You've met Remus," Layden bites back. "Does anyone ever *let* him do anything? He just flew off, and we haven't heard anything for hours. And you weren't around, taking off to play hero like that."

"We need to be working on a backup plan. Remus isn't exactly reliable! Maybe that's why the spirit left. He knew he'd accomplished the end of the world in a different way than expected because the Devourers are eating the sun as we speak."

"I came back up so we could try to make another circle to call the Devourers back," Phoenix rushes to say. "We brought them in; we're responsible for ridding this plane of them and sending them back where they came from—"

I can't handle listening to them anymore. My heart is a double drumbeat, whispering two names over and over. *Remus. Romulus. Remus. Romulus.* I spin away and run down the hallway, bursting out into the courtyard and staring up at the gray sky.

Where are you, my beloveds?

I know being out here won't bring them back any quicker, but still, I close my eyes and pray. It worked once...

Please, God or whatever deities may be out there... including my beloveds... Please. Please bring them home to me. Please let them be safe. I never deserved them the first time, but I beg you, please bring them home, and I swear I'll never take another moment for granted.

I look up toward the sky.

It's foolish, childish, really, that I expect to see the huge black wings extending from my glorious beloved's back flapping as he comes down.

All I want to see are his hands held out and that huge, slightly wild grin on his face.

I fall to my knees and weep, my hair around my face.

I don't know how long I kneel there, weeping, before I hear a voice.

"My mortal beloved, behold!" a voice shouts. "Your god is here among you!"

I swing my head up so fast that my neck cracks. It's him!

I jump to my feet, joy bursting from my chest as history repeats itself. The god I prayed for descends from the sky just like he did that first day in the plaza. Except there's clearly something different about him. Is he... *glowing*? He's so bright I have to shield my eyes.

I don't care. I still reach my arms out and run toward him as he descends the last ten feet, nearly bowling him over as he touches the ground.

He wraps his arms around me and squeezes me tight to him. I can *feel* the light inside him. It vibrates, hot and so bright I have to squeeze my eyes shut.

"Remus!" I cry, burying my face against his neck, in part to shield my eyes and to prove to myself he's actually real. Actually here.

"I'm home, my love," comes his voice, deeper and somehow more mature sounding than it used to. It's like it reverberates from deep in his chest and echoes back again. "You gave me strength when all was lost."

"What happened?" I cry.

"I vanquished the foe. We are safe."

I squeeze him even tighter. "We have to tell everyone. They're still terrified the world's about to end."

"In a moment. I must hold you first."

He does, continuing to hold me tight. At first, I just feel the warmth from his light. I still don't open my eyes because even through my closed eyelids, the brightness feels like it's all but burning my retinas. And then I realize it's not just my eyes that are burning. My whole chest suddenly feels on fire everywhere I'm touching him.

"Ow, Remus, let go," I start, but he holds me tighter still.

"Do not be afraid, beloved," he says calmly, bending his head over mine as he clutches me tight. The heat becomes so intense—

"It's burning! It's burning me!" I cry, starting to struggle in his arms. Useless against his strength. What's happening? Why is he—?

But right as I begin to scream from pain, the heat becomes cool, like icy tingles across my skin. Except that's not all. There's a humming heat now in my chest.

Remus finally releases his arms, and I break away from him, stumbling back with a confused cry, tears in my eyes.

But I can finally open them without pain to look at him. Is he not glowing as bright?

Which is when, holy shit, I look down at my own chest and realize that now *I'm* glowing too. "What did you do?" I cry.

"I have shared my life spark with you," he says, stepping close. "Today, I realized how easy it would be to lose you. After absorbing power from the Devourers when I destroyed them, I saw so many things clearly."

The look in his glowing eyes is wilder now than I've ever seen, which is saying something when it comes to Remus. He steps closer, and I hold still as he reaches out and caresses my face. When his fingers make contact, it sizzles but not with pain. I hiss out in shock at the intensity of the feeling.

"My brothers and I are more powerful than even we realized. Without knowing it, they bestowed extended lifespans upon their wives when impregnating them with offspring."

I feel my eyes widen.

"But I could not wait for that chance with you. And an extended life is not enough. I cannot lose you."

I look again at my chest. "What does this mean?"

Remus grins. "You will now live forever with me."

I about choke on my tongue. "Forever?"

He nods and then bows his head. "If you'll have us."

From the back of his bowed head, I can see Romulus awake and blinking at me. "We love you. It can be us, together. Forever."

I blink in shock. I may never know all of what happened up there when Remus battled those creatures, but I have the feeling it was something momentous if Remus has found peace with his brother.

Remus peeks up at me again. "Well? Will you have us?"

I grin and throw my arms around him. "Forever," I breathe out happily.

* * *

I'm still glowing—both literally and metaphorically—when Remus and I head back inside. Romulus stays awake a little while longer as we're welcomed enthusiastically by the group when he recounts his victory. Romulus only rolls his eyes a couple of times, I note, but otherwise actually looks *happy* to celebrate his brother.

Luna starts whining and Ksenia and Kharon stand up to bounce her. Abaddon gets up, too. "Well, I think it's time we took our leave. Thank you, Vlad, for your hospitality. We will never forget your kindness in this time of need and consider you true allies. Should you ever need the favor returned—"

But Abaddon doesn't finish talking before Vlad speaks up. "Oh, not quite yet. That one"—He points a sharp fingernail-tipped finger at Remus—"struck a blood oath with me, the terms of which have not been fulfilled."

"What are you talking about?" Remus snaps irritably. The glow from his chest flares slightly, and Vlad's sons shy back from the light as if it pains them, but Vlad stands unmoved in front of Abaddon.

"You drank of my sacred blood," Vlad says.

Phoenix gasps in horror.

"What?" Remus says, arm tightening around me. "We struck a bargain."

"What did you give in exchange?" Abaddon asks, obviously not happy.

"Hey, take it easy on him," Romulus speaks up in defense of his twin—a first by the look of surprise on Abaddon's face. "He just stopped an apocalypse, if you'll remember."

"Something my blood may have helped with," Vlad inserts. "It may have fortified him beyond his own abilities so he was able to take on the Devourers and actually defeat them."

"In that case, it was to your own advantage that you gave it to him," Abaddon growls at Vlad, who only just smiles a razor-sharp grin in response.

"That's not how a blood oath works."

"I gave you your fee," Remus says, and when Abaddon turns on him again, he just holds up his hands. "Just some information."

Vlad laughs. "Only a fool would think the eldest living vampire would give his blood for such a piddling fee. No, by imbibing my blood, you made an unbreakable pact with me that you and all your blood kin are bound to until it is paid."

"That's bullsh—" Remus starts, flaring brighter again, but Phoenix steps forward, hand out.

"It's true," she says, her face pale.

Vlad just continues grinning. "Your family is bound to me in blood until the debt is paid."

Abaddon grits his teeth. "And how exactly do we do that?"

Vlad looks at Layden. "It's quite simple, really. You give your brother to my granddaughter in marriage so she might bear me an heir. Only then will the blood debt be considered paid."

"Grandfather!" Phoenix explodes, spinning toward him.

I'm shocked too. I thought Vlad hated Layden. At least that was the vibe I got from him whenever Layden and Phoenix were close. But maybe now that he knows how powerful their family is…

Layden steps up, an unreadable expression on his face. "I will do it…" Phoenix's mouth drops open as he looks over his shoulder at her stunned face, "if she accepts."

"I— I—" she stutters. "You don't have to do this."

Layden walks over and clasps her hands, looking deep into her eyes. "We both know I do."

"He does," Vlad snaps. "And so do you."

Blinking several times, and looking back and forth between Vlad and Layden, Phoenix finally nods. "All right. I accept."

"Excellent," Vlad looks around at the rest of us. "Your family is welcome to stay the month while we prepare for the blessed nuptials." He claps his hands. "Now, I'm starved. It's feeding time. Come on, boys." He looks around to his sons. "Let's go see if there are any looters breaking curfew."

I shudder and step back as several of his sons grin and rub their hands together as they follow their grandfather out of the room.

Remus squeezes me tighter and puts his body between me and them as they pass.

"I'm so sorry," I hear Phoenix apologizing to Layden. "I had no idea he was going to do that."

"I don't look forward to being in-laws with him," Abaddon says, "but nothing forges a true alliance like a marriage if you're both willing."

"We are," Layden says firmly. If I'm not wrong, I think he's actually blushing as he glances over at Phoenix, who still seems a little distressed about it all, even as she nods vehemently.

But Remus is apparently done with family time. His arms come around me. "I don't know about you, but I'm ready for some alone time," he says in my ear.

"Me too," Romulus echoes, and I struggle not to giggle, the light in my chest flaring a little in response.

"Brothers," Abaddon calls toward Remus and Romulus as they lead me from the room. "We need to have a long chat soon."

"Fine," Remus growls over his shoulder. "Just don't come knocking too soon if you value your life."

Abaddon's chuckle is the last thing I hear as Remus carries me out of the room.

Chapter Thirty-One

ROMULUS

Several days later

"You're really okay with this?" I ask, facing forward and in full control of our body—everything except for our mostly regrown new tail—as I sit on the bed holding up a hand mirror. I can see Remus's face on the back of my head in the reflection of the corresponding hand mirror he's using our tail to hold up.

Lo-Ren's shower spray from the bathroom provides white noise in the background.

"If you want to keep arguing it," Remus growls, "I'm happy to switch back."

"No, no," I say quickly. "I'm just surprised, that's all." But then again, I've been surprised about a great many things since I woke up a few days ago. I don't know exactly what happened since we don't share memories anymore, but apparently, my brother single-handedly defeated an undefeatable interdimensional threat and absorbed its life force, which has given us a shit-ton of new power.

Which, for some equally unknown reason, he's decided to share by *willingly* taking turns switching out control of our body with me. We have control over when we switch now. And he'll actually give it up to me on a prearranged schedule.

Along with using his new power to give Lo-Ren immortality, it means we'll never have to suffer her withering and dying in the scattered handful of years most mortals get.

It's all so. . . unsettling. You go for thousands and thousands of years thinking you know a person, and then. . . this? Remus goes and commits multiple selfless acts?

Yes, giving Lo-Ren immortality wasn't strictly selfless, but he did have to give up some of his new power for it, and I know all that new power meant he had the choice he always wished for. He could have destroyed me. Certainly, he could have put me to sleep for a century or two at least. Instead, he's suddenly willing to *share*?

"Did you get a personality transplant out there in space?" I ask.

Our shorter, barely regrown tail comes around to slap me in the face. "Hey!" I glower, rubbing my cheek. "I'll take that as a no," I mutter.

This whole being conscious at the same time as him business—and not just for a few moments when we're having sex—is a whole new thing, too. I glare at him distrustfully in the mirror, but he just looks bored. It's so bizarre to be able to talk to him relatively face to face rather than just passive-aggressively through action and waiting to see what he does next in memory.

We're not both awake all the time. God, that'd be a real nightmare. But Lo-Ren suggested we carve out times like this to communicate directly.

"So, what do you want to talk about?" I ask.

"I don't know," he says as he picks the mirror back up with our tail. "How big an asshole you are? Cause from back here," his eyes glance down, "I can see just how big and phew!"

"I'm sitting down, you knob, you can't see shit."

He just chuckles, and it's odd to feel it shaking our shared body. I sigh. I'm not sure this is accomplishing what Lo-Ren hopes. Mostly, it's just us exchanging insults. Or each of us looking at the little calendar in Lo-Ren's phone, working out who's going to be awake when and making sure we both get equal time with her. It's all so... civilized.

Which is what I don't get. When I'm in control, I can feel the power inside us. And if my brother was the self-absorbed, narcissistic, power-hungry asshole I always assumed him to be...

"Why am I still here?" I finally just ask it straight out.

"Ughhhh," he makes a long-suffering noise and rolls his eyes in the mirror. "What the fuck is this, feelings hour?"

I stay quiet, not responding.

He shakes our head and then says, "Fine. You really want to know?"

"Yes."

He sighs again. "You see how she looks at us. You think she'd look at me even half the same way if I'd shown back up after killing you? Everyone else only saw a monster, but she looked at me and saw more. So I could finally *be* more, okay?"

Wow. And damn. "I get it," I say solemnly. "And I'm sorry for not giving you the benefit of the doubt sooner. We didn't have to live so long with all that acrimony and suspicion between us that Father put there all those years ago. You're a good man, and I see that finally."

"Don't start that now and make me regret keeping you around," he says. Again, our tail smacks me in the face—or tries to.

I catch it and toss it away, standing up as I laugh. "Don't be so predictable. Your enemy will see it coming a mile away. But you're getting pretty good with the tail. So why don't we see if Lo-Ren wants some company in the shower?"

"Finally, something worthwhile comes out of that mouth."

I stalk into the steamy bathroom to surprise our woman, tail whipping excitedly behind us.

* * *

Did you miss how Abaddon and Hannah met? Check it out here in MONSTER'S BRIDE!

Don't miss Kharon & Ksenia's love story either, available here! THING

And coming this Spring, Layden and Phoenix:

When Phoenix ran away from her controlling vampire grandfather, the last thing she expected to stumble upon was an angel with shorn off wings who'd given up all hope. As she nurses Layden back to health, she begins to dream of a life beyond the one her grandfather has pigeon-holed her into. One where she can live—and love—for herself.

But her grandfather's reach is strong, eventually tearing her and Layden apart.

Fast-forward ten years later, now it's become expedient to Grandfather Vlad to force her into an arranged marriage with the last person she wants to see: Layden.

Phoenix has moved on. Without Layden. She doesn't need him. She doesn't want him. It's better when he's not there to confuse and cloud her senses... isn't it?

Because now with him back in her life—in her bed—suddenly Phoenix is rethinking everything she thought she knew.

Did you miss how Abaddon and Hannah met? Check it out here in MONSTER'S BRIDE!

Don't miss Kharon & Ksenia's love story either, you can find it here in THING!

And coming this Spring, Layden and Phoenix:

When Phoenix ran away from her controlling vampire grandfather, the last thing she expected to stumble upon was an angel with shorn off wings who'd given up all hope. As she nurses Layden back to health, she begins to dream of a life beyond the one her grandfather has pigeon-holed her into. One where she can live—and love—for herself.

But her grandfather's reach is strong, eventually tearing her and Layden apart.

Fast-forward ten years later, now it's become expedient to Grandfather Vlad to force her into an arranged marriage with the last person she wants to see: Layden.

Phoenix has moved on. *Without* Layden. She doesn't need him. She doesn't *want* him. It's better when he's not there to confuse and cloud her senses... isn't it?

Because now with him back in her life—in her *bed*—suddenly Phoenix is rethinking everything she thought she knew.

About the Author

STASIA BLACK grew up in Texas, recently spent a freezing five-year stint in Minnesota, and now is happily planted in sunny California, which she will never, ever leave.

She loves writing, reading, listening to podcasts, and has recently taken up biking after a twenty-year sabbatical (and has the bumps and bruises to prove it). She lives with her own personal cheerleader, aka, her handsome husband, and their teenage son. Wow. Typing that makes her feel old. And writing about herself in the third person makes her feel a little like a nutjob, but ahem! Where were we?

Stasia's drawn to romantic stories that don't take the easy way out. She wants to see beneath people's veneer and poke into their dark places, their twisted motives, and their deepest desires. Basically, she wants to create characters that make readers alternately laugh, cry ugly tears, want to toss their kindles across the room, and then declare they have a new FBB (forever book boyfriend).

* * *

Join Stasia's Facebook Group for Readers for access to deleted scenes, to chat with me and other fans and also get access to exclusive giveaways:

Stasia's Facebook Reader Group

* * *

Want to read an EXCLUSIVE, FREE novella, Indecent: a Taboo Proposal, that is available ONLY to my newsletter subscribers, along with news about upcoming releases, sales, exclusive giveaways, and more?

Get **Indecent: a Taboo Proposal**

When Mia's boyfriend takes her out to her favorite restaurant on their six-year anniversary, she's expecting one kind of proposal. What she didn't expect was her boyfriend's longtime rival, Vaughn McBride, to show up and make a completely different sort of offer: all her boyfriend's debts will be wiped clear. The price?

One night with her.

* * *

Connect with me on social media!

Website: stasiablack.com

tiktok.com/@stasiablackauthor
facebook.com/StasiaBlackAuthor
twitter.com/stasiawritesmut
instagram.com/stasiablackauthor
amazon.com/Stasia-Black/e/B01MY5PIUH
bookbub.com/authors/stasia-black
goodreads.com/stasiablack

Also by Stasia Black

REVERSE HAREM ROMANCES

MARRIAGE RAFFLE SERIES

Theirs To Protect

Theirs To Pleasure

Theirs To Wed

Theirs To Defy

Theirs To Ransom

Marriage Raffle Boxset Part I (Boxset)

Marriage Raffle Boxset Part II (Boxset)

WHO'S YOUR DADDY

Who's Your Daddy

Who's Your Baby Daddy

Who's Your Alpha Daddy

FREEBIE

Their Honeymoon

DARK CONTEMPORARY ROMANCES

VASILIEV BRATVA SERIES

Without Remorse

STUD RANCH SERIES

The Virgin and the Beast

Hunter

The Virgin Next Door

Reece

Jeremiah

Breaking Belles Series

Elegant Sins

Beautiful Lies

Opulent Obsession

Inherited Malice

Delicate Revenge

Lavish Corruption (Coming soon...)

Dark Mafia Series

Innocence

Awakening

Queen of the Underworld

Persephone & Hades (Boxset)

Beauty and the Rose Series

Beauty's Beast

Beauty and the Thorns

Beauty and the Rose

Billionaire's Captive (Boxset)

Love So Dark Duology

Cut So Deep

Break So Soft

Love So Dark (Boxset)

Taboo Series

Daddy's Sweet Girl

Hurt So Good

Taboo: a Dark Romance Boxset Collection (Boxset)

Freebie

Indecent: A Taboo Proposal

Monsters' Consort Series

Monster's Bride

Thing

Between Brothers

Draci Alien Series

My Alien's Obsession

My Alien's Baby

My Alien's Beast

Made in the USA
Monee, IL
25 October 2024

68627722R00138